SOLOMON'S PORCH

ENDORSEMENTS

A compelling story with characters who will become part of your life forever, *Solomon's Porch* reminds us that hope often comes in unusual or unexpected packages, that although other people may overlook your acts of kindness, God sees—He remembers, and He rewards. This book will keep you going through the dark nights and give you hope to face the toughest of days.
—**Ken Abraham**, *New York Times* bestselling author

Whether penning a feature article or writing a devotional, Janet Morris Grimes is a gifted writer with a keen understanding of the ties that bind us all. Her skills are on full display in her inventive new novel, *Solomon's Porch*, where she breathes life into an interesting cast of characters and draws readers into an intriguing tale. The town of Ginger Ridge comes to vivid life in her skilled hands. She has a way of making the reader care deeply about her characters as she pulls you further into their world. It's an auspicious debut not to be missed!
—**Deborah Evans Price**, author of *Country Faith* and *Country Faith Christmas* and winner of Country Music Association's Media Achievement Award

Solomon's Porch is a great read that you won't be able to put down. Janet Morris Grimes is an excellent storyteller, weaving character arcs and plot twists all into a setting that will make you feel like you're experiencing the book along with everyone in it.
—**Brian A. Klems**, author of *Oh Boy, You're Having a Girl*

SOLOMON'S PORCH

Janet Morris Grimes

ELK LAKE PUBLISHING INC
PUBLISHING THE POSITIVE
Plymouth, Massachusetts

COPYRIGHT NOTICE

Cover and Interior Design: Rhonda Dragomir, The Dragomir Group, Derinda Babcock

Editor(s): Sue Fairchild, Deb Haggerty

PUBLISHED BY: Elk Lake Publishing, Inc., 35 Dogwood Drive, Plymouth, MA 02360, 2021

Library Cataloging Data
Names: Grimes, Janet Morris (Janet Morris Grimes)
Solomon's Porch / Janet Morris Grimes
310 p. 23cm × 15cm (9in × 6 in.)
ISBN-13: 978-1-64949-339-2 (paperback) | 978-1-64949-340-8 (trade paperback) | 978-1-64949-341-5 (e-book)
Key Words: Dementia, Family, Social Work, Health Care, Communities, Mystery, Single Parents
Library of Congress Control Number: 2021944504 Fiction

DEDICATION

To Daddy. Thank you for the fairy tales. I so wish they'd been real. But through my stories, I can hear your voice. For now, that will have to be enough.

To my mother, Jeannine. You never flinched, and here we are. Against all odds, your faith and diligence gave us an advantage in life. Thank you.

To my sister, Jeanna. My biggest cheerleader, despite often telling me to shut up.

To my husband, Thomas. These are the imaginary friends I've been telling you about. Without your support, spunk, and frequent flirtations, I'd probably never leave the basement. Thank you for making life so fun.

To Crystal, Andrew, and Malloree. You are my story. In a weird plot twist, God used you to raise me. He's tricky like that. Traveling beside you now, as adults, is my definition of happily-ever-after.

To my readers. Where have you been all my life?

I hope you find yourselves traveling the sidewalks of Ginger Ridge, and finally realizing how much your own story truly matters.

We need each other.

And that is more than enough.

Please post a review to share on social media and drop me a line to let me know how you're doing. You may find me at http://janetmorrisgrimes.com/

I can't wait to hear your story!

ACKNOWLEDGMENTS

To my Elk Lake Publishing Family, Deb Haggerty, Sue Fairchild, and the entire team—thank you for taking the isolation out of writing and for showing me how it's done.

All I ever wanted was a chance to succeed and a great product. You have given me both.

I'm honored to sit on your shelf.

To Andrew Ramirez and Heidi Cook, I found you at a breaking point. Thank you for helping me rediscover my purpose in writing, connecting, and changing the world, one delicious story at a time.

The little girl in me is giddy. She always believed this was possible.

Bless her heart.

She was right!

CHAPTER ONE

Time.

Solomon was running out of it.

He rarely made wise choices when pressed for time.

He ached to get home in time for dinner. Sweat trickled from his forehead as he battled the stifling beat-down of the afternoon Georgia sun. At the ivy-covered iron gates to the cemetery, he shielded his eyes and considered his options.

From either direction, the route led home. He was sure of it.

Why couldn't I find their tombstones today?

Tombstones and rituals were all he had left.

Except for Sadie Beth. I must hurry!

He loosened his bow tie as he thought about a tall glass of Sadie Beth's sweet tea. She would be getting worried soon. He checked his watch. The second hand hadn't circled the dial in years. Still, he couldn't force himself to remove the timepiece. Sadie Beth had surprised him with it when he'd dropped her off at college.

Always on my mind. Love, Sadie Beth.

He smiled as he remembered the engraving.

As a shiver ran up his spine, he realized the sun had dipped low in the sky. He wiggled his cap back on his head and gripped his cane, using his finger to trace the names etched into the handle. Winnie on one side. Silas on the other. Another gift from Sadie Beth.

Better hurry. Sadie Beth will be waiting.

He winched himself up from the bench and took off at a pace he couldn't handle. Soon, each breath brought an intense wheeze.

A shiver ran through him.

The paved driveway led to the street, he knew that for certain.

At the end of the drive, he expected to see a stop sign to his left. To the right, down the road a piece, should be the water tower which boasted the high school football legacy of the Ginger Ridge Eagles, state champions from 1997 through 1999. Visible from any direction, he trusted the beacon of the water tower to guide him to Main Street.

But the tower was nowhere in sight.

Solomon chose the road to the right, though it proved more winding and narrower than he recalled. Still, he felt certain the turnoff ahead would fork to the left halfway down the hill, past the faded billboard that read:

GINGER RIDGE—HOME OF FORT BRYCE
WELCOME HOME, SOLDIERS.
WE'VE BEEN WAITING FOR YOU!

Ginger Ridge deserved an updated sign. Fort Bryce shut down a decade ago.

His heart climbed out of his chest, pounding hard.

"I've got to get home in time for dinner." Solomon's raspy words dissipated into the weight of the late summer humidity. "Sadie Beth will be mad as a hornet if I'm late again. I'll stop at the pay phone on the corner to call home."

The last rays of sunlight took a nosedive behind a thick row of pines. Deep shadows dominated this stretch of road, and darkness was never kind to Solomon.

He groaned and patted his pockets for the flashlight he kept with him.

Nothing.

I must have left it on my dresser.

A whimper escaped his throat. He pressed on, his strength and determination draining with each step.

A rock wedged into one of Solomon's loafers, biting him in the foot. He braced himself against his cane to check his shoe. His ankle cracked, and a couple toes wiggled through a hole at the edge. He pried the rock out with his finger.

I need to polish these shoes first thing in the morning.

He zig-zagged to the center of the lane and took off as fast as his gimpy legs could carry him in a desperate hunt for the blasted water tower.

CHAPTER TWO

Raphael Henry found himself perched atop an unknown bluff which offered a brilliant view of Atlanta. Each breath was shallow and intense, bringing a new stab of his own betrayal.

He propped himself up against his old-school Mustang convertible—its black vinyl top open and retracted as if bowing to the skyline that reigned supreme in the distance. Raphael's gaze rested on the second largest building on the horizon—Wilburn & Hessey Towers. The sun reflected off the windows in the evening, casting a peaceful glow of gold across the crowded streets of the city.

Raphael had overseen construction on that project not long ago. His first as a foreman.

The project also proved to be his last.

He gripped a fistful of thick hair, still damp from another stifling day in a half-constructed building. The familiar blend of perspiration and construction dust taunted his nostrils. He couldn't wait to take a shower, normally a daily ritual once he entered the welcoming front doors of home.

But not today.

Home was the last place he wanted to be.

He unzipped his blue coveralls, revealing a white tank top glued with sweat to his browned skin. He clutched the lime green construction hat against his chest. Both the coveralls and the hat read Majestic Construction in reflective block letters across the front. A name he'd always worn with pride.

Until an hour ago.

He tossed the hat into the passenger's seat in disgust and caught sight of the blue and white packet presented to him before quitting time.

Time.

Raphael was running out of it.

He relived the painful moment that had led him to the overlook and the complete shock and betrayal he'd seen in his immediate supervisor's eyes when he'd escorted Raphael off the premises.

Late that afternoon, a lady Raphael recognized from the CEO's office had approached him in the hallway. With no explanation, she'd handed over a folded letter. Underneath the official Majestic letterhead, the note read: *Please report to the CEO's office ASAP.*

By the time he'd raised his head, the messenger had disappeared.

He remembered wondering why they hadn't used his radio to summon him and checked the walkie talkie to be sure it was working.

It worked fine.

A sense of dread crept over him then. Raphael had followed the maze of connected hallways and stairwells leading to the management wing. The last time he'd been summoned to that floor had been for a promotion.

Today's meeting felt the opposite. As he walked, Raphael wracked his brain to recall the name of their recently promoted CEO. When he arrived, the lady who had hand-delivered his letter now waited at her desk in expectation. She motioned him toward an intimidating closed door a few feet away. He followed her lead but chided himself for not paying more attention to the CEO's nameplate by the door.

As soon as he entered the room, Raphael recognized the man from publicity photos in the newspaper.

Roscoe something ... or was it Monroe?

Next to the nameless CEO stood a tattooed chunk of a man known as Boomer, Raphael's immediate supervisor. Raphael often thought of him as an older brother but, in that moment, they were strangers. Boomer avoided eye contact. Both men's hands rested on their hips like linebackers trying to catch their breath between goal-line plays.

Between the two of them stood a dark-skinned man in a business suit with gold-rimmed glasses. Raphael cleared his throat and reached to shake each man's hand to introduce himself, hoping they'd do the same.

No one returned the favor. Raphael thought he might choke on the uncomfortable silence that fell across the room.

He'd been with Majestic for ten years. Rumor had it, the company had even bigger plans for him.

Rumors. Construction sites were full of them.

He shoved his hands in his pockets and waited, taking in a gulp of involuntary air. He coughed it out as best he could.

The one in the business suit spoke first—his voice much deeper than Raphael expected.

"Mr. Henry, I'm Agent Marcus Dixon—Department of Homeland Security."

Raphael's stomach gurgled then. Out of the corner of his eye, he located the nearest trash can in case his Thursday meatball lunch special from the corner diner came back to haunt him.

The detective handed a packet of information to the CEO, who covered his mouth as he read. Boomer focused a penetrating stare out the window and appeared to be holding his breath.

When the CEO tossed the packet onto his desk, Raphael caught the title, written in bold letters across the front.

Immigration and Customs Enforcement Case #908766 Raphael Henry

Raphael's mouth felt parched, and those meatballs continued to climb their way up his esophagus. He forced out the only words he could think of.

"Please, sir, can we discuss this matter in private?"

Certain words from a guilty person.

The agent nodded and ushered Raphael into an adjacent conference room.

"Take a seat," Agent Dixon said.

"No thanks. I'll stand."

Agent Dixon presented the results of a year-long investigation—Case number 908766. The unquestionable proof of Raphael's violations summarized in black and white, like a crisp slap in the face.

"As you can see, Mr. Henry, I work with the ICE Task Force, and our records show your H-1B Visa expired four years ago. Since there's been no attempt to renew it, this violation can no longer be resolved legally. You must prepare for deportation to Mexico within the next thirty days."

There was no sense arguing the point. Raphael knew it to be true and had no one to blame but himself. Year after year, his legal status in the country, or lack thereof, had slipped to the back of his mind.

Immigration laws were barely enforced in this region, or so he believed.

Still, he had no excuse. All along, he fully intended to launch the process to become a legal citizen, but there were always more pressing ways to spend his money. More important things to do, such as marrying the girl of his dreams and building the perfect home for their family. Bringing their sons Xavier and Zander home from the hospital. And now, anticipating the birth of their first daughter. He couldn't wait to meet her.

Will I even get the chance?

The detective intruded on his thoughts. "As it states, Mr. Henry, September fifteenth is your mandatory date of deportation. You may turn yourself in at our regional headquarters in Atlanta at the address listed." Agent Dixon pointed to a highlighted area at the top of page two.

"But my baby's due in October," Raphael argued, as if it made a difference. The thought of not being present for the birth of his daughter kicked him in the gut. Hard. Raphael folded his arms across his stomach.

The ICE detective presented a pamphlet with a list of numbers for government agencies that offered assistance. As if Raphael trusted such things.

How do I seek help from the same justice system I've avoided my entire life?

When the agent pointed to a signature line, Raphael gulped, signed on the dotted line, and then shuffled his feet toward the exit.

"Please. Am I free to leave?"

Agent Dixon nodded.

Raphael thrust open the first door he could reach. In a back hallway, Boomer waited with arms crossed over his chest. He grabbed Raphael's arm, and the two of them moved together to the parking lot in complete silence.

Once outside, Boomer rushed them toward Raphael's classic Mustang. His mint condition muscle car had long been the envy of everyone on their team. Today, it felt like a dumpster—a place for Majestic Construction to drop off their trash.

Boomer's eyes were bloodshot. "I'm sorry, Raphael. I think the world of you, but you're banned from the premises of any Majestic Construction sites. I must take possession of your badge."

Raphael's brows drew together as he deferred, removing the badge from a belt loop and handing it over.

Boomer's voice cracked. "Our legal department advises no further contact. Because of your actions, Majestic will face a stiff penalty for our hiring practices. Goodbye."

Boomer took off in a jog toward the employee entrance to the building.

Message delivered. Career ended. No response required.

Raphael paced at the top of cliff now as he tried to shake off the biting memory of it all.

Raphael jumped when his phone rang. He checked the number and answered on the second ring.

"Hello. Yes, this is Raphael Henry. Thank you for calling me back so soon."

He gripped the phone to his ear, wincing at the questions the caller asked. The welfare of his family depended on his ability to close out this sale.

He patted the hood of the car. "Yeah man, she's ready to go. As you recall, I never intended on selling my Mustang, right?" He kicked at the tires and waited on the response.

"I remember," the caller said. "Your car's a beauty. You sure you're ready to sell?"

"Yeah. Change of plans. The wife's got another bebé in the oven. Guess it's time to sell *my* baby if you know what I mean." He caressed the windshield's edge as if consoling the vehicle while he planned its demise.

"Count me in. Call me when it's ready, and I'll take it for a spin," the caller replied.

"Sounds good. I'll call you early next week."

Raphael hung up and squared his shoulders. Surrender didn't come easy even in the worst of circumstances. Isabella had been begging him to sell his prized possession for months, ever since she announced she was pregnant with their third child.

Baby Evelyn was due in six weeks.

According to Homeland Security, Raphael would be a rightful citizen of Mexico by then.

Truth. Brutal and terrifying.

He checked his surroundings, unable to recall the route he'd driven to arrive at the dangerous crags of this bluff. A few wrong steps, and he'd topple off the edge, never to be heard from again.

That might be best.

He hung his head and hurled a rock off the cliff, letting out a long, piercing scream which echoed in painful layers.

Why God, after all these years?

Raphael sighed. He'd already missed dinner and Isabella was blasting his phone with one message after another, but he had no idea how to respond. Instead, he sent a quick text.

RAPHAEL: Tied up at work. Will be awhile. Sorry.

Another lie in a long series of them, but at least it bought him time to get his story straight.

The sky had morphed into a deep shade of purple as the sun's rays poked through the clouds like a hidden stairway.

An incredible setting for such a dismal day.

He pounded his fists against the hood of the car before dropping into the driver's seat. Tears filled his eyes and tires squealed as he backed onto the winding country road. The distorted grays of twilight slinked across the sky. Raphael flipped on his headlights and took off faster than usual. He sped past an overgrown cemetery on his left and had to jerk the steering wheel to return to the proper lane.

Out of control, like everything else in my life. At this point, what does it matter if I get a ticket?

He pounded the steering wheel and pressed harder on the gas.

Raphael bit his lip and ignored the speedometer as he raced down the hill, wiping tears with the back of his hand. As he rounded a bend, the headlights of an approaching car that had veered way over the center line lit him up. Raphael tapped the brakes and swerved to avoid hitting the other vehicle.

His tires hit the grassy edge of the narrow shoulder of the road which bordered a deep embankment on the right. He yanked the steering wheel in the opposite direction, sending the car into a back-and-forth swerve. He gripped the wheel tight to regain control.

In his rearview mirror, he caught a glimpse of an old, powder blue Ford Ranger as it tore up the hill, clacking as if it had lost half a muffler along the way.

As he turned his attention back to the road in front of him, a feeble old man loomed—mouth wide open and stiff-arming a cane, as if it might protect him from the impact.

Raphael's foot punched the brakes and his tires squealed.

"No!" The man rumbled across the hood, smashed against the windshield, flipped into the air, and landed face-down in a heap upon Raphael's back seat.

Raphael's beloved Mustang came to a halt and he peered tentatively into the back seat. Blood pooled across the white leather as it oozed from a deep gash in the man's head.

Raphael leaned his head over his door and relinquished those meatballs.

CHAPTER THREE

Detective Cameron Sterling blocked the wind from the Air Medic helicopter with his suit coat as the pilot maneuvered the chopper into place on the roof of an abandoned fire station. The helipad, still partially marked from a past decade, hadn't been operational in years.

Down below, the parking lot exploded with flashing blue and red lights of emergency vehicles from every agency in Madison. He even noticed marked state vehicles among the throng making an appearance where they didn't belong. Cam dropped his sunglasses from the top of his bald, dark head to shield his eyes and chomped on a wad of pink bubblegum as if life depended on it. Across the street, news crews filed in to film live footage for the evening news.

Great! Just what we need. Another breathless reporter exploiting the latest tragedy to gain a few extra viewers.

Cam no longer had patience for such things. He'd seen too much in his twenty-five-year career with the police department. His supervisors up the chain-of-command often accused him of being jaded, but Cam chalked his cynical attitude up as a stark requirement for survival.

When the pilot of the chopper cut the engine into standby mode, Cam approached the aircraft and spoke into the voice recorder on his phone.

"Elderly white male hit-and-run victim dumped at the old District 3 fire station on Dixie Highway. No ID on the victim. No known witnesses. Time of anonymous 911 call,

8:10 p.m. First car on the scene, 8:17 p.m. Air Medic unit arrived at 8:31. Transporting victim in extreme critical condition. Awaiting to confirm further details."

Cam knocked on the cockpit window and flashed his badge. When the pilot slid the pane of glass to the side, Cam's lip curled into a snarl. His sergeant often reminded him to tone down the attitude, but Sergeant Lewis was out of town for a couple more days.

Maybe I'll have this case solved by the time he returns.

He yelled over the idling engine. "Good evening. Detective Cam Sterling with Madison PD. Can I get your name and badge number for my report?"

The pilot handed him a business card. "Jake Easton. Air Medic One. I'm the only pilot covering the eastern half of Georgia tonight."

Cam made a few notes on his clipboard. "Thanks. Where are you taking our victim?"

"They've rerouted us to Savannah Regional. Atlanta's trauma unit is full due to an afternoon bus crash on I-85."

Cam pointed his pen at the pilot in response. "Doesn't sound like our victim stands a chance, but I'll follow up with the hospital."

The pilot lifted his chin. "Challenge accepted. I'm always ready to save a life. You should try it sometime."

Cam shook his head and allowed his lip to finish a full snarl.

Fire department and medical personnel are so cocky.

A team of paramedics clanked up two stationary ladders attached to the building, carrying the victim on a stretcher with swift and careful movements. They had him loaded and ready to go within a minute. Cam took cover while the Air Medic unit lifted off and noted the time on his watch. When he raised his head, the paramedics had already cleared the side of the building.

Impressive.

Cam peered over the edge as they dropped to their feet, skipping the last few rungs on each ladder. Their agility and teamwork intrigued him, even if they were considered fire department personnel.

In my college football days, I could have scaled that ladder with arm strength alone.

These days, he wheezed with every breath.

Day five without a cigarette. Cold turkey, fully engulfed in the jittery and miserable phase. He'd already packed on a few pounds which complicated the next goal the departmental physician had laid out for him:—lose fifty pounds by the end of the year.

Make that fifty-two pounds.

Time.

Cameron was running out of it.

He shook his head, unwrapped another piece of bubblegum, and pressed the record button on his phone. "Air Medic left the scene at 8:34 p.m. en route to Savannah Regional Trauma Center. Victim's current condition is a serious Code 3. Not likely to survive."

Harper Phillips swiped her access card and poked her head out the employees only door to the rooftop of Savannah Regional Hospital. After an afternoon bus crash in Atlanta redirected most rural patients to their trauma unit, she desperately needed a few minutes to herself. Seeing no one, she pushed through the door and out into the stagnant night air. Her long, golden waves dangled over one shoulder as she approached the makeshift oasis she had created with a few coworkers using thrift store patio furniture. The evening humidity took her breath away—she removed her sweater and tossed it on the back of a wrought iron chair. She brushed at a stain on her purple scrubs she'd acquired from an earlier catastrophe with a patient in the ER. Noting the smell of the clothes, she gave up on the stain.

Taking in the 360-degree view of Savannah's night sky, Harper detected a medical helicopter on the horizon, most likely headed to the roof diagonally across from her with an incoming patient. It had been that kind of day.

Do you mind? This is supposed to be my hiding place.

She pressed her lips together, checked her watch, and sent a quick message to her teenage daughter.

HARPER: Sorry I'm late. Be home in an hour. Feed Brewster. See you soon.

She knew better than to expect an immediate reply from Presley, who was likely in the process of changing her outfit for the tenth time. Teen problems.

Harper dropped to a cushioned love seat and leaned back to stretch her neck and close her eyes. Latin music blared from a Mexican restaurant a couple of blocks over. A car horn chimed in, and a whiff of grilled goodness from the local steakhouse wafted past her nose. Harper welcomed the urge to order takeout.

She opened her eyes and lifted a piece of mail from the pocket of her sweater.

You are cordially invited to the Harbor House annual banquet, featuring guest speaker Harper Phillips.

Harper sighed and rolled her eyes. "Yikes. I guess I'd better get a speech ready. As if I really have time for this."

A message pinged through on her pager. Harper grabbed her sweater and rushed inside as the helicopter came in for a landing on the roof opposite where she had been sitting.

Inside the elevator, she checked her reflection in the shiny doors. She stifled a yawn and noticed her tired eyes—not as bright as they used to be, but still honest, determined, and sincere. She'd take that any day. Those traits hadn't come easily.

Her phone jolted her with an unexpected response from Presley.

She grinned at her daughter's exuberant, open-mouthed expression in the photo that popped up with her text. Presley Rose recently celebrated her sixteenth birthday and went out of her way to be the complete opposite of her mother. Except for those transparent blue eyes. With her brunette hair and fearless approach to life,

Presley carried a flare for the dramatic and enjoyed the spotlight. Thankfully, her impatient spirit balanced an acquired sense of understanding and pride in her mother's chosen career.

PRESLEY: Feed Brewster? What about me? We've got one last can of soup in our pantry. We're pitiful.

Harper shrugged but couldn't argue. She recalled the inviting scent of steak from their favorite restaurant.

HARPER: I'm about to order steak. Just call me Mother of the Year.

Harper paced in circles in the elevator while she speed-dialed the number and placed their usual order.

On the pediatric floor, she reached her hand under the sanitizer dispenser and then hurried to her patient's room. The scent of rubbing alcohol tickled her nose as she nudged the door handle and entered the room of little Wallace Higgins. This sterile space inside Savannah Regional Hospital had served as his home for the past three months.

She broke into a smile as Wallace scampered toward her.

"I'm gonna miss you most of all, Miss Harper." He threw his arms around her neck and squeezed tight.

She swung him back and forth and grinned at his parents, perched side by side on his bed. "I'll miss you too. You've been my best buddy, but my favorite thing to do is send patients home where they belong. Aren't you excited to go home?"

He shook his head. "No, not really."

His father gasped and Harper grinned as she lowered Wallace to the ground. "Are you kidding me? Why not?"

He pointed to the pedal fire truck in the corner.

"Because I don't have a fire truck at my house."

Roger Higgins laughed. "Oh, we'll see what we can do about that." He turned to Harper. "What time will we be discharged tomorrow? Looks like I need to make a run to the toy store."

Wallace jumped up and down and clapped his hands, then climbed into the fire truck and circled the room, making siren sounds.

Harper focused her attention on Roger and Claire Higgins. They held hands and their eyes sparkled in anticipation of bringing their son home.

"Let me say how happy I am to see you both supporting each other through these trials. Sometimes these situations rip families apart. I'm thrilled this hasn't been the case for you."

Claire grinned. "If anything, his illness made us stronger. Our only goal is for Wallace to remain in remission, gain strength, and enjoy life. Whatever it takes, you know?"

Harper gave a thumbs up. "That's my goal as well. As his case manager, my job is to assist you through this transition and ensure you receive the same level of support at home." She handed over a yellow folder stocked full of information from various agencies in the community. "This contains contact info for Leukemia support groups."

Roger interrupted. "We're happy to be done with the hospital for a while."

Claire touched Harper on the arm. "Do you think it's safe to travel? We're hoping for a Florida vacation over Christmas, since we postponed our trip this summer."

Harper nodded. "By all means, take the trip. But consider driving. That would expose him to fewer germs than flying. He'd benefit from the Vitamin D, and warm climate. And if you don't mind, please take me with you."

Roger and Clair cut their eyes at each other and chuckled.

Harper's pager buzzed. "If you'll excuse me, that's the emergency room. We'll go over any last-minute questions tomorrow before discharge." Harper stooped to give Wallace a high five and shifted to the hallway.

She checked the urgent message from her friend Lazarus.

LAZARUS: Report to ER Bay 7. New patient with no ID. Elderly John Doe. Extreme critical condition.

Harper set her shoulders and took the steps down two flights to the ER. Entering the chaos, she maneuvered past guests gathered in the wide hallways with her head down, focused on the next task at hand as if traversing an obstacle course.

I bet our steaks are ready.

She sighed, and almost bumped into a short Korean man with glasses.

"Whoa, sorry, Laz. What's up?"

"Harper, did you see that fireman at bay three? He was checking you out. I could totally picture you with a fireman."

Harper rolled her eyes. Laz's receding hairline grew in direct proportion to his keen sense of humor.

"He can't check me out. I'm not a library book."

Laz crossed his arms. "Whatever. One of these days, I'll unearth your deep secrets to figure out why you've sworn off dating."

"Who has time for dating?" She pointed to the clock on the wall. "It's two hours past the end of my shift, Presley is nibbling on stale crackers for dinner, and my best bud Lazarus can't wait to assign me a fresh case." She patted him on the arm to confirm the tease.

Besides, she didn't have the energy to deal with the exposed nerve he struck.

I haven't sworn off men. Just the mean ones.

Laz grimaced. "Fine. Moving on. We've got an elderly hit-and-run victim dumped at an old fire station. We can't go any further with treatment without permission from next of kin. Do we keep him on the ventilator or let him go? He's not strong enough to withstand surgery, but if we find DNR papers, we'll have to discontinue treatment."

"Don't say that, Laz."

Laz shrugged his shoulders and raised his prominent eyebrows. "You're the best detective this side of the Mississippi."

"Laz, have you ever seen the other side of the Mississippi?"

He shook his head. "No, can't say that I have. Unless you count Korea."

Harper gave him a stern look.

Laz winked. "This side of the Mississippi. Heard that phrase in a John Wayne movie once. I'm gonna be just like him one day, Pilgrim."

"Yes, of course. The resemblance is uncanny. Now, where did this guy come from?"

"Chart shows they transported him from Madison. EMTs turned his clothes over to the police. On-scene tests indicate a traumatic brain injury plus seven broken bones and a punctured lung. I took his vitals. Everything's in the chart."

"There must be a reason he's still hanging on. Perhaps he's waiting to say goodbye to someone special."

"That's where you come in." He handed over the chart. "Good luck."

"Gee, thanks." Harper skimmed the notes, crammed her hands into latex gloves, and backed through the curtain.

The old man's appearance stopped her in her tracks.

His body—swollen, scraped, and battered—barely made a lump in the bed. His head was completely encased in bandages and a patch covered one eye. Tubes protruded in every direction. The skin on his arms looked paper thin—almost see-through—and was freezing cold to the touch. Pre-existing bruises mixed with new ones already formed near his IV.

His breaths remained slow and shallow, controlled by a ventilator. His face, what she could see of it, kept a pleasant appearance. If he could speak, Harper suspected he'd elbow her like old men do after they've said something clever.

Grabbing a blanket from the warmer, she covered his arms and spoke gently. "Good evening, sir. Looks like you've had a rough evening. I like to call people by name. How about Grandpa Doe?"

She scrawled his given patient name at the top of his chart and lifted the covers to confirm what Lazarus had documented for his height.

"About five foot three," she said aloud. "Weight, one hundred and twenty-seven. That's not enough, Grandpa

Doe. You clearly haven't been taking care of yourself, have you?"

In Harper's opinion, men didn't tend to live this long without a healthy dose of stubbornness and a wife.

"I don't suppose there's a Mrs. Doe is there? If she existed, she'd have the entire east coast on alert looking for you by now."

The permanent indention on his finger confirmed he wore a wedding ring but didn't necessarily corroborate a current marriage.

"I consider this a sign you once loved someone deeply. Right, Grandpa Doe? Your wedding ring must be with your belongings with the Madison Police Department." She made notes to check his personal items for clues to his identity.

Harper stretched his lips apart to examine his teeth around the hose of his ventilator. Dental records often proved vital when identifying unknown patients, usually after a pronounced time of death.

She shuddered at the thought and bit her lip as she logged into the computer. Laws were strict for releasing confidential information, but she documented enough details to flag the system state-wide when someone reported him missing. Nothing popped up as an immediate match, but surely someone would notice he was gone by morning.

She stood to leave, peering over her shoulder with regret. A part of her longed to stay.

"You remind me of a kind old man who used to wander around my hometown. Neither me nor my daughter would be here today if not for him. Promise you'll hang with me while we figure this out, okay? We'll move you to intensive care when a bed becomes available."

Harper sighed. She'd been in this position many times, feeling helpless and bothered by the lack of support her patients experienced outside the hospital. This case already felt different—more personal and frustrating.

The end result seemed inevitable.

"I may not be able to save your life, Grandpa Doe, but I promise to do everything I can to end it on your terms, surrounded by people who love you. May God bless your sweet soul, whoever you are."

CHAPTER FOUR

Raphael backed into one of the darkened bays of a random car wash. His heart raced with the memory of dumping the old man at the fire station two towns over. At the time, groans had escaped from the old man's bloody mouth.

A good sign.

After propping him against the entry door to the old fire hall, Raphael had hidden behind a hedge in a church parking lot down the road until an ambulance passed.

I'm sure he'll die tonight, but at least it won't be like an animal on the side of the road.

He'd accept the moral victory which provided a twisted sense of comfort.

Raphael clenched his fist and exited the car by jumping over the door—the feature he'd miss most about owning a convertible. He ran his fingers through his hair and circled the car. Quick breaths echoed off the metal walls of his hiding place, and he stepped into the light long enough to notice blood splayed over his coveralls and undershirt.

A new stream of tears found their way down his cheeks. The scene of the accident replayed on a loop in his mind, growing more vicious each time.

The thunk of the car smashing into him.

The look of terror in his eyes when he flipped into the air.

His pained moans when he landed.

The feel of the old man's hand as it brushed across Raphael's face.

Blood. So much blood.

The marginal weight of his lifeless body as Raphael lugged him across the fire station parking lot.

"It was an accident. I swear," he uttered into the darkness.

His cane! What happened to the old man's cane?

He looked through the back seat with no luck. He'd placed the old man's flat cap beside him at the fire station. Why? He'd never know. Everything had happened too fast.

Dead men don't need caps.

Raphael's phone buzzed with another call from Isabella. He declined it. She'd know something was wrong by the sound of his voice.

It's the worst day of your life, Isabella, and you don't even know it yet. Our lives have shattered since I kissed you goodbye this morning.

Headlights from a passing car stretched across the metal wall behind him, picking up the reflective lettering on his coveralls. He dropped to his knees. The last thing he needed was a bystander to place him, the Majestic uniform, or his jacked-up vehicle in the area.

His eyes widened.

My gym bag.

He popped open the trunk and removed his work boots, stepping out of the car wash bay to survey them under a streetlight. Droplets of blood mixed in with oil and dust from the job site.

I might as well throw these away. Won't need them anymore.

He hurled the boots one at a time into his trunk and changed into shorts, a tank top, and tennis shoes. Stuffing his coveralls and shirt into the gym bag, he tossed it on top of the boots until he could figure out how to dispose of them.

He squeezed his eyes shut and prepared to check out the damage to his car. The glass on the passenger's side of the windshield was punched in like the eye of a hurricane with a perfect indention of the old man's head. Cracks spiderwebbed out from the indent. The front grill had a noticeable chunk missing, and a heavy dent defaced the hood. Blood pooled across the white leather of his back seat forming streaks where Raphael had hoisted the old man out of the car.

Still, the car remained drivable. A plus.

Raphael dug through his toolbox to find a mallet and pounded out the dent in the hood. He opened the hard-core cleaning products provided by Majestic and scrubbed his back seat from top to bottom. Tying the bloody rags into a plastic bag, he added it to the growing pile of guilt in his trunk.

Pushing the button to extend the convertible top, he fished out enough coins from his console to run the car through the automatic wash. He turned the key to start the engine and soon, streams of water crashed around the vehicle, jarring it back and forth. The fruity scent of soap drifted through the air vents, and Raphael let out a scream.

I almost killed a man. I'm here in this country illegally. What am I supposed to do? Flee to another state?

He lifted a photo from his visor of his family posing on their front steps for this year's first day of school. All four-and-a-half of them. Isabella's hand rested on her tummy in the photo. Zander looked over his shoulder to show off his new backpack for kindergarten, and Xavier stuck out his tongue. In the photo, Raphael beamed with pride.

Was this only two weeks ago?

Raphael tucked the picture in place as the car wash chugged through its last cycle. His head dropped in shame.

Truth. My family deserves the truth.

Water trickled down the windows as he drove out the other side. He lifted his phone to call home. Isabella answered on the first ring.

"Raphael, are you okay? I've been trying to reach you for hours. Boomer finally answered but could only tell me you'd left work early."

"Hey, baby, I'm sorry I'm so late. Are the kids in bed?"

"You know they are. They've got school tomorrow."

"Okay. I'll explain everything when I get home. I love you."

He ended the call before she peppered him with questions.

Raphael took the long way home, crisscrossing his route to swing past garbage bins and disposing of one item at a time from his trunk.

He hoped getting rid of the evidence might put his mind at ease.

No such luck.

Harper inched through the side door to her kitchen and slipped off her shoes. "Hey, Squirt. Why is every light in the house turned on?" She glanced into the living room and rolled her eyes. "And why are your clothes scattered everywhere?"

No answer.

Harper bounded up the stairs to her daughter's loft bedroom. She knocked on the door, bumping it open without waiting for a response. Brewster, a teacup Yorkie, launched himself off Presley's bed to greet Harper.

Presley, cuddled under a slew of pillows, took her time tugging yellow earbuds out of her ears.

"Hey, there," Harper said, reminding herself not to sound too irritated. "Did you happen to do any of the things I asked when I texted you?"

Presley shook her head. "Wait, I did let Brewster out, but in my defense, you got home quicker than I expected." She painted on a smile of innocence.

"Well, I brought us steaks. Meet me downstairs." Harper pursed her lips when she noticed the gray ears of an old stuffed bunny protruding from the covers. "Where did you get that bunny?"

"From a box in the garage. Next week is Spirit Week at school, so I was rifling through old Halloween costumes. Sidney and I are trying to match. I found him in a carton of yearbooks. He's so cute."

"That's Ginger. And he's a she."

"Fine. Ginger is staying with me. She's deserves better than living in a box."

Harper shrugged. "Maybe Ginger can help you put away your clothes. If your closet isn't big enough to contain them, it might be time to give some away."

Presley smirked. "I agree completely."

Harper twisted her mouth in response. "Yeah, sure you do. See you in a minute. I want to hear about your day."

Harper arranged the steaks in the oven to keep them warm and tender before settling on the sofa. She called out to Presley, "You remember my stories of a man named Solomon from when I grew up? I think he died years ago, but I met a patient tonight who reminds me of him."

No response, other than the sound of Presley singing at the top of her lungs to old Elvis songs, one of the few loves Harper had passed down to her daughter. Typical teenager—glued to her earbuds as if they provided oxygen through her ears.

Harper thumbed through a stack of junk mail on the table. Her eyes felt heavy, and she propped her head on her fist. Within seconds, she'd drifted off to sleep.

Easter 1987

Five-year-old Harper gripped her parents' hands and skipped between them, pigtails flopping from side to side to the rhythm of the ringing church bells. The scent of her mother's lemon perfume tickled her nose. Her father marched beside her, tall and serious in his dark blue army uniform. Her mother's heels clicked against the sidewalk. Mama was blonde, shorter, and rounder than Harper's father. Wearing a flowered dress and a fancy hat, her mother stopped to fiddle with the massive bow on Harper's head.

"Be still. Your bow is lopsided, sweetie."

Harper wrinkled her nose but did as she was told.

A large brick building loomed on a hillside overlooking the town of Ginger Ridge. Next to the bell tower stood three wooden crosses, the center one draped in purple. The sign along the edge of the street read, "On the third day, He rose. Join us on Easter Sunday for the rest of His story."

At Harper's request, Mama read those words aloud every time they passed the church. Now, Harper had them memorized and announced them in a series of dramatic voices. She switched to her schoolteacher voice.

"On the third day—"

"Hush, child," her father scolded. "You are such a chatterbox."

Harper stuck out her lip. Mama offered a nervous laugh and intervened. "This church has an outstanding program for kids. Today, they're holding an Easter egg hunt and a potluck dinner on the grounds after church."

"What kind of luck? And what if the new kids don't like me?" Harper asked.

"Don't be ridiculous," her father snapped. "It's not our job to make people like us."

Mama patted her on the head. "Holy Moses, Harper, how could anyone not like you? You are stunning from head to toe. People love to be around pretty girls."

Her mother repeated those words often, but they confused Harper every time. What if someone didn't think she was pretty? Would they still be her friend?

Harper spotted an older gentleman carrying a basket on one arm and poking a cane around the bushes with the other. She pulled free from her parents' grasp to scurry toward him.

"Hi, mister. My name's Harper. What's yours?"

"Well, good morning, Miss Harper. My name's Solomon. Nice to meet you."

"I'm new here. Why come you gotta walk with that cane? Is this your church? Do you live close by?"

He kneeled to look her in the eye. "Wow! So many questions." He pointed to a house behind the church. "That's where I live—the one with the big front porch.

My leg hasn't worked the same since I was injured a long time ago, so I use this cane to keep my balance. I've been coming to this church for the last decade."

"A decade? Is that a hundred years?" she asked.

He gave a full belly laugh. "Feels like it, sometimes. I've experienced many lifetimes and traveled across the world, but there's no place I'd rather be than right here in Ginger Ridge. Are you staying for the Easter egg hunt?"

Harper bobbed her head and clapped her hands.

Solomon continued, "Wonderful! They asked me to hide a few of these eggs." He lowered the basket for her to peek. On top lay a large, golden egg, twice as big as the others. "The golden egg contains the best prize."

Harper's blue eyes widened. "Wow! Will you put it somewhere I can reach?"

Solomon winked. "You bet. You'd better get to Sunday school. Just follow those steps."

"Harper, get over here!" her father yelled, causing her to jump. "How many times have I told you not to speak to strangers? You'll wear them out, talking so much."

She stuck out her lip. "I gotta go, Mr. Solomon. Daddy says I talk too much when I get nervous. Thank you for being my first friend here at Ginger Ridge."

A few hours later, following a yummy picnic with fried chicken and biscuits, Harper stood in triumph on the top step beside Solomon in front of the red church doors.

"And now I present this Easter basket to Miss Harper Phillips for finding the golden egg. May God bless you with the many gifts of the story of Easter."

Harper wrapped her arms around the old man's neck. Inside the Easter basket was an oversized, lop-eared stuffed bunny with big blue eyes. Harper hugged the gray bunny and buried her face in it. Someone jumped in front of them to snap their picture. She grinned, and Solomon lifted his cane into the air.

"Thank you, Mr. Solomon. I'll name my bunny Ginger, after our new hometown. We already love it here!"

Harper woke to the slam of the oven door. Her mouth had grown dry, and so had the trail of slobber that leaked from one corner onto the pillow Presley must have settled beneath her head on the sofa. She squinted to check her surroundings and propped to a sitting position.

"Sorry, Mom. I ate without you. I figured you needed sleep more than food." Presley clapped a set of oven mitts together. "Yours is still warm if you want me to bring it to you."

"Yes, please. What time is it?"

"After ten."

"I definitely need both. Sleep and food. I was just dreaming about that old bunny you found in the garage. I haven't thought about Ginger in years. The bunny or the town I named her after."

Presley dropped a fork and giggled as she bent to pick it up. "Five-second rule."

Harper spread a blanket across her lap. Presley handed over the tray of food and a bottled water. She snuggled in next to her mother and put her feet on the coffee table, making Harper's suspicions arise.

"What is this? You're choosing to spend time with your tired old mama?"

Presley smirked. "I'm one of the few who still claim to enjoy it. But speaking of Ginger Ridge. I've been looking through your old yearbooks. When are you going to let me in on all your secrets? Why haven't we ever gone back for a visit? You look so happy in all your school photos."

"Goodness, Squirt. I can't think straight enough to face your stream of questions tonight. One of these days, I'll fill you in, when the time is right. But know this. Looks can sure be deceiving."

CHAPTER FIVE

Pulling into a spot reserved for clergy, Brock Timberland took one last gulp of his morning thirst-quencher from the local Drive & Shine market. After a few weeks into his new role as an official minister, he considered this another habit he should kick.

Extra caffeinated cola for breakfast? In a cup larger than my head? What could be biblically wrong with that?

A few religious terms came to mind. Gluttony, laziness, and a growing sugar addiction sent the wrong message. The buttons on his shirt tightened around his belly in agreement.

In the safe confines of his silver pickup, he tucked a New Testament in his shirt pocket and checked his reflection in the mirror. Brown hair thinned in front, but choppy spikes did their best to hide the evidence. Squinting his deep blue eyes, he wondered if they'd ever recover the mischievous twinkle he often used to his advantage. His smile still felt forced most of the time.

Divorce has that effect on people.

Brock sighed. His would become final within days, with or without his signature. Kelly filed papers long before he saw it coming, and his brain still struggled with a future he didn't choose.

One thing he knew for sure. Kelly would no longer be a part of that future.

Kelly.

Her name still knocked him senseless. A fresh reminder of what a fool he'd been. He shook his head and tried on a pair of glasses—on and off until he decided to keep them on.

Deacon says they make me look smart, like a preacher.

Brock shut the visor and tensed his shoulders. He set an alarm on his phone with a reminder to pick Deacon up from kindergarten. Time management had become an ongoing struggle since his honorable discharge from the US Army. He still found unsettling that the military no longer dictated his every move. Turned out, he craved the stiff sense of direction and preferred a set of defined expectations for each day.

Instead, here he was, making it up as he went along—in search of a sense of purpose or someone who needed prayer, whichever came first.

I'd choose sunrise PT drills any day.

Brock skulked out of the truck and slammed the door on the angst that begged him to abort the mission. His steady stride took him through the main entrance of Savannah Regional Hospital in no time. With his untucked shirt and lightly distressed jeans, he resembled more of a rock band front man than a broken man in his late thirties posing as a minister.

At the front desk, he broadened his public smile and waited his turn.

"Good morning. How may I help you?"

He took in the nameplate of the unnatural redhead perched on a stool and dug out a business card with an upturned corner from the pocket of his jeans. "Good morning, Rosie. I'm Brock Timberland, a minister from a town called Ginger Ridge, about forty miles northwest of here. I promised a lady at church I'd pray with her mother this week. She's supposed to be a patient here."

She peered over a set of librarian glasses at him with her fingers at the ready on her keyboard. "Her name?"

Brock winced. "About that. Funny story."

Rosie cocked her head and didn't appear to agree with him.

He whipped out a crumpled piece of paper to show her. "See, I wrote down her name, but my son scribbled over my notes. Her first name is Nancy and her last name starts with a W. She's in ICU." He shrugged. "I drove an hour to pray for someone named Nancy, so I will do it."

Rosie raised her eyebrows. "You're asking me to find someone named Nancy for you to pray over? Is this correct?"

Brock gave her a slow nod.

"I'm sure I can find someone for you. I guess you and God can work out the details later." She pursed her lips and scrolled through her computer screen. "How about Nancy Werther? Sound familiar? She's in room 833 in ICU."

Brock thought it over, then took off his glasses to lean in close.

"Does it matter Werther she's the right one or not?" He used air quotes around the word Werther and grinned.

Rosie remained emotionless. "You're new at this preacher thing, aren't you?"

"Yes. What gave it away? I can assure you I'm a better pastor than a joke-teller."

"I should hope so."

He straightened. "Ouch, Rosie. You hurt me. Just for that, I'll add you to my prayer list. What's your last name?"

"Would you remember if I told you?"

Brock crinkled his nose and backed toward the elevator. "I guess I deserved that. Rosie, you're the funniest person I've met this week. Thank you."

Impressed with her spunk, he pushed the up button and waited. Finally, a set of doors opened at the far end of the elevator bay.

By that time, he'd forgotten the room number. He poked his head around the corner and called out to his new friend.

"Rosie, what was the room number again?"

She brought her finger to her lips to shush him and approached in angry strides. "Here you go, Pastor Timberland. Don't lose it on the elevator." She passed him a card with the requested information scrawled on it.

He detected half a smile as she shifted away.

That's the kind of direction I've missed since my discharge from the army.

He pressed the button once again and waited as a genuine smile spread across his face.

Harper breezed in from the parking lot.

"Good morning, Rosie. I hope you got my note. Please tell me Grandpa Doe is still with us ..."

A red-headed fixture at the front desk, Rosie was repositioning herself in her chair. Her expression never changed, and her voice remained strong even in the direst circumstances. Harper often bragged every trauma center in the country should have a Rosie guarding its doors.

She looked at Harper. "Good morning. Yes, he's here. Grandpa Doe has relocated to the Intensive Care Unit. Room 815."

Harper clapped her hands. "Oh, thank goodness. I'm not too late. You know where to find me."

Rosie gave an understanding nod. "I'll take any messages, as per usual."

Harper scurried to the elevators and pressed the up button. She tossed her head forward to gather her damp hair into a loose bun before it frizzed.

She heard the doors drag open before she was ready.

"Going up?"

Harper caught a man with glasses poking his head out at the far end. She rushed to jump on as the doors lurched closed.

"Yes, thank you. Eighth floor, please."

The man ran his fingers through his choppy, disheveled hair. "That's where I'm headed. Here to see a friend, I guess you could say."

Why does this stranger assume he owes me an explanation?

She humored the man and kept a pleasant expression, reminding herself not to treat him as an annoyance.

Lazarus often accused her of blowing men off if they came on too strong. Of course, her first goal was to prove him wrong.

The stranger continued, "I'm a member of the clergy, according to your reserved parking signs. Here to visit the mother of one of my church members."

Harper squeezed her eyes shut before he caught them rolling. She forced a smile. "That's so kind of you."

She took in a deep breath and gritted her teeth as the elevator chugged past the fourth floor.

Halfway there.

The man continued to fill the silence. "My name's Brock Timberland. I had time on my hands and thought I'd drive to Savannah."

Harper took her eyes off the light that outlined the number eight to return the favor. "Harper Phillips. Nice to meet you. I'm a case worker here at the hospital." As the elevator dinged on the eighth floor, she breathed a sigh of relief. "Here we are. Have a lovely day."

She leaned forward to make her escape and almost crashed into the doors that stammered open at their own pace.

"Wait. Could you point me to room 833?"

"Sure. Right this way." Harper took off with long strides.

"Are we in a hurry?" the stranger asked, hustling to keep up.

"Most of the time, it seems. Sorry about that." She slowed to fall in stride with him as they passed the room of Grandpa Doe. "I'm playing a waiting game, so I'm not even sure why I'm hurrying. Nervous energy, I suppose. Forgive me for being rude."

"No problem. I'm former military. I'm drawn to rude people." His eyes grew wide, and Harper drew her head back in surprise. She couldn't help but grin.

"You caught me off guard with that one, but I deserved it." She stopped in front of room 833 and motioned for Brock to enter. "Here you go. I hope your friend gets better soon."

Brock rested his hand on the door handle. "Thanks. This shouldn't take long. Got anybody else you need me to pray for while I'm at it?"

Harper paused for a moment and snapped her fingers, causing him to flinch. "I sure do. You say you've got time on your hands, right?"

The stranger tilted his head. "Lay it on me."

"Great. Meet me in room 815 when you're done. I've got the perfect patient for you."

Brock eased into the room, careful not to disturb the lump in the bed known as Nancy Werther. He leaned in to confirm that it was indeed an elderly lady with her eyes closed. The room remained eerily quiet.

"Please tell me you're still breathing," he whispered, kneeling beside her to close his eyes. "Dear God, please be with Nancy, who is obviously struggling with health issues. Hopefully, she's the mother of one of our church members. If not, please bring her peace and comfort. We could all use an extra dose of that. Amen."

He opened his eyes to discover a bald doctor had tiptoed in to wait by the door.

"Sorry to interrupt. I need to check Ms. Werther's vital signs."

Good. I'm not sure she has any.

Brock stopped himself from blurting out his thoughts. Another habit he planned to get under control soon.

"Yes, please do."

The doctor cleared his throat in that condescending way he must have learned in medical school. "That was quite a prayer. I've got to ask—do you even know this patient?"

Brock shrugged. "I guess I do now. I'll show myself out. Thank you."

He avoided the eyes of the doctor and escaped into the hallway. Pausing in front of room 815, he peered through the window and tapped on the door. Harper motioned him to enter.

"That was quick. Thank you," she said.

In a loving way, she ran her fingers across what little skin was visible on the patient's face as if he belonged to her.

"This unidentified patient was brought in last night. I refer to him as Grandpa Doe. He's a hit-and-run victim dumped at a fire station." She spoke faster as she shared his story. "It's my job to find out who he is and where he belongs. As of now, no one knows he's here, so he could use a visitor and extra prayers, Reverend Timberland."

A sense of urgency shadowed her face.

"Please call me Brock. I'm no reverend and may not be a minister long enough to earn an official title."

Harper tilted her head, as if requesting more details. "So, you're new to the business, I take it?"

Brock lifted his hands in an overstated shrug. "Interim. It's a long story I won't burden you with today. But yes, I've got time, and I'd be thrilled to sit with your friend."

She scooted a chair to the bed. "Perfect. Have a seat and tell my friend here whatever you want. He's a great listener. I've been reading to him and playing music. Studies show patients can hear us, even when in a comatose state."

Brock wiggled in the chair until he got comfortable. "Well, I can talk with the best of them, so I guess I'm your guy."

Harper grinned. "I noticed. I'll be back in an hour. I've got to discharge a patient."

She scurried out the door.

Brock clasped his hands behind his head and launched into a dialog with the old man.

"Nice to meet you, Grandpa Doe. You and I have something in common. Like you, I seem to have hit a rough patch in life. I guess I'll start at the beginning." He propped his feet against the lower bedrail. "Until six months ago, I served as a chaplain in the United States Army, on month three of a nine-month stint stationed in

Germany. I left behind a beautiful, loyal wife named Kelly and the best five-year-old who ever lived, Deacon."

Brock's stomach burned as he recounted the memories. He stood to pace, letting out pent-up energy. His voice grew louder as he went on.

"One morning, first thing, I opened my phone to find a message. 'I'm done. Deacon is at your mother's. Sorry it didn't work out between us.'"

The cruelty of his story caught him off guard and his eyes filled with tears. He drew in a deep breath.

"I later discovered she'd ridden off into the sunset on some guy's motorcycle. Got a better offer, I guess. Haven't heard from her since, but her lawyer often sends his regards."

He checked the old man for a response. The silence in the room overpowered the beeps from machines, making Brock uncomfortable. He kept talking to fill the silence.

"I took an honorable discharge, retrieved my son, and my divorce will be final in a few weeks." He nodded as if the old man responded in some way.

"How did I become a minister, you ask? Funny story. With no job and no home, I found a dying church embroiled in a frantic search for a leader. At one time, this church was vibrant—the hub of a town called Ginger Ridge. I guess I'm their last gasp attempt to save themselves. In return, they provided a place for Deacon and me to live for one year. I see no signs of life in our church, but it buys time to get my act together."

Brock patted the old man's hand.

"I know what you're thinking. That really sucks. You'd be correct with that assumption."

Brock rubbed his hands together. "Are preachers supposed to say sucks? Sorry. I haven't located my Minister Manual. I'll add that to my list of habits to break."

The tension in Brock's shoulders relaxed. He checked his watch and stared out the window.

"Thanks for listening, Grandpa Doe. My apologies. I'm slowly teaching myself to focus on others. Mind if I pray for you?"

CHAPTER SIX

Standing in line, waiting for the public library doors to open, Raphael lowered the brim of his ball cap. The previous night, he'd stored his Mustang in a friend's garage where he often worked on vehicles. Borrowing a clunker in the meantime, Raphael assumed he'd have the library to himself on a Friday morning, but a group of slow-moving senior citizens beat him to the punch.

He pretended to scan a magazine before grabbing the last available computer desk in a back corner.

Old folks and free Wi-Fi ... I should have known.

With a gnawing sense someone might view his screen, he scrolled through national news sites before launching his search for replacement auto parts. He decided to purchase online rather than in person where security cameras might do him in. And he'd chosen to come to the library instead of using his home computer, providing a brief respite from Isabella's constant stream of questions.

Raphael made his selections, paid for expedited shipping, and shoved his credit card into his pocket.

I've got twenty-nine days left. Expedite everything.

He lowered his head and exited through a side door, never taking a breath until he settled into the borrowed, two-toned Pinto. He pushed the button on his phone to return a missed call from his wife.

She answered immediately. "Raphael, where are you?"

"I had some business to take care of, but I'm heading home. Why don't we take a walk by the river? I know you have many questions after our talk last night."

"Okay. I'll get ready."

Gravel popping like popcorn bounced beneath him as he traveled the long, winding driveway to their log cabin. Built to Isabella's specifications by his own hands, the wrap-around porch was currently littered with shoes and toys. The crown jewel inside was the massive island in the kitchen where Isabella created the most amazing dinners— better than any he'd ever tasted from a restaurant. An upstairs hallway led to the bedrooms where the boys found ways to sleep anywhere except their own rooms. Dormer windows spread across the front, which allowed natural lighting down below. Behind the house stood a detached, three-car garage and a treehouse, a zip-line, and several acres of woods with a creek for them to explore.

True paradise.

Isabella waited for him on the front steps, topping the view off to perfection. Her long, dark hair rested over one shoulder as their eyes met. Despite everything he'd thrown at her, she still carried a spirit of trust.

I don't deserve this woman.

Her expression changed to one of confusion when she noticed the car he drove. He pulled to a stop and stuck his head out the window.

"Raphael, where is your Mustang?"

He gulped. "At Jason's garage. I'm getting it repainted, so he let me borrow this junker."

She rolled her eyes. "That thing's dreadful. Let's take my car instead."

Half an hour later, they strolled on a paved trail at the riverfront. Raphael slowed his pace for Isabella as she recapped their conversation from the previous night.

"Now that I've had time to absorb it all, let me get this straight." Isabella turned to face him. "Your true name isn't Raphael Henry?"

Raphael cocked his head. "Yes and no. My H-1B Visa and driver's license, which are official documents, both show Raphael Henry. My original name on my Mexican Consular Card shows Enrique Raphael. I reversed the names and Americanized the last name to Henry."

Isabella gave him a blank stare. "It's too much to comprehend. What about your parents? Is this why we never visited them in their Mexican beach town?"

Raphael's heart sank.

Oh. I'd forgotten about that one.

He shook his head. "There are two truths I need to set straight here. First, I don't recall my parents ever being together as a couple. Second, they never lived in a hideaway resort town. I barely remember my father. I firmly believe if he'd stuck around, I would have stayed in Mexico."

Isabella wrung her hands and stared across the water that shimmered like diamonds under the morning sun. A tear rolled down her cheek, and Raphael caught it with his thumb.

His voice cracked when he spoke. "Isabella, when I crossed the border in El Paso, I was a terrified sixteen-year-old. I'd been plotting my escape since I was a kid."

Isabella held up her hand to stop him. "I know that, Raphael. But you're illegal, and you've been lying to me all these years. What am I supposed to do with this information? It no longer affects only you."

Raphael shrugged. "You can do what I'm doing with it. Focus on the things you know to be true about me. On the person I am today."

"But that truth is all built on lies."

Raphael held her shoulders and drew his face close to hers. "No, it's not. You know the man I turned out to be. For Zander, Xavier, and soon, Baby Evelyn, I am the father I always craved. The father I always needed. I used my pain and emptiness to make their lives better."

Isabella bit her lip—her sign she was about to lose it. Raphael led her to a nearby bench. Her silence freaked him out, so he spoke faster as if it might keep her tears at bay.

"In Mexico, I roamed from town to town, on my own since I was twelve. The wrong crowd had their eyes on me. One gang tapped me to be their leader, which required me to kill a man for the fun of it. So, I fled. I wanted something different. I found work at construction sites. One of my supervisors took me under his wing, taught me what I know today, and encouraged me to come to America—the land of dreams." Raphael's voice faded at the memory of it.

Isabella sat in silence, refusing to look at him. "You should have told me," she whispered.

Raphael threw his hands into the air. "If you knew my background, would you have agreed to marry me? Would your father have allowed it? Your family is close, supportive, and you've got that fancy college degree. You deserved someone as good as you are, and I believed I could grow into that person. To be the kind of man who deserves such a woman." He caressed her cheek. "Look at the life we've built together. I never dreamed it could be so wonderful."

Isabella jumped up in a huff, stumbling when her sandal caught the edge of the sidewalk. Raphael grabbed her elbow to steady her, but she jerked away.

"Stop it." Her voice quivered. "Now is not the time to remind me how great our life is. You're making it worse since I'm about to lose you."

Her words brought a well-deserved kick in the gut.

"Raphael, you got us into this mess, now what are you going to do about it? How are you planning to fix it?"

He had no answers. Yet.

Isabella knew it. She waddled up the embankment and paced in angry circles beside her old sedan. He'd never seen her so angry.

It takes her a while to process. She needs time and space.

He said nothing, unlocking the passenger's side door for her. She slammed it hard, narrowly missing his fingers as he yanked them out of the way.

As Raphael settled into the driver's seat, he popped on his sunglasses and tried to change the subject. "You hungry? Want me to swing through a drive-thru before we get the boys from school?"

Isabella shook her head and reached for the knob on the radio, turning it up loud to keep him from talking.

Raphael had it programmed to talk radio, which he credited for teaching him to speak English. As a result, he often forced the use of large vocabulary words where they didn't belong. Under normal conditions, Isabella called him out on this practice and giggled until he guessed the right meaning for each word he'd used in error.

It's worth a try.

"Do we agree on a bipartisan motion to discuss this at a later time?"

Facing the window, Isabella shook her head. She turned the radio up another notch as the mid-day news kicked in.

"Authorities are seeking information on the driver of a vehicle used in a hit-and-run that left an eighty-year-old man in critical condition last night. They believe the accident took place near Madison and currently have few clues to go on. Please call the Madison Police Department—"

Raphael shoved in a CD and started singing along with Xavier's favorite nursery rhymes, cutting his eyes toward his wife. Isabella rested her hands on her oversized belly and kept her eyes closed.

She's either praying or plotting my demise. There's no way I can tell her about the old man right now. One battle at a time, and the radio said they have no leads.

He patted his wife on the leg to reassure them both.

Maybe I won't have to tell her at all.

CHAPTER SEVEN

Harper rubbed at a ball of tension forming in her neck as she returned to the eighth floor. Brock Timberland remained where she left him—beside Grandpa Doe with one leg crossed over the other as if they were watching a ballgame together.

"Hello. You're still here? I figured it out. I think I'm going to call you Rev. Does that sound okay?"

"Sure. Why not?" Brock checked his watch. "By the way, you said you'd be back in an hour. That was three hours ago. At first, you came across as an honest person." He flashed a mischievous grin. "I guess first impressions can be wrong."

"I apologize. My day gets away from me quickly. We discharged a four-year-old pediatric cancer patient today, so we threw together a celebration parade for him on his way out."

Brock's tone grew more serious. "I'm sorry. I have a son about that age, and I can't imagine him being sick."

Harper shook her head and changed the subject. "Thank you for staying with Grandpa Doe for so long. If nothing else, you made *me* feel better."

"We had much to discuss. I presume this old guy is filled with wisdom, and it did my heart good to talk to him. Let me show you something."

Brock moved to a table at the foot of the bed and flipped open a spiral-bound journal to the first page. "At the gift shop, I picked up this notebook and pen. I left a message with my name and cell phone number."

Harper's eyes filled with tears. "Thank you. I'll hang your message on the wall so he can see it if he wakes up."

Brock's watch beeped. "I've got to pick up my kinder-monster. That's what I call him, though Deacon is the best kid around. He's at a new school, and we made a deal I'd always be near the front of the pick-up line. He'd never forgive me if I'm late."

"Oh, I remember those days well. My daughter will be driving soon, so I've graduated to much bigger concerns."

"No, thanks. I'm content with my five-year-old battles." He grabbed the door handle and looked over his shoulder. "Do you have a direct line? Could I call to find out how Grandpa Doe is doing?"

"Of course." Harper jotted down her cell number on a business card. "I'm never at my desk. Feel free to leave a message on my cell phone."

She ushered him to the elevator as they spoke.

"All right, I'll touch base in a few days. I'll have our congregation in Ginger Ridge pray for Grandpa Doe on Sunday."

Harper gasped.

"Miss Phillips, are you okay?"

A gurgling noise rattled from her throat. She bolted to the water fountain and gulped down enough to buy her some time. Her head buzzed with a montage of memories of Ginger Ridge. She finally raised her head to discover Brock standing wide-eyed with his mouth open.

"What did I say?"

"I apologize. You said you're from Ginger Ridge?"

He gave a slow nod as if afraid to answer.

"I haven't heard my hometown mentioned in ages. I took off after high school and never returned."

Brock leaned closer. "You aren't the only one who left. Ginger Ridge has become a ghost town since Fort Bryce shut down. That doesn't bode well for my church."

Harper winced. "I know that church well. My first Sunday in town, I found the golden egg during the Easter egg hunt and won a big stuffed bunny. After that, I was hooked. Not all memories from Ginger Ridge are bad I suppose."

Brock dug his hands in his pockets. "I hope not. The church contracted me for a year as a minister to rescue the congregation. We have that enormous, boarded-up sanctuary. There's so few of us, I had to drive an hour to find someone who needed prayer, and I'm not even sure I got the right person." Brock shrugged and rubbed his hand across his chin.

Harper raised her eyebrows, and a smile escaped before she realized it.

Brock interrupted her thoughts. "I'd love nothing more than to return the church and the community to its former glory." His watch beeped again, and he squeezed into an elevator as the doors snapped shut. "I'm sorry I upset you. Keep in touch. Talk to you lat—"

"Bye, Rev. Nice to meet you," Harper called out.

She stared at the doors long after he was gone, chastising herself for becoming so emotional.

What has happened to you, Harper Phillips? Get your act together.

She sighed and returned to room 815. With a sheet of paper from the notebook, she crafted a name tag to fasten outside the door to match the other patient rooms.

She scribbled a note of her own and added it to the wall before dashing out the door for her next appointment.

Dear Grandpa Doe,

My name is Harper, and I'm honored to be your friend. You remind me of an older gentleman in my hometown who I once loved dearly. He knew how to guide me in the right direction.

I wish you'd do the same. Show me how to help you and where to find your family. They must miss you terribly.

I promise to do my best if you'll keep fighting along with me.

Harper

MARCH 1965

Solomon stood in a daze, heartbroken. His dark suit was now drenched due to an unexpected afternoon shower, which he barely noticed.

Sadie Beth buried her face in his neck. Solomon moved her to the opposite hip and brushed his hand through her hair. Both of them had run out of tears.

"We're going to be okay, Daddy. We still have each other. Maybe God needed Mommy and Baby Silas more than we did." Her voice sounded much wiser than her years.

He hated that for his young daughter. She deserved the carefree innocence of youth like every other child.

They were the only ones remaining at the mound of fresh dirt on side-by-side graves. Solomon had asked the minister for a few minutes alone, but an hour passed, and he wasn't sure how to leave.

The abyss waiting at home terrified him.

So, he remained in place. Frozen. Unable to move forward. Unable to move at all. Instead, he relived every moment shared with Winnie.

They were in grade school when she first asked his name on the playground. He remembered rope jumping off a tire swing in the creek as teenagers and teaching her how to drive in a vacant parking lot. He'd left her to join the army, but soon returned to present her with an engagement ring at Christmas.

Winnie had convinced him their marriage was more important than a wedding. "I want to be with you, Solomon. Wherever that takes us. The sooner, the better."

One Friday evening in June, after an impromptu wedding at the church she'd grown up in, they loaded everything they owned into a pickup truck he'd bought off the corner lot with six months' worth of paychecks. Instead of a honeymoon, they made their first voyage as husband and wife to the married housing unit of Fort Lansing in Missouri.

The ten years since had passed swiftly.

Military life had not been easy, but Winnie remained a trooper—stronger than any soldier he'd ever known. She believed in Solomon and tackled each transition with loyalty and pride in his accomplishments.

She never shined brighter than the day a grenade sent him reeling, leaving him severely burned and unable to walk. He gave Winnie credit for praying him back to life. His recovery had been long and tortuous, but his limbs were intact, so they were fortunate.

He'd never forget waking up in a military hospital in the states to see her face after a few months apart. Her hair had grown long and curled more than he remembered. Tears poured from her eyes, but she beamed with pride.

"My husband is home safe, my prayers have been answered, and all is right with the world!" she'd announced as if none of what had happened was up for discussion.

Solomon had taken her hands in his, feeling the urge to taper her enthusiasm. He still had a long road ahead and hated for her to gloss over the seriousness of his injuries. But he was no match for the one-two punch of Winnie and her God. Nobody was.

She'd placed her finger against his lips.

"Hush, now. This is a place of miracles and healing. Keep your negative thoughts to yourself, and let's focus on our future."

Her eyes glistened as one hand rested against her stomach. It took him a few moments to grasp what she was trying to tell him.

He gasped. "Winnie, we're having a baby?"

Her eyes twinkled as she kissed him around the bandages on his face. Solomon held her tight and sobbed in her arms.

"I'm still alive, and we're having a baby!"

She cupped his chin in her hand. "Now you're talking. We are blessed, and every day we get to spend together is a gift."

Wisdom fell from Winnie's lips with little effort.

After their daughter was born, Solomon fought hard to regain his strength and recovered to the point he only walked with a limp. His injuries kept him stateside, and he transferred to a long-term assignment at Fort Bryce, where they finally bought a house.

They'd barely gotten settled in their new home in Ginger Ridge when Winnie announced she was expecting again. Sadie Beth had just turned five. Solomon and Winnie threw their energy into preparing their third bedroom as a nursery, letting Sadie Beth choose the colors. Winnie never doubted this one would be a boy, and even crafted the name Silas on the door in blue and gold block letters.

One day, Solomon had caught sight of his wife as she and Sadie Beth painted the walls in the corner. Sun filtered through the window to illuminate her face, and Solomon didn't like what he saw. Her eyes were weak, her skin ashen.

"Winnie, let's move outside for some fresh air. You don't look so good, darlin'."

Winnie didn't put up a fight. "That's a good idea. My doctor cautioned me about low iron in my blood test results, so he switched my vitamins. I'm sleepy, as usual, but I'll be fine."

Solomon led her to the front porch. Sadie Beth hurried ahead of them to hold the door open. Winnie rested in a rickety patio chair they'd picked up at a garage sale and drew in slow, deep breaths while fanning herself with a magazine.

"Let me get you a glass of lemonade." Solomon scurried to the kitchen and returned with a frosty glass of her favorite beverage.

Winnie smiled as she sipped it. "So refreshing. Thank you."

Solomon sat across from her. Sadie Beth crawled into his lap, causing the table to wobble between them.

"This patio set has seen better days, for sure."

Winnie lowered her eyelashes. The twinkle slowly returned to her deep-set eyes.

"You know what this porch needs? A swing. Right over there in the corner. And a rocker on this side."

"Yes, a swing." Sadie Beth clapped her hands. "That way, I can do both of my favorite things at the same time. Swing and read books."

Solomon tapped his foot. He never stood a chance when his girls teamed up against him.

"Okay, I'll find a porch swing first thing tomorrow."

And he did.

They spent the next couple of months swinging together each evening, going over plans for the baby's arrival.

One afternoon, Winnie called him in a tizzy. She had gone into labor while sitting on that swing. Solomon rushed home from work, bumping the oak tree when he careened into the front yard a few minutes later. They made it in plenty of time to the hospital at Fort Bryce, which boasted the best doctors in the world.

He'd never fully understand what went so wrong after that. The doctors used medical terms like grand mal seizure and limited oxygen supply, but the words made no sense to him.

Women have babies all the time. How could he lose them both?

Winnie had been right, as usual. It was a boy.

Solomon named their son Silas as she wished. But instead of bringing them home to nestle in the rocking chair he'd given her, Winnie and Silas rested on a hill underneath a tree at the Gardens of Ginger Ridge.

Side by side. Forever.

Solomon no longer remembered how to breathe, much less how to pray.

For Sadie Beth's sake, he had to figure out a way to do both.

"Sweetheart, are you ready to go home?"

She held his face in her hands like her mother used to do and gave him a nod.

"Mommy loves it when we take walks together. We can visit her every day."

CHAPTER EIGHT

At the hospital, Presley followed her mother up the escalator to the second floor, each sipping their favorite drinks from the coffee shop near their home. Presley wore sweatpants cut off at her knees and an old shirt from church camp. Her hair fell in braids over her shoulders, causing her to look more like a twelve-year-old than someone ready to get her driver's license. Sometimes, Harper preferred this version of her daughter. Life changed so swiftly these days, and she was nowhere near ready to allow Presley to tackle the world in a car all by herself.

Harper stepped off the escalator and jogged toward her office, speaking over her shoulder.

"I promised you a mani-pedi before cheerleading tryouts on Monday. Let me check on a couple patients first. I'll only be a few minutes." Harper retrieved a couple of folders from her desk. "I assume you want to wait here?"

"No, take me with you. I'd love to check out what you do around this place."

"Outstanding! I've got the perfect job for you."

"As long as it's not giving somebody a sponge bath, I'm in."

Harper nudged Presley as they strode to the elevator. "No, Squirt. Follow me."

On the eighth floor, Harper led her to the room of Grandpa Doe. She handed Presley a journal and pointed out the notes others had posted on the wall.

Harper whispered, "This is Grandpa Doe—the one I mentioned earlier. Can you write this sweet man a note?"

"Sure," Presley answered, "but why are we whispering? I thought you wanted him to wake up."

Harper shot her a stern look and raised her voice. "When you put it that way, I'm not sure." She swatted at her daughter's arm. "I've got to check on my families. Wait here, so my friend won't be alone. I'll be back soon-ish."

"Famous last words," Presley teased.

Harper blew her a kiss on her way out the door. "Patience is a virtue, and so is forgiveness, right?"

MAY 1966

Solomon clutched a bouquet of roses and held Sadie Beth's hand as they strolled past the Main Street Bakery. A trail of cinnamon wafted through the air to beckon them inside.

"Something smells yummy, Daddy. Can we get a cinnamon bun? Please?" She flashed her irresistible grin.

"After we visit your mother and Baby Silas, the day is all yours."

Sadie Beth's frizzy hair swayed in a messy ponytail behind her head.

The two of them had fallen into a respectable rhythm of day-to-day existence, and fixing Sadie Beth's hair the way her mother did would never become part of their routine. Her blonde waves were so thick, she winced when he combed through them. Once the summer humidity took over, her ringlets tangled into a lion's mane around her face. Solomon found the hair product aisle at the grocery overwhelming, so he simply avoided it.

Sadie Beth needed a trim, but he knew better than to cut her hair too short.

"Winnie would come back to haunt me, for sure." Solomon was surprised to hear a chuckle escape from his lips when he said those words aloud.

Winnie always had Sadie Beth looking as if she'd stepped straight off the pages of a Sears & Roebuck catalog.

But it had been a year. Priorities change. Survival required it.

Solomon took pride in the fact they'd made it through the first Thanksgiving, Christmas, birthdays, and Easter. To him, each day felt the same. He still had to conjure up enough motivation to get out of bed, and to perform mundane tasks such as dishes or laundry.

None of it came easy. Would it ever?

Solomon's search for peace intensified over time. Now, at least twenty pounds lighter, he'd lost both the skill and desire to talk to people about the weather or any other form of frivolous drivel.

Instead, he focused on Sadie Beth's future, her prom, her wedding day. He laid awake at night, reassuring Winnie he'd keep their daughter safe.

He formed a habit of dressing the same every day—knickers, suspenders, a white dress shirt with a bow tie, gray socks, and black loafers. Sadie Beth chose that outfit for him on their first outing after the funeral, and he'd donned a similar version of it ever since. Solomon realized his wardrobe was outdated, but Sadie Beth thought he looked fancy.

"You're a hero from one of my story books," she said with pride in her voice. "I can always find you in a crowd of other parents."

Solomon wasn't one to argue, and wearing the same outfit day after day required less effort on his part. One less decision for him to make by himself. More importantly, his choice of clothing proved he had control over something. Anything.

The door to his son's room remained closed with S-I-L-A-S still splayed in blue and gold letters above the doorway. Perhaps, on a subconscious level, Solomon clung to the hope of one day peering in to find Winnie and Silas cuddled snuggled together in their rocking chairs— that same rocking chair he'd so carefully assembled the week before they left for the hospital. The chair had yet to serve its purpose.

Such disappointment. Such emptiness. Solomon only held his son for a moment—not long enough to say goodbye. He should have taken more time to absorb his baby's scent, his lips, and his chin dimple. Those eyelashes curled as if painted on. His perfectly oval eyes.

Eyes that never opened.

The entire scene played out before Solomon, blurred by a fresh pool of tears. Winnie never got the chance to hold Silas. She lay dying in the next room. Solomon had handed the baby off to a nurse and chose to be with Winnie.

Had he made the right choice?

What did it matter? He'd lost them both.

Solomon dropped his shoulders. Rather than open that bedroom door, he'd rather pretend Winnie and Silas were in there together, where they belonged.

His grief counselor described this behavior as unhealthy and suggested he divert his energy into moving forward rather than looking back.

But the experts didn't live in his house or sleep in his bed at night.

Solomon taught himself to count his blessings.

And there she was. A tiny blonde angel who celebrated life as if she already had one foot in the door of heaven.

In fact, it was Sadie Beth who had gotten them this far. She had a better understanding of death than any grief counselor he knew.

She tugged on his suspenders, bringing him back to the present moment.

"What is it, Lightning Bug?"

Her freckle-covered nose crinkled when he called her by her nickname. "Mommy says she and Baby Silas are having a picnic today. We should have one too, so we can eat together."

"That sounds great, m'dear."

Her mouth spread into a toothless grin.

She let go of his hand and skipped the cut-through path that led to the back gates of the cemetery. Within a few moments, she'd stopped at the final resting place of Winnifred and Silas Thomas.

"Good morning, family! I hope you slept well. Did you hear the story I read last night? *Beauty and the Beast* is one of my favorites. Belle likes to read as much as I do. She even had her own library in the castle where Beast kept her against her will."

Sadie Beth's exuberant chatter echoed off nearby headstones. Solomon wondered if the other citizens of the cemetery looked forward to her visits. He shook his head at the odd thought.

Grief had a way of blurring the lines between life and death. Most days, Solomon was no longer sure which side of that line he traveled.

He joined his daughter at the gravestones. He'd ordered a stone bench to place at the foot of the graves. Last he checked, the shop was engraving it with Winnie & Silas's names, her favorite Scripture, and a carved teddy bear like the one still waiting in their rocking chair.

This was the only way he had of telling their story—a stone-cold bench. It had to be perfect.

Solomon drew in a deep breath and scooped up his daughter. She wrapped her arms around his neck and held on tight while he spun her in circles. She squealed with delight, and he giggled along with her.

Progress.

He followed the path to the exit and kissed his daughter on the forehead. She took his face in her hands. "Daddy, I miss going to church. Can we go in the morning?"

Solomon froze as Sadie Beth gazed up at him expecting an answer.

He pursed his lips and fought back a sigh. "I'm sorry, Lightning Bug. I'm just not ready. I'm not sure what to say to God these days. Besides, church was your mama's thing."

Sadie Beth nodded as if she understood, and then quickly changed the subject. "What about those cinnamon rolls?"

Solomon grinned. "You bet. We'll get a blanket and sit underneath that big oak tree at church."

"After that, can we go to the library?"

"Oh, we'd better hurry then. Sounds like you've got a busy day planned for us."

He twisted her around to his back.

"Giddy up, horsey!" she called out, tightening her arms around his neck. Solomon took off in a gallop, jostling her around.

"Daddy, tell me the story of why you call me Lightning Bug."

Solomon grinned. She'd heard it hundreds of times.

"Because you're tiny, like a bug, but you glow so bright, you illuminate the world around you when it grows dark."

"I love that story, and so does Baby Silas. He wants you to give him a nickname too."

Solomon sighed. "I wish I could, Lightning Bug. I wish I could."

CHAPTER NINE

Brock Timberland wiggled the outside door which led to a lower-level classroom at the church building. Closest to the parking lot and restrooms, this location made as much sense as any for their abbreviated worship service. The room held a maximum of twenty-five people—still a lofty attendance goal.

The high for the day was predicted to hit below ninety for the first time in weeks, bringing a welcome reprieve. Brock hoped the temperature drop might entice a few churchgoers to venture out of their air-conditioned homes.

On his heels, Deacon mimicked Brock's every move. Like his father, his son's dark hair formed a series of unruly cowlicks that bounced as he walked. His big blue eyes sparkled through a new set of glasses. He often scrunched his nose to keep the spectacles in place. Both Timberlands wore jeans and tennis shoes with an untucked plaid shirt, topped with a dark colored vest. Their Sunday best.

Brock propped the door open with a chair and stepped inside.

"Shhh. Can you hear that?"

Deacon held his hand to his ear. "Sounds like someone is taking a shower."

"We cut the water and electricity to most of the building. Where can all that gushing water be coming from?"

Brock peered into the darkened hallway. The swishing sounds grew louder. The only source of light filtered through windows on the back wall. He tucked Deacon on his hip and took off running. Grabbing his phone, he flipped it into flashlight mode and handed it to his son.

"Buddy, I need your help. Hold this light and show me where to go."

Deacon pushed his glasses up his nose. "Okay. I'll be your helper."

They turned down one hall and followed another, chasing the threatening sounds. As they drew close to the source, Deacon's light picked up a stream of water coming from the ceiling and pooling on the floor.

Brock set Deacon on the floor a safe distance away.

"Looks like a pipe burst. Don't move unless the water seeps toward you. Got it?"

Deacon clapped his hands together, twisting the light in every direction.

Brock splashed through the puddle toward a maintenance closet. He fiddled with his keys until he found the right one and wrenched the door open. It took both hands to jerk the control valve to the off position. The flow of water in the hallway slowed to a trickle, as droplets of water rolled from Brock's hair toward his mouth. He stuck out his tongue and coughed out the taste of hair gel he'd caked on earlier that morning.

Deacon stood on his tiptoes and held his breath—his default stance when he got too excited. Brock caught the look of anticipation on his son's face and broke into laughter—an extended snigger that brought tears to his eyes. Deacon followed his father's lead with the contagious laugh of a child. They both doubled over until the moment passed.

"Why are we laughing?" Deacon asked, with eyes wide open.

Brock caught his breath. "We've either got to laugh or cry. Today, you helped me choose to laugh. Thanks, I needed that."

Deacon grinned. "We fixed it, didn't we?"

"For now. We make a terrific team, you and me. Let's take a quick look around."

Brock carried Deacon through the puddle to a door with a sign that said LEAD PASTOR. The sound of dripping water echoed from within, though the drips slowed as they drew closer.

"This must be my office. I hope it didn't wash away."

"Cool. I didn't know you had an office."

"Me neither."

Brock poked his head in. Streaks of sunlight broke through the skewed blinds on the windows and illuminated the dreary room that now served as more of a storage closet. The few ceiling tiles that remained in place sagged with the weight of water from the burst pipe overhead. Carpet, old and moldy, ripped at the seams. Towers of stacked classroom chairs lined the walls. Boxes of hymnals formed teetering piles of unwanted history. The only salvageable items were several framed photos on the desk, bubble wrapped for protection.

Other than the photos, the entire room was a massive pile of soaking-wet debris.

"Everything is ruined. I'll rent a dumpster and clean this place out."

Brock wondered if it might be better to bulldoze the entire building. Complete sections of it were in a state of disrepair, and the church couldn't handle the financial burden if anyone got injured on their property. The elders had discussed selling the building, but even with real estate values at an all-time low, they weren't likely to find a buyer in this town.

He stopped himself from following his own dark train of thoughts.

I'm supposed to be the one demonstrating an abundance of faith, right?

A trail of voices echoed down the hall. Brock checked his watch.

"Nine thirty? Yikes!"

Brock threw Deacon on his shoulders and gathered the framed photos under his arm. He took off running through the slippery corridor.

"Hold tight, Son."

A breathless Brock thrust the classroom door open where his church guests gathered. He slid Deacon to the ground and positioned the photos against the wall. When he reached for the sermon notes in his shirt pocket, he drew out a dripping wet piece of paper.

Great. One of my best sermons yet. Soggy and unreadable.

He painted on a smile and greeted the fifteen people who waited in rows of chairs he'd lined up the day prior. An awkward silence filled the room. No one spoke to one another.

Church shouldn't feel like a waiting room at the doctor's office.

Brock cleared his throat.

"Good morning. My name is Brock Timberland. I apologize for my appearance, but a pipe burst this morning. To make it worse, I had a terrific sermon prepared for you today, if I do say so myself, but now I can't read my notes." He held up the dripping piece of paper and shook it off. "I think we'll try something different."

Brock stood at the lectern and tried to regain his composure. His eyebrows tingled with hardening hair gel that dripped from his forehead.

"Let me tell you about a new friend of mine, someone I met while visiting the Intensive Care Unit at the hospital in Savannah on Friday." Brock stepped away from the podium. "I don't know this gentleman's name. No one does. He was hit by a car last week and is registered as a John Doe. But he's elderly, alone, and in desperate need of support for his last days here on earth. I kept thinking what he needs most is the love of a church family to surround him."

Brock picked up a box with sheets of paper and pens and passed them down the rows. "The definition of the word 'worship' means 'to honor.' What better way to honor God than to encourage someone who can never repay us? Do this unto the least of these. Isn't that what Jesus told us in the book of Matthew?"

Deacon gave his dad a thumbs-up sign when he sauntered past.

"Let's take a few minutes this morning to write a note of encouragement to this stranger. A favorite Scripture, prayer, or even a picture from the kids. If this man were to wake up this afternoon, I'd like him to know he's not alone."

The audience sat in silence for a minute to ponder his words. A few scooted their chairs together and opened their Bibles to share ideas.

Brock couldn't help but smile as a spirit of unity spread across the room. The stack of framed photos caught his eye. He carefully unwrapped each one, stopping to answer questions from the crowd.

The first photo depicted soldiers and their families scattered across the lawn on blankets, each person waving a handheld American flag. The caption read: *Fort Bryce Welcome Home Picnic, August 5, 1975.*

The next showed an outdoor nativity scene at Christmas, complete with live animals, kids dressed as angels, and adults donning Bible character costumes. The bell tower resembled a Christmas tree. Most impressive was the number of townspeople in attendance, despite a slight dusting of snow on the ground. A train of horses and buggies waited at the front steps, offering rides to each family. Even the horses wore angel halos. *Christmas Eve Service, December 24, 1979.*

Brock beamed at the level of creativity.

This church once served as a hub of activity for this entire town. Is it possible to do it again?

For the first time, Brock believed this church might have a future.

The next photo displayed at least two hundred kids dressed in Halloween costumes posed on stacks of hay bales in what looked to be the church's parking lot. In front of them was a dance floor with square dancers and a musical group with banjos and guitars. A banner hung from the bell tower that read: *Ginger Ridge Fall Harvest Festival, October 27, 1983.*

Somehow, they'd acquired an aerial shot, possibly taken from atop the courthouse on Main Street.

The next photo was a collage that depicted a hillside dotted with children dressed in pastels. By the bell tower were three wooden crosses, the center one draped in purple. In a separate inset at the top, an older gentleman presented a basket to a cute little blonde girl. She hugged a stuffed bunny as big as she was. Brock estimated at least eight hundred in attendance that day. *Easter Service Egg Hunt & Picnic, April 1987.*

A bunny? Could this be Harper Phillips? Didn't she mention winning a bunny on Easter Sunday?

He did his best to calculate the years, and they seemed to match up with what he guessed to be her age.

I'll have to show these to her. Maybe she can help me fill in the gaps.

Brock assembled the photos on a table as a wave of sadness overtook him. In his own desperate battle for survival, he'd not taken the time to grieve what the town of Ginger Ridge and this church had lost. He'd forgotten to stand in their shoes—to see Ginger Ridge from their point of view.

He squared his shoulders with renewed determination. Those in the audience finished their projects and some rose to come look over the collection of pictures. Comments scattered across the room.

"Look, there's Aunt Lucy when she was a little girl."

"I remember this. My grandmother brought me to the Christmas Service every year."

Brock cleared his throat to get regain their attention. "Some may say we are a forgotten church from a forgotten town. But it doesn't have to stay that way, does it?"

CHAPTER TEN

Harper and her daughter huddled in their standard front-row seat of the balcony at the Savannah Church. As a little girl, Presley Rose had selected that exact spot their first Sunday visiting that church. She loved to watch the choir and wave at the people down below.

A smile of satisfaction spread across Harper's face as Presley nestled in beside her, doodling on a note pad like she had when she was little.

I must have done something right.

Presley Rose was the ultimate motivation for overcoming each obstacle life tossed her way. Her daughter's friends often commented how Harper rocked it as a single parent, but she knew the truth. From the start, Presley was the one who gave them strength. She asked a million questions, always keeping Harper accountable and focused. With Presley, Harper enjoyed the family life she always craved, even if it had been just the two of them all these years.

That was no accident. It had to be God's plan in action.

On the stage, the minister paced as he shared anecdotes about the innocence of children.

"In the book of Proverbs, the Bible tells us to 'Train up a child in the way she should go, and when she is old, she will not depart from it.' Through many generations, those words have proven to be true. Many of us wouldn't be here today unless someone had taken the time to influence us—to show us what it means to serve God by loving others."

Harper's gaze drifted to the dazzling reflection of the sun through the stained-glass windows. Solomon again crossed her mind. Without him, Presley Rose wouldn't be here, nor would she have been given that name. Two of Harper's favorite memories combined into a constant source of strength to pull from when she needed it most.

JULY 1987

Harper skipped along the sidewalk with a messy ponytail bouncing against her head, lugging Ginger the bunny under one arm. Music played in the distance, and the sound grew stronger as she headed up a slight hill and rounded the corner.

Solomon's eyes lit up and he waved from his porch, motioning for her to come over.

"Hi, Solomon. Remember me? Where's that music coming from?"

"Good morning, Miss Harper. That's Elvis music playing inside the house. I've got the window open so I can hear it while I work. I prefer his hymns."

"He sounds sad, but I like it."

Solomon nodded. "Me too. Would you like a glass of lemonade?"

Harper clapped her hands and scuttled up the steps where he handed her a plastic cup and straw.

"Whatcha doing today, Solly? Is it okay if I call you Solly?"

"I'd love it. I'm a big fan of nicknames."

"Why come you still have on your church clothes?" She pointed to his neck. "I've never seen anyone wear a bow tie on a Tuesday."

He shrugged. "I try to look nice every day. New folks move to town often because of Fort Bryce, and I want to make a good impression."

"Fort Bryce? That's where my daddy works."

"I figured that's what brought you to town. What do you think about Ginger Ridge?" Solly eased into the porch swing, holding it still for Harper to climb up. She squeezed Ginger between them.

"Ginger Ridge is fine, I guess." Harper pointed to the church across the street. "Church is my favorite, but Daddy likes to stay home on the weekends so he can yell at us. I hear the church bells and remember how much fun I had. I'd love to go back one day."

Solomon patted her on top of the head. Harper slurped the last drops of lemonade and handed over the empty glass.

"Thanks." She snuffled. "Why does your porch smell so nice?"

"Those are my roses. We've had a lot of rain lately, and my roses are letting us know they're happy about it." He pointed to the pink and white flowers surrounding the house. "There are hidden thorns on the branches. You can smell, but don't touch."

"Okay. I promise." She took in a big whiff and swung her legs back and forth. "I like being with you, Solly. You make me feel special."

"You are incredibly special, Harper. Drop by anytime. I'm usually here on my porch. My heart is always ready to listen."

Harper gave a big belly laugh. "Hearts don't have ears, Solly. Are you being silly?"

He shrugged his shoulders. "I suppose I am. Just call me Silly Solly."

Harper tried to pronounce it through her loose front teeth. "Silly Solly. I like that."

"Here, let me show you something." Solomon led her to the opposite corner of the porch and knelt in front of a bookcase. He lifted a hard, plastic cover. "You may borrow any of these books as long as you bring them back in good shape."

Harper gasped and shuffled through the books. She chose a heavy one with Bible stories and colorful pictures.

"Solly, I forgot. I can't read yet."

"It's okay. These books will help you learn."

"Where did you get so many books? Do you have kids in your house?"

Solomon shook his head, but his face tightened in a way that made Harper wish she hadn't asked. Daddy often scolded her for talking too much. Harper should have known better.

Solomon cleared his throat. "These books are important to me, but I enjoy sharing them with children who will appreciate them."

Harper accepted his explanation and reminded herself not to ask so many questions.

"Solly, I'd better get home. Mommy's probably looking for me." Harper picked up Ginger from the swing.

Solomon helped her down the steps. "Harper, ask your parents if I can walk over to bring you to church sometime."

"Okay. I'll try to remember."

Solly waved goodbye and craned his neck to watch until she could no longer see him.

She clutched the book to her chest and swung Ginger by the ears, skipping down the hill to reach her house. In the old days, Mama would have been waiting on the front steps ready to visit the park. But she was nowhere to be found today. Harper opened the storm door and scampered in to find her mother still asleep on the couch.

Her mother had explained the new medicine she was taking would often make her drowsy.

Mama hadn't seemed sick until she started taking that blasted medicine, but her mother insisted it made her better. Every time Daddy came home from overseas to announce they had to move again, Mama got worse.

Harper rummaged through the pantry to find an opened bag of potato chips. Outside, she rested her back against a shade tree and snuggled Ginger in her lap. The two of them finished off the chips, and she opened the storybook. She tried to sound out the letters of the name written inside the front cover.

"S-A-D-I-E- B-E-T-H. I don't know who that spells."

She flipped the pages until she recognized pictures of Noah and the Ark. She held the book so Ginger could see as she interpreted the story.

"Once upon a time, there was a man named Noah. He had a long beard. Noah loved animals and wanted to take them for a ride on his new boat ..."

Harper soon slammed the book shut and left it for Ginger to read on her own. "What's that sound? Do you hear it? I'll be right back."

She wandered into the back yard to stand along the creek bank. The water rolled past, making pretty white bridges over the rocks. Harper kicked off her sandals to dip her toes in.

Harper followed the path of slippery rocks to wade to the middle, giggling as the rushing water tickled her feet. The current came so strong it knocked them out from under her. She fell hard on her bottom to roll with the flow of the water. Harper yelped as her head went under. She popped up in time to grab a tree branch and managed to swing her body until her toes stretched far enough to touch the safety of the bank.

Covered in mud, she put her hands on her knees to catch her breath, but a smile spread across her face. She hustled back to where she first started and followed the same path.

"Harper Gail Phillips. What on earth are you doing?"

Harper froze in place at her mother's angry voice. Her eyes grew wide.

She turned to face her mother who held the back door open. "I'm just playing in our new creek."

"You have ruined your clothes. Get in this house right now. Pretty girls don't play in the mud, sweetie."

"Yes, ma'am."

"Why don't you find a few friends to play with instead?" Her mother made it sound so easy.

Harper dropped her head and trudged toward her mother, turning over her shoulder to take one last look at the creek.

"I have found a new friend. The creek!"

CHAPTER ELEVEN

Harper drove to work with a renewed sense of purpose. With no medical explanation why Grandpa Doe still hung around, she assumed he must be waiting for something, or someone. She'd seen it too many times—a supernatural will to make things right as death drew near.

Time.

Harper was running out of it.

She must dig deeper to discover what might bring Grandpa Doe peace.

How can we help you if we don't know what you need?

Solomon once asked her that question and she'd come back to it frequently throughout her adult life.

Wise man, that Solomon.

She took one last swig of lukewarm coffee from a local drive-thru and fiddled with her phone, selecting a number she'd not used in years. She winced while it rang, not sure what to expect.

"WAGA-TV, this is Aaron Foster speaking."

"Hi, Aaron, it's Harper Phillips at Savannah Regional. I know it's been a while, but I'm hoping it's a slow news Monday and you could use a remarkable story to share."

"Harper Phillips. Can't say I ever expected to hear from you again. How have you been?"

"Same as usual. Doing my best to keep up with my daughter. How about you?"

"Great. Tell me what you've got."

"Can you be at the hospital at ten this morning? We've got that elderly hit-and-run victim from last week. We've nicknamed him Grandpa Doe. He's still unconscious, but that hasn't stopped him from making new friends. Strangers leave notes on his wall. We hope to identify him and locate his family before it's too late."

"Sure. Sounds like a tear-jerker, a wonderful way to end a newscast. I'll bring my cameraman and notify a reporter from the newspaper."

"Thanks. You're the best."

"If that's true, why won't you date me?" He paused long enough to make the moment awkward. "Just kidding. I moved on long ago, but you called me, so you deserve it. I'll see you at ten."

Harper's mouth twisted and a nervous laugh escaped her lips. "Thank you, Aaron. See you soon."

If I knew the answer to any questions about dating, I'd be happy to share it.

Instead of delving into her entrenched habit of running from commitment, she prepared for the scheduled interview by rehearsing some talking points at each traffic light. The phone rang, causing her to jump. She pressed a button on the steering wheel to answer.

"Hello?"

"Miss Phillips? This is Detective Sterling."

"Yes, great. I was just about to call you. I've got a press conference set for ten."

"Perfect. I'll be there. Where shall we meet?"

"Inside the main lobby. Surely someone out there knows this precious man."

"Sounds good. See you in about an hour."

Harper ended the call and continued to practice her lines. By no means was this her first press conference, but the camera had a way of melting the professional, protective bubble she'd built over time. Once the spotlight landed on her, she defaulted to her natural coping skills: nervous and chatty, emotions evident. Never comfortable with such a level of vulnerability, Harper cleared her throat and switched to her official speaking voice.

"They brought this unknown patient in Thursday evening after being hit by a car, possibly in the Madison area ..."

Wait. The detective can explain that part. I'll take it from there.

"We've got an elderly white male, approximately eighty to eight-five years old, estimated about five feet two inches and one hundred and thirty pounds. His injuries are life-threatening, and he remains unconscious. If anyone has information about the accident or the identity of Grandpa Doe, please contact Savannah Regional Hospital or Detective Sterling with the Madison Police Department."

She pulled into the parking lot and informed the attendant to be watching for the detective. Harper steered into a space reserved for staff, refreshed her lipstick, and scuttled into the hospital. She darted first to the eighth floor to check on Grandpa Doe.

No sense holding a press conference if he's no longer with us.

Harper's heart beat faster as she entered his room and she paused to catch her breath. The patient's chart showed a significant rise in temperature and pulse rate, a strong indication that pneumonia was settling into his collapsed lung. When she scanned the room, she realized the number of letters on the wall had doubled, which brought a sense of satisfaction.

For a change of position, she raised the foot of his bed. Then with a washrag, Harper cleaned his swollen mouth, and dabbed petroleum jelly on his chapped lips. She stepped back to check his appearance, which resembled most little old men she'd seen, and clasped his hand in hers.

"Stay with me, Grandpa Doe. I'm spiffing you up for when your family arrives, hopefully by the end of the day."

Detective Cameron Sterling maneuvered his black police SUV through the narrow streets of Savannah. He hadn't allowed enough time to deal with the slower pace of tourists.

He checked his reflection in the mirror. Day nine without a cigarette. So far, he had yet to experience any of the fantastic benefits his doctor promised. Bloodshot eyes revealed his struggle to sleep through the night. He guzzled the last drops of his umpteenth cup of coffee and tossed it to the floorboard with the other empty cardboard cups.

At least my coffee game is stronger than ever.

A newspaper from the town of Serendipity, Alabama lay on top of his passenger's seat. The cover featured a photo of his much-adored twin brother.

[start headline]

Deputy Fire Chief Grayson Sterling Saves Family in Overnight Blaze

[end headline]

The picture showed Grayson carrying an unconscious toddler in his arms, with open flames behind him. A photo op so perfect it must have been staged.

"Way to go, Little Brother," Cam muttered. "Mom and Dad would be so proud."

I need to cancel my subscription to this stupid newspaper.

Cam found himself slugging through a low point in a once stellar career. He'd been with the Madison Police Department for nearly twenty-five years. Recently passed by for a promotion, the powers-that-be drew his attention to documented anger issues which confirmed what he already suspected to be true.

I never measure up to expectations. Unlike my brother.

Cam gritted his teeth. Even in their high school days, Gray found his way to the cover of every local sports page. As a quarterback, his brother had a way of attracting glory. He raked in one award after another, unscathed from injury or setbacks.

Cam had played defensive end and had suffered numerous broken bones and concussions throughout his career. Still, he considered their state championship to be worth the extra pain he'd endured.

Cam blocked many memories from his teen years. Sometimes, he wondered if his brain suffered lingering effects.

Too many concussions. Still, I'd give anything to return to those days.

Offense versus defense. Brother versus brother.

The brothers hadn't spoken since their mother's funeral ten years ago. Keeping Gray at a comfortable distance was the only way Cam knew to pull himself out of his current slump. Solving a case or two might help. Maybe a front-page photo and a headline of his own?

Sure, I'd take that any day.

The John Doe hit-and-run case wouldn't accomplish that for him. If anything, it only agitated him further, pulling resources away from higher profile crimes.

After lunch, he was due in court on a separate case, a preliminary homicide. Lacking hard evidence and unable to find anyone willing to testify, the judge planned to release their suspect to his own recognizance, adding a check mark to Cam's loss column.

Another failure.

Cameron sighed.

He'd already paid a hefty price for this job he once loved. Now divorced with a son he never got to see, Cam's blood pressure often skyrocketed without warning. He hurled himself into each case with more anger than technique or skill like he once did on the football field.

Cam checked the time on his dashboard display, punched the steering wheel, and stomped on the gas.

Ugh! Late too. Can't I get anything right?

Harper Phillips made it sound like their John Doe was near death, so this press conference was probably a waste of time. But he knew the compassionate social worker hoped for more when she'd requested his assistance. He clicked on his recorder to confirm what they knew thus far while reminding himself he was a talented, seasoned detective.

"The location of the victim was not the scene of the accident. Whoever dropped off the victim made sure he was visible to passing cars. Is this a sign of remorse? Was the person who dropped him off the same one who hit him? Or someone who chose not to get involved for other reasons? The vacant fire station was on the south side of town next to many boarded-up buildings. No active security cameras in that area, so the driver was possibly familiar with that part of town. The passerby who called 911 had nothing more to offer, though he had the decency to stay with the victim until help arrived. Whoever hit him should show damage to their vehicle, though none of the local repair shops have reported any suspicious cars with front end damage."

He pumped the brakes. "Missed my turn. Thanks a lot, Savannah." Cam muttered under his breath. He turned off the audio recorder and tossed the phone into his passenger's seat in disgust.

I need a cigarette.

Harper frowned as she read through an urgent message on her pager. She hurried to the elevator and punched the button for the third floor.

It's never a good sign when we readmit a patient. Especially not little Wallace Higgins.

She forced a reassuring smile and entered room 350. Roger and Claire Higgins huddled in the corner, facing the window. They struggled to hide signs of disappointment from their son, who once again laid in the bed attached to an IV pole and oxygen tank.

"What's this I hear? You came back to see me so soon? How lucky am I?" Harper ruffled Wallace's thickening hair and clasped his hand. "Tell me what happened, buddy."

Wallace's eyes still shone. "It's not the 'kemia this time. It's the 'monia."

"Oh no. Not the 'monia," Harper said. "Well, doctors around here are experts on treating the pneumonia, so I'm sure they're taking great care of you. Can I get you anything?"

Wallace gave a big nod. "You already know."

"A purple popsicle, right? But only if your parents approve."

A huge grin spread across his face. "You guessed it."

His parents nodded their approval, and Harper excused herself to retrieve one from the kitchen and promptly returned.

"Roger? Claire? Can we take a walk? I think Wallace will be fine with his popsicle while we're gone."

They followed her into the hallway and Harper led them to a private waiting room.

"How are we doing, Mom and Dad?"

Claire let out a heavy sigh. "Trying to stay strong. We've been through this before, and I keep telling myself it's just one small setback. Another obstacle on our course. Honestly, being home together for the weekend was magical."

Roger wrapped his arm around Claire's shoulder. "I bought a fire truck and he helped me put it together on Friday after his goodbye parade. He was so excited to show the neighbors. He drove it down every sidewalk in the neighborhood. Perhaps we shouldn't have allowed him to go outside. His cough came back fierce the next morning."

"Don't blame yourselves. All you can do is handle one day at a time." She did her best to guide them through uncharted territory. "You remember there is a chapel on the first floor. Make sure you take care of yourselves as well. This has been a lengthy battle, and I sense you're exhausted."

Roger cleared his throat. "May we have a few minutes alone? We must get our bearings."

"Of course. You have my number. Please call if you need anything at all."

CHAPTER TWELVE

Cam entered the lobby and approached a petite blonde pacing in front of the vending machines.

"You must be Harper Phillips," he said. "Sorry I'm late. I blame Savannah. Tourists barge into the street with no warning around here."

She reached to shake his hand with a firm grip.

This woman means business. Intense.

"Good morning, Detective. I appreciate you driving so far to get the word out." She checked her watch. "We've got the media set up in a conference room. You can cover details of the accident, and I'll touch on his condition."

She spoke at a rapid rate. Faster than his ears could listen, even in his overly caffeinated state. She launched down the hall and he scrambled to keep pace.

No sense looking for trouble with this one.

The press conference kicked into gear as soon as they entered the room. Cam read what details he could release. When Harper took over, he stepped back to observe and take notes.

"This gentleman, whom we've affectionately nicknamed Grandpa Doe, doesn't have long to live. We need to determine who he is and where he came from. Our goal is to locate his family, so he'll be surrounded with loved ones."

Tears filled Harper's eyes and her voice quivered. She bit her lip but continued. "In the meantime, he's made quite a few friends. We've loaded his wall with encouraging notes, so he's not truly alone."

She wiped at a tear and stepped away from the microphone, making a brisk exit, catching Cam off guard.

He stepped to the podium to answer remaining questions off camera, repeating the phone numbers for the hospital and the Madison Police tip line. Soon, the reporters scattered, and Cam was left to gather his thoughts. The whole thing had taken less than five minutes.

In his notebook, he'd written only one word.

Compassion.

What Cam first interpreted as intensity proved to be sincere kind-heartedness. Harper Phillips genuinely cared for this patient, which made him wonder if that's what he'd been missing in his life. He made a few notes and wandered around until he found a coffee machine—police officers had a sixth sense about such things.

After obtaining another cup of coffee, he strode to the information desk and waited for the middle-aged redhead to acknowledge him.

"How may I help you?" she asked without looking directly at him.

He flashed his badge. "Do you know where I can find Harper Phillips? I'm working with her on a case."

"She'll be back after lunch." The lady paused and motioned with her head toward a flat-panel screen on the wall. "But it looks like you can catch her on the midday news. Would you like to leave her a message?"

"No thanks."

Cam stepped aside and studied the film clip that rolled as a teaser. Even with the volume muted, Cam noticed the marked difference in their expressions.

Misery vs. Passion.

The difference rattled him.

Cam rushed for the exit to make his escape, but something forced him to turn around.

"Excuse me, ma'am. Can you give me the room number for the John Doe case we're working on? The elderly man?"

"Yes, sir. Grandpa Doe? He's in room 815, in the ICU."

Cam checked his watch and hurried to the elevator.

"Thank you. You've been most helpful," he called out as an afterthought.

He had no time to visit a comatose patient with no information to offer. Still, it seemed the right thing to do. Seeing his victim in person might spark that passion that once drove him.

Baby steps. My therapist would be proud.

Raphael Henry had no trouble finding the executive offices of Wilburn & Hessey on the top floor of Atlanta's newest skyscraper. In the waiting room, he paced and took turns smoothing out wrinkles from the white dress shirt, gold tie, and khaki pants Isabella had purchased for the occasion. After processing their predicament, she'd shifted into Mama Bear mode, throwing her energy into finding a way to beat it. Just as he'd hoped.

A black leather portfolio marked Majestic Construction rested underneath his arm. Raphael gripped it so tightly his hand cramped. That portfolio marked his promotion to foreman—a priceless keepsake from an impressive career.

Regrets. Raphael had acquired a long list of them in such a short amount of time.

His only choice was to confess and find a legal way to fix this mess.

"Raphael Henry?"

He jumped out of his daze.

"Right this way." A young woman in a business suit escorted him to a room filled with countless rows of identical books. Behind the desk was a massive wall of picture windows that overlooked the city.

Raphael knew that view well. He and his team had installed each of those windows with careful precision.

Bart Wilburn stood facing him with his arms folded across his chest. Raphael recognized the man from a series of "Let me fight your battle" commercials where he showed up in court dressed like GI Joe in army fatigues. His thick head of hair matched the color of Raphael's deep brown shoe polish he'd used that morning.

When Mr. Wilburn reached to shake his hand, Raphael wiped the sweat from his palms on his stiff new pants and offered a firm grip.

"Hello, sir. I'm Raphael Henry. We spoke on the phone about my immigration case. I've been advised to get a lawyer, and you came highly recommended. I definitely need someone to fight this battle with me."

The man never changed expression. "Bart Wilburn. Nice to meet you. Please have a seat."

The door closed behind Raphael and he dropped into an oversized leather chair that made him feel like a school kid waiting to go into the principal's office.

He cleared his throat. "My company—I mean, my former employer, Majestic, built these towers. I wondered who'd end up in the penthouse suite. I never thought I'd be here as a client."

Shut up, Raphael! You're paying by the hour. For God's sake, let the man speak!

"Can I review your citation and papers? My assistant will make copies."

Raphael handed over his portfolio. Isabella had fastened a family photo inside the front cover.

"Since I arrived in this country, I've done everything by the book. I take my family to church every Sunday, and I've worked hard to make a difference in my community. We own our home that I built with my own hands. I love it here."

Mr. Wilburn acknowledged his words with a forced smile and absorbed several costly minutes reading through Raphael's paperwork.

"Nice family," he commented without looking up.

Raphael winced.

Salt in the wound. Please read faster, dude.

Mr. Wilburn tapped his finger against his chin. "Tell me this. What is your best-case scenario? How would you like this to end?"

Raphael froze for what felt like a full minute. He'd not allowed himself to think that far into the future. He shifted forward in his chair and shut his eyes for a moment.

"Ideally, I apply for citizenship, stay with my family, and can be at my wife's side when our little niña is born in a few weeks. I'd love to return to work for Majestic as a foreman and help my wife open the bakery she's always dreamed of. Bella's Best. We've got big goals, I guess you'd say."

Wilburn rubbed the corners of his mustache. "Sounds like it." His tone sounded less than comforting. The silence that followed, even worse.

Is he taunting me now?

Wilburn cleared his throat. "Mr. Henry, I'm going to be honest with you."

Raphael braced himself. The muscles in his neck tensed. "Please."

"Immigration laws are less than lenient in cases like yours. If you were in the country legally, I'd file a petition to adjust your official status. But you arrived under false pretenses and created a fake identity, which leaves me little to work with." He stood to pace behind his desk, making Raphael even more nervous.

Wilburn continued. "Since we have no lawful standing, protocol requires you to return to Mexico. Because of the infraction, you're banned from reentry for ten years. Even then, your application for entry won't be easily granted."

Raphael felt the swift kick of the attorney's words in his gut. He understood enough of the legal mumbo jumbo the attorney threw at him to double over.

Ten years? I think I'm gonna throw up.

In ten years, Xavier and Zander would be in high school, almost ready to drive. He'd miss it all. Teaching them to ride a bike, watching Baby Evelyn learn to walk, visits from the Tooth Fairy, Christmas mornings, and running in at the last minute to church to get to Bible class.

How did I let this happen?

Wilburn stopped pacing and placed his hands on his hips. "You seem shocked. I apologize, but I want to give you the most valuable advice I have to offer."

Raphael felt himself nodding against his will.

"OK. Here it is. The truth, and nothing but." Wilburn sauntered around his desk to confront Raphael, barely three feet from his face. "I hate to be so harsh, Mr. Henry, but none of what you mentioned is legally possible. I can see that you love your family. If I were you, I'd take this next month and do what's right for them. Open that bakery for your wife. She'll need the income. Sell your house and find a cheaper place to rent, so you can pay in advance and someone else can be responsible for the repairs. Plan for your family to grow up without you. Do what makes sense for them."

Raphael leaned back against the chair. His head dropped, and he struggled to breathe. The room swirled around him.

When he looked up, Wilburn was closing his folder to hand it back to him.

"That's it? You can't do anything to help me?"

"I'm sorry. Not with the way Homeland Security has tightened restrictions. With a fake ID, I have no basis for the fight, and I'd hate for you to waste your money on a lawyer."

Raphael wondered if he'd chosen the wrong lawyer.

What if Wilburn is a racist? What if he hates immigrants?

He bit his lip hard enough to sway the urge to punch the haughty lawyer in the nose.

"Listen. I'm not one to give up easily. I have much to be proud of, and I'm willing to do anything to stay with my family. Can you recommend anyone who can help me?"

Wilburn shook his head. "No. I'm doing you a favor. Fighting this in court would cost you a fortune and you'd likely end up with the same result—with you being barred from reentry for an extended period. The best advice I may offer, legal or otherwise, is to save your money. Make the necessary preparations. Use the money to provide for your family."

Raphael backed away from the desk as if a snake coiled after him. Bile rose to his throat, but he set his chin to accept defeat.

"Thank you for your time. Have a nice day, Mr. Wilburn."

Raphael exited with his head held high. The receptionist looked up as he passed.

"How much do I owe?" Raphael spoke through clenched teeth.

The receptionist shook her head. "He normally charges $350 an hour, but he's elected not to charge for your preliminary consultation today."

He didn't enjoy being a charity case. He threw a one-hundred-dollar bill on the desk and exited before the lady could stop him.

In the lobby by the elevators, he pressed a button, but experience told him it would take a while for one to reach the top floor.

Raphael elected to take the stairs—all fifty-two flights of them. He needed to burn off excess energy and preferred to avoid any awkward elevator moments with strangers who took this country for granted.

By the time he made it to the ground floor, he had worked up a sweat. His shirt tail had come untucked and cockeyed, his necktie curled in his fist as he entered the main lobby. Raphael stooped over a water fountain and splashed himself in the face, no longer caring what impression he made. Taking a minute to catch his breath, something caught his eye on the wall of twelve panel televisions in the atrium. He stepped closer and concentrated on the audio of the midday news.

"Madison Police and officials at Savannah Regional Hospital seek help from the public to identify an elderly gentleman, the victim of a hit-and-run on Thursday evening. Dropped off at a vacant fire station in Madison, officials haven't determined where the accident occurred. To date, there are few clues to the identity of the victim or any suspects in this case."

A pretty blonde appeared on the screen.

"This gentleman doesn't have long to live ..."

Her voice quivered. The video footage cut to a detective who repeated that they had no leads in the case.

Raphael's heart beat as if sprinting for an unknown finish line. He turned his head from side to side, waiting for his vision to clear. The world moved in slow motion around him. No one else seemed to be paying attention to the midday news.

A uniformed security guard met his gaze as the man patrolled past the front entrance doors.

Does he know?

Raphael felt the weight of the glass atrium about to crash down around him. As he burst through the external doors into the roasting August heat, tears rolled down his cheeks.

He's still alive? I can't believe he's still alive. I've got to go see him.

CHAPTER THIRTEEN

Harper rushed to her car and followed the back entrance from the parking lot, chiding herself for losing her cool in front of Aaron Foster and the cameras. She typically presented herself in a professional manner, but nothing about this case felt normal. Grandpa Doe weighed heavy on her heart. She suspected it was brought on by leftover guilt she still carried for not keeping up with her old friend Solomon Thomas.

The last time she'd seen him was when he visited her in Savannah a few months after Presley was born. Within a few years, her letters to him were returned, stamped as undeliverable. She'd heard Ginger Ridge had become a ghost town and assumed Solomon had either moved or passed on.

How did I allow myself to lose touch after all he did for me? Why did I refuse to visit Ginger Ridge while he was still alive?

Regret. Harper knew it well.

She recalled his words: "You can only use the past to change the future. Find a way to pay it forward."

Which brought her back to Grandpa Doe. Soon, they'd reach the limit on what measures they could take to keep the old man alive. Tests revealed brain activity, but his organs showed preliminary signs of shutting down. Medically, there was no reason he'd survived this long.

Still, Harper preferred to focus on the person behind the statistics. He'd already proven to be a fighter, but if nothing changed, she'd be forced to sign the directive to discontinue life support.

A chill ran down her spine.

I'm nowhere near ready to make that decision.

At a red light, the car next to her honked and jolted her from her thoughts. She looked over to catch a bushy-haired man winking at her as he brushed his hands through his extensive beard.

"Hey, baby, come here often?" He laughed at his own question.

Harper rolled her eyes. The light changed and she hit the gas pedal, driving faster than usual to catch Presley in action at cheerleader tryouts. They were more of a formality for those who'd been on the squad the previous year and took place in front of the entire student body to test their ability to pump up the crowd. Presley never came across as nervous in her element at Lancaster Heights, a costly private school.

To Harper, the price and sacrifice were worth Presley having a better school experience than she'd had. Harper had considered taking a second job to cover tuition in the early years.

She remembered the notice she'd received about Major Garrett Phillips III dying unexpectedly from a massive heart attack at the age of sixty-two. More shocking than his death was the realization he'd never followed through on his threat to remove her from his will. No one was more shocked than Harper to learn her name was listed as the lone beneficiary to her father's hefty life insurance policies.

Though she considered the windfall to be tainted, the financial gain brought a level of desperately needed provision and peace. Harper acquired enough to cover Presley's private school tuition through high school and halfway through college. She'd also yielded a down payment on a comfortable two-story house in a gated community.

Shelter and safety. Priceless.

Leaving her in his will was the best gift her father had ever given her, but she'd never know if it had been intentional. After he'd kicked her out of the house the week she'd graduated from high school, she'd had no reason to stay in Ginger Ridge or to keep up contact with her father.

She shuddered at the memories.

Some mysteries weren't meant to be solved.

The only person who might answer those questions was her mother.

And she was gone as well.

AUGUST 1996

Harper changed into three different outfits before deciding, by default, on a black skirt with a polka dotted white button-up blouse and tennis shoes. Sporty, yet cute. Or so she hoped.

To her surprise, her mother waited by the door in a pink bathrobe that swallowed her whole. That robe had been a gift for Mother's Day not long ago. At the time, it fit perfectly, and her rosy cheeks had glowed in the same color as the robe.

But today, her mother's eyes were vacant as she handed over a folded paper bag. Harper peeked inside the bag to make sure there was something inside.

"Bologna. Thank you, Mama." She bit her tongue to hold back a reminder that this was high school, and she'd rather buy her lunch. She appreciated the gesture, and the concentrated effort it took for her mother to be awake so early in the day. She bent to kiss her mother on the cheek.

"Thanks for seeing me off. How do I look?" Harper spun around and didn't wait for one of her mother's cryptic answers. "You know how hard it is to make friends with kids my age. Maybe that will change now that I'm in high school."

Her mother swatted at her arm. "Oh hush, child. You are still such a chatterbox when you get nervous. Like

I told you, everyone likes the pretty girls. I would have given anything to be so lovely. Instead, I was always the ugly duckling with buck teeth and braces."

Harper took in her mother's appearance and noted the thinning hair that exploded wildly over her head—clearly not brushed or washed for several days.

"You're pretty now, Mama," Harper reassured her with a syrupy tone.

Her mother's bloodshot eyes burned a hole out the front window. She seemed lost in a haunted past, unable to break free.

"Maybe things would have turned out differently ..." She barely spoke above a whisper.

Harper rolled her eyes, wishing her mother had stayed in bed instead of using this day to reinforce her disappointment in life.

Depression is such a selfish disease.

Harper snapped her fingers to jolt her mother to the present.

"I know one thing, I'm determined not to be late this year. I set my own alarm this morning. You were right. It's my job to get myself up and ready for school."

She spoke louder than necessary, but her mother didn't respond.

"Mama, why don't you eat some breakfast and take a shower? It will do you a world of good. I've got to run."

Her mother ignored the suggestion but chimed in with one of her own. "Can you pick up a gallon of milk on your way home? I'll never hear the end of it if your father has to drink sour milk again."

"Sure, Mama. See you this afternoon. I'll be home by four o'clock. Let's take a walk, like we did when I was little."

Her mother brushed past her and meandered in a daze toward the permanent indention in the sofa that matched the shape of her body. Harper yielded any hope for a response and closed the door behind her.

She skipped a step on her way to the sidewalk and tried to shake off the suffocating sense that hung in the air. These days, Ingrid Phillips only left the house to go to the doctor or drug store to pick up stronger medications.

Harper gritted her teeth. She knew they wouldn't go for a walk this afternoon nor anytime soon.

Her father dealt with the situation the only way he knew how—by treating her mother like an insubordinate soldier who had no place under his command.

Emotions were his kryptonite. He had no tolerance for them.

Harper often wondered if her father would have done better with a son—perhaps a Garrett Phillips IV. Someone to mold into the perfect soldier.

Harper recalled the night she confirmed her parents would never truly be okay.

She was nine—old enough to recognize when it was best to hide in her room. Home was a place filled with enough tension to set off a bottle rocket at any given moment, and she taught herself to never be the reason for the next outburst.

Military orders had arrived with news of another faraway destination—someplace Harper had never heard of. Starting over felt like jumping off a cliff, but never landing. Even Harper understood what a toll moving took on her family over time. The moving truck was scheduled to arrive the next morning, and most of their belongings were already packed into boxes that waited in perfectly constructed rows against the living room wall. Except for their full set of dishes, stacked neatly on the table waiting for the proper carton to arrive.

From what Harper could tell, her father had brought home the wrong box. Or had forgotten altogether. Whatever happened, the end result was a loud, angry, and out-of-control mother. But at least she wasn't passed out on the couch.

Curse words and accusations were hurled in every direction.

Along with the dishes. Every last one of them.

Harper cowered in fear in her upstairs bedroom, burying her face in the fur of Ginger the Bunny.

Earlier that afternoon, she'd stopped in to tell Solomon goodbye. Music escaped from the open front windows. Elvis Presley's "Love Me Tender." Solomon's favorite had become hers as well.

"Solly, can I go inside and pick a song?"

He shook his head. "You know the rules. No one is allowed in my house. Never go into other people's houses alone. It's neither wise nor safe."

Solomon must have his reasons for being so stern. Harper respected his boundaries and had run out of time to uncover his mysteries. She trusted his judgment and changed the subject.

"You know what I'll miss the most, Solly?"

"What's that?"

"Your porch. It's the safest place I've ever been. No one can hurt me here."

Solomon patted her on the head. "My porch will miss you, too. You are welcome here anytime, m'dear."

He escorted her to the sidewalk and presented her a gift in a bag with tissue paper. Harper peeked inside to discover purple stationary with her name written across the top. She gave him one last hug. "Thank you. I'll write letters all the time. I promise."

"I look forward to it."

At her bedroom window, Harper squeezed her eyes shut and tried to recapture those feelings of safety from Solomon's porch.

Another dish crashed against the wall beneath her. She bounded into bed and buried herself under the covers. The moon shone through her window and made her feel as if someone was watching over her.

"I sure hope so."

Harper turned on the lamp and lifted a page of stationary and an envelope from her gift bag. She scribbled the beginnings of her first letter.

Dear Solly,

I miss you and your porch already ...

Sirens wailed in the distance, growing steadily closer. Too close. Red and blue lights splashed across the light purple of her bedroom wall. Harper jumped to her feet and stood on tiptoe, clutching Ginger to her chest. All she could see was the angled roof beneath her window, but neighbors gathered in small groups to either side of her house.

Harper noticed the screaming downstairs had stopped. Tears poured from her eyes.

Two police cars pulled up at the same time and parked at opposite street corners. The officers inched toward one other and met in front of her house, out of her line of vision.

Her mother was taken away in an ambulance that night.

And her father was furious.

After the police left, well past midnight, Harper snuck out of her room to listen from the top step. The sliding sounds of a broom cut through a million pieces of shattered glass from the dishes. But she detected the muted sounds of something else. Sniffling? Moaning?

Is Daddy crying?

She couldn't be certain, but the thought sent her scampering to bed.

The next morning, Harper poked her head around the corner and saw her father waiting at the kitchen table past the time he normally left for work. Both the living room and kitchen were spotless, as if nothing had happened.

He stared out the window, speaking as soon as she entered the room. "Your mother hurt herself and needs to spend a few weeks in the hospital. She'll be fine, but she's not allowed any visitors." His voice was authoritative, never allowing room for questions.

Harper froze in place, unsure of what he wanted from her.

"Do not discuss this with anyone. Do you understand?" He looked her in the eye and waited for a response.

She swallowed hard and forced a nod. "Yes, sir."

The day before, Harper had said a lengthy goodbye to the kids in her class. But she went on to school in mismatched clothes and without brushing her hair, as if it was normal. She pretended to discover she'd accidentally left her lunch at home, and the teacher was nice enough to provide lunch money.

The ability to ignore red flags and act as if everything was fine would get her into trouble later in life, but on this day, she was proud of herself for not discussing it with anyone as her father had ordered.

That evening, her father brought home a new set of dishes, identical to their previous set.

He stood ramrod straight and glared at the wall as if reading words from the flowered wallpaper. "I've extended my job assignment. We're staying in Ginger Ridge indefinitely."

Harper's heart leapt for joy, but her father's expression reminded her to keep her level of excitement contained. She helped him unpack the boxes exactly the way he said and not once did she get in trouble for doing it wrong. By the time they'd washed and put away the final dish, Harper never felt so close to her father.

She told him goodnight and hurried up the stairs to finish her letter to Solly.

Dear Solly,

You're never going to believe it, but we get to stay in Ginger Ridge!

CHAPTER FOURTEEN

Brock Timberland grabbed the folder full of the hand-crafted cards from his church members and headed toward the hospital entrance. He noticed the bounce in his step despite the burst pipe from yesterday and the recent arrival of divorce papers.

Time to move forward.

His son and the prospect of a revived church provided enough motivation for him to figure out his future. Single Dad. Pastor. Divorced. Dazed and confused. Party of two.

Brock ignored the gnawing emptiness in the pit of his stomach as he poked his head through the door of room 815.

"Hey, Grandpa Doe. Remember me?"

The old man remained in a similar position as when he'd left him on Friday. Brock reached to touch his hand which was a disturbing shade of purple.

Brock tucked the old man's hand under the covers.

Why do they keep it so cold in hospitals?

Brock shook off the chill and caught sight of his note still clinging to the wall. He noticed at least ten other similar notes scattered about. He began taping up the additional letters from his "flock"—an awkward term he'd have to get used to.

When he finished, he lifted his phone to call Harper. No answer.

"Hello, Harper Phillips, this is Brock Timberland from the Ginger Ridge Church. I saw your story on the news.

Great job! I stopped by to deliver a few letters from my congregation to our friend. Let me know if you think of anything we can do to help. Bye for now."

Brock stepped back to salute the old man. "Until we meet again, Grandpa Doe. I'll pray for you, and I'd like you to do the same for us. For me, my son, our new town, and our church. I suspect your prayers rise all the way to heaven and don't get stuck somewhere near the ceiling like mine sometimes do."

APRIL 1977

Solomon rounded the corner with a grocery bag in each arm to find Sadie Beth pacing on the porch. A teenaged version of her mother, Sadie Beth's long curls bounced in the evening sun as Elvis music echoed through the open windows. She loved to listen to Elvis albums while she studied, closing her eyes and using her pencil as a microphone for a big finish. Half the time, she never realized Solomon was watching.

But Sadie Beth clearly wasn't studying. Her footsteps were heavy as she nearly stomped across the porch and back again.

Also like her mother.

If either of them were troubled, it revealed itself in their countenance and expression. Solomon sighed. If something had rattled Sadie Beth's cage in this way, the rest of the world better run for cover. She had always been the strongest and wisest girl he knew.

She's a woman now.

He often had to remind himself that she'd recently celebrated her eighteenth birthday.

The more he studied his daughter, the more distraught she became. She hugged a magazine to her chest as if it was her last prized possession. Her heart was clearly in turmoil, and Solomon trusted his would soon follow. He held his breath in dreaded anticipation of whatever she was working up her nerve to confess.

Solomon waited at the edge of the sidewalk for her to notice him, but her eyes squeezed shut so tight she never looked up. She mouthed a series of words as if practicing a speech.

He cleared his throat to get her attention.

Sadie Beth flinched, and her eyes popped open. The normally translucent pools of blue revealed a carefully guarded secret. She rushed to greet him, taking one of the grocery bags while still clutching the magazine against her body.

"Oh, hey, Dad. I've been waiting for you. Dinner is in the oven. We're having breakfast casserole tonight. Your favorite!"

Another sign of serious trouble.

"I thought I detected the scent of bacon. It smells delicious. Thank you, Lightning Bug."

He cocked his head in her direction and followed her to the kitchen. Her royal blue graduation gown hung from a hanger in the open doorway of the dining room, freshly pressed and ready for action. Graduation portraits were scheduled first thing in the morning, launching a series of last acts as a high school senior.

Thankfully, any life-altering decisions were behind them. Sadie Beth had registered at the local community college. She preferred to live at home and planned to knock her general education credits out of the way before deciding on a major. This carefully thought-out plan had been her choice from the start, and Solomon knew better than to argue.

Few parents could say that of their eighteen-year-old daughter.

Winnie would be so proud of her ... of them, but Solomon still gave Winnie the credit, even after all these years.

Solomon studied Sadie Beth out of the corner of his eye as she bustled about the kitchen, putting the groceries in their proper place. She'd laid the magazine in a chair, face-down.

She filled the room with nervous chatter. "I thought about making biscuits and gravy, but I can never get it quite right. My gravy is too lumpy or too runny. Never in between."

Solomon shook his head and changed the subject. "How much time do we have? I was about to prune the rosebushes."

Sadie Beth checked the stove. "Twenty minutes. Um, I'll help you."

Solomon threw on his golf cap and made his way outside. Sadie Beth appeared with two sets of garden shears and their gloves—hers pink, his dark blue.

"All right, Dad. Show me how it's done." She tossed him a grin that melted his heart. She already knew the answers. She'd heard them all her life, but he appreciated her asking.

"Well, the reason we prune the bushes is to give the roses room to breathe. They need air and circulation, which protects them from disease. If they get too crowded, it suffocates the blooms." He lifted a couple of branches. "See here? Any place the limbs rub together can damage the roses, which limits their potential."

Solomon glanced her way, but her eyes were squeezed shut as her lips continued to move through a well-rehearsed speech. He worked in silence around the sharpest thorns to cut stems at a forty-five-degree angle as the worst possible scenarios of her looming announcement rolled through his mind.

Has she gotten a tattoo? Is she married, pregnant, or joining the army? Selling drugs on the side? Becoming an atheist? A nun? Quitting school? Planning a hitchhiking trip across Europe or Africa?

Winnie's face popped into his head, giving him a stern look that warned he had crossed the line.

How could I think such things about our daughter?

Elvis's voice chimed in with a familiar tune: "Suspicious Minds."

Solomon couldn't help but chuckle at the ludicrous ideas rolling through his mind. He dove headfirst into the pool of awkwardness between them.

"What is it, Lightning Bug? What's troubling you?" He rested his hand on her shoulder.

Her eyes met his, and he could see the look of terror.

"Daddy, they called me to the office today at school."

He raised his eyebrows, absorbing the long, uncomfortable pause that followed. "And?"

Her words came bubbling out—too fast, and probably not the way she practiced.

"A few months ago, they held a college fair at school. I strolled through the gym and spoke to different representatives from universities around the south. They encouraged us to turn in applications, primarily for the experience. I filled out several at once. I wondered if the bigger schools might accept me, or if I'd get lost in the shuffle."

She took his hand in hers and led him to the swing. "I'd never given it a second thought, because we'd already figured out what was best for our family. But these people wooed me with pictures of beautiful, multi-level libraries, and I couldn't resist."

Solomon leaned against the swing, and Sadie Beth's head naturally fell onto his shoulder. "So, why did they call you to the office today?"

She sighed and patted his leg. "Two reasons. First, to inform me I'm the valedictorian of the Class of 1977, so now I must prepare a speech for graduation."

A wave of relief fell across Solomon. His shoulders relaxed, and he squeezed her in a side hug. "That's terrific, Lightning Bug. I'm so proud of you!"

She gripped his hand but refused to meet his gaze. "But that's not all."

He pursed his lips. "Okay, what's the other terrible thing you must tell me?"

"I'm afraid Perkins University has awarded me a full-ride scholarship in their new program for neuroscience majors."

She fell apart in a heap of tears in his arms. He kissed the top of her head and rubbed her back until she calmed.

Why is she so afraid of letting me down? Have I put too much pressure on her to stay close to home without realizing it?

Solomon knew his daughter well. She desperately wanted to accept the offer, but also wanted to honor his wishes. He was the reason her heart had ripped in two.

He lifted her chin toward his and held her face between his hands.

"Sadie Beth, you are a treasure of a girl. Beautiful and brilliant, like these roses. But what do you think makes them so pretty?"

She thought for a minute and forced a half-smile. "You do. You anticipate their needs."

Solomon shook his head. "Maybe I do, but I told you if they get too crowded, they suffocate. The bloom of the rose is special because it opens itself up to the rest of the world. That's the only way it can flourish."

He kissed her on top of the head.

"Lightning Bug, we both know what you should do. To become a perfect rose, you must bloom on your own. Far be it from me to hold you back. I won't stand in the way of your dreams."

"Oh, Daddy, you are the reason I even have dreams. You've shown me how to overcome obstacles and stay true to who God created me to be."

He hugged her close. "That's exactly why you must go. To stay true to yourself. It's settled then, but I do have a couple of questions."

Her eyes widened as the twinkle he so adored slowly returned.

"Go ahead. Ask me anything."

"How far away is Perkins University? And which state is it in?"

"Four hundred and seven miles from our front porch to the Duchess Library, which is where I'll spend most of my time. A six-hour drive or an eight-hour bus ride. I've got a catalog that explains everything, and I've already been assigned a room in the honor's dorm!" Her smiled faded slightly as she asked, "Now, what's your second question?"

Solomon's tone grew serious. "For the love of all things holy, what does a neuroscience major do?"

Sadie Beth doubled over in a fit of giggles like she had when she was little. Solomon suspected it was as much from relief as thinking he was funny.

"It's in the catalog. I can't wait to show you, but first, I've got something for you." She reached behind the swing.

Solomon noticed a shiny piece of dark wood with a bow wrapped around it. "Oh my. What is this?"

"It's a cane. I had it made just for you, since your limp has gotten worse and the doctor suggested you might need it for balance as you get older. If I'm going away to college, I can't worry about you falling."

A tear rolled down Solomon's cheek. "You know I hate getting old, but it's simply beautiful. Thank you."

She took it from him and removed the bow. "You haven't seen the best part. Look, I had it engraved for you, right at the hook."

"Winnie and Silas. You put their names on it? That makes it even more special. Thank you, Sadie Beth."

CHAPTER FIFTEEN

Presley ran into Harper's arms. "Mom, did you hear? They elected me cheer captain, and I'm only a junior. That never happens!"

Harper squeezed her daughter tight. "I'm so proud of you, Squirt. Remember, being a leader brings great responsibility. Use that power wisely and include others in your decisions."

"I know. Walk in other people's shoes. You've taught me to do that my entire life."

The gaggle of girls that made up the cheerleading squad surrounded her and soon Presley disappeared in their midst. Twelve girls, somehow moving as one unit.

They're off to an impressive start.

Harper took the long way to her car. She enjoyed being outside for a change, and the school grounds were lovely. A ringing bell soon shattered the silence, and teenagers bubbled over into the courtyard with not a care in the world.

She spotted a couple in the corner strolling hand-in-hand. The guy was tall, stocky, and wore a blue football jacket despite the rising temperatures of the midday sun. His thick blond hair curled above the collar. When he stood, he provided a shade of protection over the young pony-tailed girl who stepped in stride with him. The petite young lady, tiny and trusting, gazed up at him like she might quit breathing if he ever turned away.

Harper remembered those feelings too well.

AUGUST 1996

Harper sniffed the blooms of the pink rosebushes before rushing up the steps of Solomon's porch to knock on his door.

"Solomon, are you awake? It's my first day of high school, remember?"

He stepped onto the porch carrying a cup of coffee, dressed and ready for the day.

"Yes, Harper, of course I know it's your first day of school. You've talked about it all summer long. Would you like me to walk with you?"

Harper's eyes lit up. "Would you? That would be terrific! I'm so nervous. What if no one likes me? Fort Bryce brings new kids to town all the time. I don't know why it's so hard to find friends my age. Why do you think that is, Solly? Is something wrong with me?"

Solomon held his elbow for Harper to loop her arm through his. She leaned her head against his shoulder and waited for one of his trademark answers—wise and comforting, with a gentle and loving plan of action.

"There is absolutely nothing wrong with Harper Phillips. She's deeper, more caring, and more sincere than most. She doesn't know how to be fake or let others make decisions for her. She seeks the lonely because she's been lonely herself. That's what makes her special."

Harper loved it when he referred to her this way. It helped to see herself through his eyes.

"Harper, long after these kids have moved on, you must be the kind of person you respect. Who cares what they think? The only opinion that matters is yours."

She remained silent, trying to think as deeply as Solomon did. They stopped atop the hill that overlooked the massive complex known as Ginger Ridge High School. Behind the school building stood a huge water tower with the name of the town in bold blue letters. School buses lined up in perfect rows like a brigade of marching soldiers while cars driven by teenagers swerved into the adjacent parking lot from every direction and parked wherever they landed.

Solomon raised his cane in the air in alarm. "That must be the student parking lot. Someone is going to get hurt around here. I wouldn't use that as a shortcut if I were you."

Harper's stomach coiled and she wished she'd eaten something for breakfast.

"Thank you, Solly, for being honest with me. You always make me feel better."

Solomon grinned. "Remember to walk in other people's shoes. We've all got a story to share." He offered a side hug and stepped away. "Would you like me to walk you down the hill?"

Harper shook her head. "No, sir. I'm a big girl. I'll take it from here. Thanks, Solly. Be careful going home."

He tipped his cap to her and pulled out his handkerchief to dab at his eyes. "Make it a great day. Stop by on your way home to tell me how it goes."

Harper waved and watched until her friend disappeared. She thought about how her father lived his life at a safe distance from others—never getting too close or too friendly. It was the military way. Without meaning to, she found herself emulating his style, always remaining on the fringes of relationships. She avoided conflict while holding her breath until the next move to the next town. Now that she was in Ginger Ridge to stay, she'd craved friends her own age. Running away was no longer an option.

My only friend is seventy years old. How sad am I?

She turned back to survey the buzzing school yard, determined this year would be different. Middle school had brought nothing but loneliness. No matter how hard she tried, girls her age were more competitive and spiteful than friendly.

"I heard her mother tried to kill herself."

"Even her own mother doesn't want to be with her."

"She thinks she's so pretty."

"Don't invite her to your party. She'll be flirting with all the boys."

Harper had heard it all—the whispers said behind her back for as long as she could remember.

She wanted to scream out in response, "I don't think I'm pretty. My mother is the only one who says that, and she's wrong about absolutely everything!"

But she kept it all in. Separated herself from the talk. Like her father taught her.

She approached high school as if she had moved to a new city. A fresh start.

First, she planned to try out for cheerleading. She'd only attended one high-school football game but fell in love with the chill in the air, the excitement and tension, and couldn't stop watching the cheerleaders on the sidelines.

Her father had insisted Harper didn't have the right body type to pull it off, while also denying Harper's repeated requests to take gymnastics to prepare for tryouts. Rather than push the issue or go through the stress of getting her mother involved, Harper had spent the entire summer in Solomon's front yard learning to do splits and working on her cartwheels and round-offs, usually while talking his ear off.

The way she figured it, if she made the squad, she would no longer be invisible.

She mentally clicked off her to-do list.

Make eye contact.

Greet everyone with a smile, but don't act like you think you're pretty.

Learn people's names and look for the lonely. A lot of these kids are new here, so they won't know they're not supposed to like me.

Harper took pride in her game plan as she marched down the hill toward the intimidating stage of Ginger Ridge High School. She passed the student parking lot and imagined the freedom of one day driving herself to school. From what she could tell, most parents handed over a brand-new sports car at the age of sixteen. That wasn't a likely outcome in her house, but it felt nice to pretend.

This year is going to be different. This year is going to be different, she repeated to herself to the cadence of her footsteps.

Once she reached the sidewalk, she kept her head up and intentionally sought the first person who stood alone. In her opinion, it was much easier to force one person to acknowledge her than to infiltrate a clique.

She found him leaning against the flagpole, facing the opposite direction. His shoulders were broad, and she had to stand on her tiptoes to tap him on the shoulder.

"Good morning. My name's Harper. What's yours?" She flashed a smile.

The guy turned around and lowered his gaze to hers. She stopped breathing for a moment, certain he must be a Greek god from one of her fantasy novels. He stared at her with deep brown eyes and eyelashes unfairly thick and plentiful. His hair matched his eyes and curled over his collar—exactly long enough to blow in slow motion with the gentle breeze that suddenly came through. Early signs of a mustache formed on his upper lip.

He's already a man. What am I doing talking to him? I think I'm about to pass out.

"Hello. I'm new to town. Julian Alexander. Official Army Brat, and the future star quarterback of your football team."

Her stomach flipped at the sound of his deep and decisive voice. She admired his confidence.

Hello, Your Majesty. You've earned the job of starting quarterback as far as I'm concerned.

He spoke again. "I've gone to a ton of schools, but my dad promised I'd get to stay in one place through high school. And I plan to take this school to the state football championship."

"Are you a freshman?" Harper heard herself ask, proud she'd used actual words.

"Yeah. My parents held me back when I was a kid because of sports. So far, it's worked out well. I turned fifteen last month."

Harper pictured him as an oversized kid with a mustache running around on the kindergarten playground. She choked at the thought of it and bent over in a coughing fit that exploded out of nowhere.

When she looked up, he was gone.

Surely that was their first and last conversation.

The school bell rang, and she ran for the front door, unsure of where she was supposed to be first.

"This year is going to be different. This year is going to be different," Harper repeated to herself as she followed signs to the principal's office.

What a dweeb I am. Recreating myself is going to require more effort than I thought.

CHAPTER SIXTEEN

Harper took the long way back to work, using the opportunity to make a few phone calls. A blurb came across the radio about Grandpa Doe, and she turned the knob up a notch.

"Police urge anyone with information on this accident to call the tip line."

Harper hoped the tip line had been flooded with clues confirming the identity of Grandpa Doe. The thought of burying him in a nameless grave in the city cemetery seemed too much to bear.

He deserves better.

She listened through a slew of voice messages and caught herself smiling at the sound of Brock Timberland's voice.

No time to talk today, Rev.

Instead, she dialed the number for Detective Sterling.

At the sound of the voice mail ding, she said, "Hi, Detective Sterling. This is Harper Phillips. I'm sorry I rushed off this morning, but I had a crucial appointment across town."

Her tires squealed as she bounced off the curb, almost missing her turn. She cringed, hoping the detective couldn't detect obvious sounds of reckless driving over the phone.

"I'm eager to see if the tip line brings a breakthrough. Is it possible for me to go through our patient's belongings to see if they offer any clues? Let me know."

Harper circled the busy hospital in search of a parking space. Finding none, she retreated to a spare lot a block down the street. After parking, she sifted through her purse for the piece of paper she'd jotted a number on earlier. Finding it at the bottom of her purse, she braced herself and dialed.

An annoyingly pleasant voice answered, as if announcing a theme park ride.

"Thank you for calling From Creation to Cremation. How may I help you?"

Harper rolled her eyes. She considered hanging up, but desperately needed the information.

"Hi, this is Harper Phillips from Savannah Regional Hospital. I'm a social worker managing the case of an unidentified elderly patient. We expect to lose him within days. At this point, there is no next of kin to claim his body. Can you help me understand the cremation process, including costs? What happens to his ashes if no one picks them up?"

Harper cringed at the words spewing from her mouth.

"I see, Miss Phillips. If no one picks up his cremains, our policy is—"

Did she refer to them as cremains?

"—we keep them for a year. After that period of time, they are scattered or disposed of."

Harper pursed her lips. "And the cost?"

"You'll find this is the most economical solution, with prices beginning at $1200."

Harper bit her lip. "You've been most helpful. I'll contact you if we decide to pursue this option. Thank you."

You've got to be kidding me! We can't scatter him in the wind, like he never existed.

Harper tossed the phone in her purse in disgust.

There's a reason I rarely leave work during the day.

She strode up the incline to the back doors of Savannah Regional. Breathless and agitated, she checked the time and headed straight for Grandpa Doe's room.

The old man's condition remained unchanged, but the notes on his wall had spread to cover a second wall. She grinned as she read a few out loud.

"God still loves you. Sorry I don't have any Scriptures memorized."

"Here is a picture of a truck. How do you like it?"

"Praying for you and your story, from the church at Ginger Ridge."

Harper detected a slight moan above the whoosh of the ventilator and rushed to the old man's side but noticed no movement. She adjusted his position, changed the radio channel, and pressed the call button to request a heated blanket.

"Grandpa Doe, I've got to check on Wallace Higgins, one of my pediatric patients. I'll be back shortly, I promise." She brushed her hand against the old man's cheek. "Hopefully, by this evening, someone will get the message you're here. If you want to leave me any clues while I'm gone, I'd appreciate it."

AUGUST 1977

Solomon pondered how Sadie Beth had convinced him to allow her to drive his truck to the well-manicured lawns of Perkins University.

Her plan started the previous evening when she'd looped her arm through his and asked him to take one last walk to the cemetery. The night ended with the two of them getting a chocolate dipped cone at the ice cream shop.

Whatever he agreed to in between, he couldn't recall.

Throughout that prior evening, he'd enjoyed her non-stop chatter. The bounce in her step. New glasses that made her look a decade older, as if she was already a college graduate with multiple degrees. Her eyes sparkled as she introduced each latest idea or discovery.

Her exuberance felt contagious, like her mother's. Solomon hoped Sadie Beth would never lose that trait.

Solomon bit his lip and let her rattle on as she leaned her head on his shoulder.

"I'll be home in sixteen weeks, in time for Christmas. I've already checked bus schedules and found the most economical way to get home."

As they strolled through Ginger Ridge, Sadie Beth stopped to hug everyone she passed. She had written the librarian a thank-you note, which she hand-delivered before closing time along with a basket of pastries from the Main Street Bakery.

He'd never be ready to send her out into the world. But it was time.

Time.

Solomon was running out of it.

To make matters worse, Sadie Beth was now in the process of launching this new chapter of her life while driving *his* truck, which was older than she was. Dented with peeling paint and rust spots, it boasted three hundred thousand miles so far. A great purchase, he and Winnie had chosen it off a corner lot a week after they'd married. They'd made several moves in that truck, loading it up and weighing it down en route to a new adventure.

The truck would see another quest now—this one with Sadie Beth at the helm. She gained confidence with each avoided pothole while Solomon calmed his palpitating heart. He gripped the handle of the passenger side door and tried to ignore the rising speedometer needle.

Two weeks earlier, the world had been rocked by the sudden death of Elvis Presley. The nation was still grieving, and Solomon wasn't sure Sadie Beth would recover. For this reason, she scrolled the radio dial in search of Elvis songs, one after another until it gave Solomon a headache.

"I didn't realize the volume went that high," Solomon said.

"What?"

"Never mind."

Sadie Beth had the windows rolled all the way down, blasting him with wave after wave of late August heat. He removed his golf cap so it wouldn't blow away, but his hair never moved, carefully chiseled into place by his morning dollop of Brylcreem. Solomon checked his reflection in the side mirror. A silver streak now made a home down the center of his head. The thick head of hair he'd always sported was getting thinner all the time as the sun bore down on his scalp.

"This is Wingate, South Carolina. A safe little college town, and Perkins University is smack dab in the middle of it."

He caught her eye and nodded. "It's lovely. It looks like the speed limit gets lower as you get closer to town." He patted her on the leg and forced a smile.

Sadie Beth tapped the brakes a couple of times and changed the subject. "We're almost there. I can't wait to show you around. My dorm room is on the second floor of Southerland Hall. Because I'm in the Honors College, I get a room all to myself. I guess they figure that's better for studying. I'm not used to sharing a room, so this will be perfect."

Solomon's thoughts burst into the open. "You don't think you'll get lonely without a roommate?"

She shook her head. "No, not at all. I know where to find the crowd. These kids are like me. Book nerds. We'll get along swimmingly. Everything will be copacetic."

"Copacetic, huh? Remind me to look that word up when I get home." He forced a smile as he surveyed the area—nothing but tattoo parlors and beer joints. The town of Wingate had yet to impress him.

Sadie Beth pulled over in a vacant parking lot to check the map. On the opposite corner was a club called Hot Legs with a handwritten sign that read: Now Hiring Pretty Girls. Dance Instruction Provided.

Solomon gritted his teeth. "Lightning Bug, this is nothing like Ginger Ridge. I don't see any charming ice cream shops or bakeries."

"Oh, Daddy, please. I made a wrong turn. I would never come to a place like this. You can trust me." She scolded him with a pointed finger like her mother used to do.

Solomon noticed her face turning red and determined not to make a big deal about it.

Sadie Beth grinded the gears of the truck into reverse and retreated down the street beside the seedy bar. "I found a church called East Ridge. It's a half mile from campus, within walking distance. They've got a great program for college students and offer free meals on Wednesday nights. You know how much I love a great church potluck."

Solomon grinned. "You always said it was the best fried chicken in the world."

Sadie Beth flashed a smile which settled his uneasiness for the moment.

Their surroundings improved drastically as the truck lurched over a speed bump and bounced into a parking place.

"Daddy, this is it. My home for the next four years." She leaned over to kiss him on the cheek. "Keep an open mind, no matter what we see, okay?"

He nodded but grew suspicious. Keeping an open mind meant trouble.

Sadie Beth pointed to a brick building in the corner. "There it is. Southerland Hall. I'll check in if you want to find a luggage cart. My room is on the second floor, but we can use the elevator. Room 298. Look at that massive front porch and swing. It's like being at home!"

A kid whizzed by on a skateboard, taking over the sidewalk. Music blared from a radio he carried on his shoulder. Solomon gulped and returned the golf cap to his head.

"I'm ready, Lightning Bug."

That was a lie, and they both knew it, but they opened their doors and braced for an unknown future. Sadie Beth jaunted up the front steps as if she knew exactly where to go.

Solomon took in the well-manicured lawns of Perkins University. In the center of campus stood an enormous fountain, surrounded by a brick walkway and cozy outdoor umbrella tables. Volunteers in matching T-shirts handed out ice cream sandwiches and bottled drinks to welcome the freshmen.

Solomon had elected to leave his cane in the truck. He took his time and lugged one of the lighter bins up the flight of stairs. In each suite he passed, mothers hovered over their daughters, decorating rooms to the hilt. Newly purchased items—bulletin boards, lamps, desk chairs, shower curtains, bedspreads, towels, mini-refrigerators, and toaster ovens—lined the hallways, as if every student had received an extra stipend for new equipment needed for college.

He'd gone over the paperwork in detail. In fact, he'd memorized it. None of those items had been listed.

Solomon sighed. Dads weren't programmed to anticipate such things.

What Sadie Beth needs most is her mother. Even now, after all these years.

Another Dad passed him. Young and muscular, wearing athletic shorts, and handling his load with ease. Solomon glanced down at his attire—the standard knickers, dress shoes, and bow tie. He resembled more of an outdated grandfather than Sadie Beth's father.

I wonder if Sadie Beth is embarrassed by my appearance. She used to be so proud I was different. If she changed her mind, she never let on.

When he reached her room, the size of it impressed him. In one corner stood a bunk bed. Opposite was a counter which would have been perfect for a refrigerator or toaster oven, if they'd known to bring such items. A corner desk with a built-in hutch was placed next to the closet. Sadie Beth would have those shelves overflowing with books in no time. He noticed there were no curtains nor a bedspread.

Sadie Beth appeared at the door. "You found it. Isn't it spectacular? With the extra bed already bunked, I have all this open floor space so I can dance to my Elvis music, and I'll use the top bunk for studying and the bottom for sleeping. I'm so lucky not to have a roommate."

She never gave Solomon a chance to respond.

"Let's get the rest of my stuff and then take a walk across campus." She glowed as she spoke.

"You left your quilt on your bed, right? Do we need to go to the store to buy comforters for your bunks?"

She shook her head. "I bought everything I need using money from after-school tutoring. I'll be fine."

"But the other girls have refrigerators."

"Relax, Daddy. You taught me to never compare myself to other people. Our story is different, and always will be. Why would that change now that I'm in college?"

An hour later, Solomon put down the final cart of boxes from the truck. Standing on an upside-down milk crate, Sadie Beth fiddled with a wall mirror to hang it on the closet door. A ponytail dangled over her shoulder. He caught her reflection in the mirror.

"There. Finished. How does it look?" she asked.

"Perfect." He smiled and vowed to never forget this image of his grown-up daughter.

Tap. Tap. Tap.

They turned their heads when they heard a knock on the door, even though it stood open.

"Hello there. I'm Spencer Patton, one of the campus safety officers. Just wanted to introduce myself and see if you had any questions about registering your car to park on campus this semester, or where to find certain buildings."

Sadie Beth's eyes grew wide as she stepped toward him. She offered her hand to shake his. "Thank you, Officer. I'm Sadie Beth Thomas. I won't have a car to keep on campus, unless Daddy wants to give me his old truck."

Solomon thought he might choke. "Not a chance, little missy." He cut his eyes toward his daughter.

Sadie Beth grinned and continued to peer up at the security guard as if she'd never met one before. Solomon could tell she was blushing, which in turn flushed his cheeks as well.

"Thanks for stopping by, Officer Patton. It's nice to know my daughter is in a safe place."

Officer Patton tipped his Perkins University baseball cap. "One of the safest campuses in the country, sir. I attended school here as well and loved it so much I decided to work here. You both have a nice day."

The officer made his way to the next door down and started the same spiel.

Sadie Beth appeared before Solomon with a glimmer in her eyes, holding something behind her back.

"I've got a surprise for you."

"What is it, Lightning Bug?"

She handed over a box. "Open it." Her feet danced as she waited.

Solomon lifted the cover off the box. Inside, a black and gold watch with a crisp leather band sat nestled inside scads of tissue paper. "A watch? Oh, Sadie, it's beautiful."

"Turn it over. Can you read the back?"

Solomon rolled the watch through his fingers and held it up to the light from the window. He squinted to make out the words.

"Always on my mind. Love, Sadie Beth."

"That's right. Perfect lyrics from Elvis himself. I think of you every time I hear that song."

Tears filled Solomon's eyes as he wrapped his arms around his daughter and hugged her as long as she'd allow. "Thank you. It's perfect." His voice cracked.

She wrapped the watch around his wrist and maneuvered the strap into place. Then she gently squeezed his shoulders and steered him toward the elevator. "Come on. Let's head to the bookstore. I want to buy you a sweatshirt. All the other dads are wearing them," she teased.

Solomon dabbed at his eyes with his handkerchief. He didn't wear sweatshirts, and they both knew it. "Oh, I can't wait," he replied with a sarcastic tone.

Sadie Beth pressed the button to the elevator looking as happy as he'd ever seen her.

"After the bookstore, we've got one more stop to make before you head home. I don't want you driving in the dark," Sadie Beth said.

Solomon checked the time on his new watch, not wanting her to know he was in no hurry to get home. There was nothing left for him there.

"One last stop? What might that be?"

"I want you to swing with me, Daddy. One last time. It's the only way I'll be strong enough to get through this year without you."

CHAPTER SEVENTEEN

Cameron Sterling propped his feet on the balcony railing of his third level condominium. Normally, he'd spend the evening snuffing out a half-pack of cigarettes, but this was day thirteen. No turning back. He took in a deep breath without wheezing and basked in the realization he'd made it up three flights of stairs without intense chest pains.

Progress.

Cam flipped open a to-go box loaded with a deluxe burger and fries from the corner deli. Not the healthiest choice for a meal.

One demon at a time.

His afternoon court appearance had proved to be a bust, as expected.

"Insufficient evidence to hold the suspect at this time," the judge announced with a resentful tap of the gavel. "Come back to me when you've got enough to prosecute."

Insufficient. How many times have I heard that?

Cam finished off his soda and crunched the can with one hand. He launched it at the trash can in the corner but missed the target.

Typical.

He shook his head and raised the cover off the evidence carton that contained the personal items of his hit-and-run victim. Harper Phillips expected him to deliver those items the following day, but he wanted to give the items one last inspection. Nothing jumped out from the inventory list—just a few generic items of clothing and a wedding ring.

Each piece of clothing was sealed in a clear plastic bag—a pair of suspenders, socks, loafers with a hole in the bottom of one of the shoes, a dress shirt, pants, and a bow tie.

A bow tie? That's the kind Daddy used to wear.

Cam checked his watch.

6:25 p.m.

Yes, of course.

OCTOBER 1980

Cameron and Grayson raced home from school and burst through the front door. Gray beat him by half a foot. Cam kept a tally of their daily battles. As the older brother, he should have won.

They'd been assigned spelling and reading homework. Gray would fly through his with ease, but Cam dreaded the extra hour it would take him to finish.

White curtains bounced away from the open front window. Wednesdays were beauty parlor days, and Mama's hair looked extra fluffy. She wore a deep red top and lipstick. Cameron remembered thinking how pretty she looked, though he was certain he never told her.

Her voice was stern. "Before you do your homework, you boys play outside until it gets dark. I can't have you rough-housing in my living room."

"Yes, ma'am," Gray said.

Always the mama's boy.

The fact that Grayson was closer to his mother didn't bother Cameron until Daddy was away like this for several months at a time.

Cameron shared the same adventurous spirit of his father. Act first, ask questions later. When Daddy returned, they always picked up where they left off—wrestling on the floor, throwing the football while they practiced spelling words, hiking through the woods to climb a tree and eat a picnic lunch, or setting out before daylight to catch fish from the banks of Shiloh Creek.

Cam never felt stupid when Daddy was around.

An afternoon game show played on the television with the volume turned down. Mama headed into the kitchen to prepare dinner.

She'd barely made it out of sight when Cam tackled Gray from behind, slamming him onto the sofa. A pillow flew across the room and a picture toppled from the mantel—a family photo from the church directory. Daddy had forced the boys to wear bow ties like his in that photo. His face beamed with pride, but the boys scowled, thinking they looked ridiculous.

Mama bellowed at them from the kitchen. "If you boys break that church picture, I will tan your hides!"

How did she know which picture had fallen?

Mama always knew.

Cam and Gray froze in place. A wait and see approach to see if she intended to chase them down.

The sizzle of frying meat echoed from the kitchen, and the powerful scent of beef hung in the air. Cameron's stomach growled in anticipation of whatever Mama was making.

The doorbell rang, interrupting a rare moment of silence.

Cam stared at the clock above the fireplace. 6:25.

The sputter from the skillet and the tick tock of that clock were the only sounds in the room.

The front door stood open where two men in uniform waited with their heads held low and arms at their side.

Cam took note of the backpacks he and Gray had left strewn by the door—something else they'd been warned a thousand times not to do. He felt the urge to pick them up, but his legs refused to move.

Mama rounded the corner, wiping her hands on a blue-checked apron tied around her waist. She stopped in her tracks as tears filled her eyes, her hands gripping the corners of that apron so tight her knuckles turned white.

The possibility that Daddy might be injured had never crossed Cam's mind. Not once. Daddy was far too smart, powerful, and confident to let anything like that ever happen to him.

Still, he sensed the truth now. The finality of it all—as if moving slow motion to a silent drumbeat he couldn't turn off.

Gray reached for his mother's hand.

Cam fought back a scream. He wanted to say, "Stop, Mama. Don't answer that door." But nothing came from his lips.

Mama faltered like a magnet drawn to the men at the front door, dragging Grayson with her. His arms were wrapped tightly around her waist, squeezing her so hard she almost tripped. Tears flowed down his cheeks.

Cam had never felt so helpless.

"Let go, son. I have to do this," Mama said to his brother with a voice that sounded like it came from someone else.

Cam no longer felt connected to his own body—taking everything in like a bystander cowering in the corner. If Daddy were here, he'd throw those strangers off his porch and slam the door behind them.

Daddy was the only one who could have stopped this from happening.

"He'll be home by Christmas. He promised," Cameron murmured.

Daddy's picture hung on the wall. A handsome man in uniform, doing his best to put a mean look on his face. But his eyes were always smiling.

Cameron seized that photo and hugged it to his chest, hoping to keep his heart from falling out.

Mama cleared her throat. "May I help you?"

One of the men handed Mama a bulky envelope and a glass case that held a folded American flag. Both men removed their military hats and placed them against their chest.

"I'm sorry to inform you ..." one of them whispered.

Mama wailed as Grayson screamed, "No, not my Daddy!"

Cam staggered to the open window and gazed outside. He'd rather be anywhere else than in this house at this moment.

Both men kept their heads down. One of them tried to hug Mama, but she pushed him away.

They stepped back, saluted her, and made their way down the sidewalk.

Cam watched as they left in a black car with letters written on the side. He wanted to throw something as they pulled away.

But not his daddy's picture which he still clutched in his hands. Now, his most prized possession.

Neighbors gathered on the street and wrapped their arms around each other. The setting sun cast a glow on the church steeple behind them.

Mama kicked the backpacks out of the way and closed the door. She leaned her back against it, sliding down an inch at a time until she rested in a sitting position on the floor.

Cam flinched at the sounds that erupted from her.

Grayson laid his head in her lap and sobbed.

Cam still couldn't cry. Instead, he envisioned his daddy's face and heard that deep voice reminding him to take care of his mother and brother.

Cameron reached for the top edge of the window and lowered it—locking it into place.

Finally, he trudged to the sofa and gazed at his father's military photo. Later that night, neighbors—the whole town of Ginger Ridge it seemed—gathered outside the Sterling house with candles. Cam could hear them singing church songs and crying together.

All while the stench of burning meat hung in the air.

CHAPTER EIGHTEEN

Harper wrapped her arm around the girl's shoulders and escorted her to the nearest chair. She grabbed a bottle of water, unscrewed the lid, and placed it in Breanna's hand.

"Take a sip of this and then take a deep breath. We can't announce children are dying up here. Not out loud. Not ever. I need you to make sure visitors sign in and show an ID. Stay pleasant and confident and, whatever you do, don't leave this desk. Answer the phone and take a name and number." Harper forced a pen into the girl's hand and set a pad of paper in front of her. "Remember to show a sense of hope. Okay?"

The girl gave another curt nod.

Harper took a deep breath and looked down the hallway.

"Breanna, where is the Code Blue? Which room?"

"Room 350."

"Oh no," Harper muttered under her breath. "That's little Wallace's room."

Breanna whispered, "He's about to die, I just know it."

Harper gave the girl an exasperated look she normally reserved for her daughter. "Remember what I said? We can't say that. That's not proper protocol."

"I'm sorry."

Harper patted the girl on the shoulder as she noticed a dazed couple huddled against the wall. "Just please answer the phones, take messages, and try to be positive and helpful."

She moved toward Roger and Claire Higgins.

His cancer is in remission. How can this be?

Wallace had been doing great on Friday when they'd discharged him. Losing a patient, especially a four-year-old, was devastating. In most cases with childhood cancer, death came gradually. Such a cruel disease, but one that usually took its time. The months of watching them suffer interspersed with moments of needed decisions created a buffer zone that allowed the family to come to terms with the inevitable.

Harper fought back tears as she touched the boy's mother on the arm. "Roger, Claire, please come with me. We'll find a place to talk."

Claire gripped her elbow. "They forced us out of the room, but we don't want to leave him. What if we never see him again?"

"It's best you don't see him like this. Let the doctors do their jobs. We won't go far. I promise."

She led them to a private meeting room with dimmed lights and no windows. Harper hated this room. Despite the comfy furniture, free bottled water, and coffeemaker with a variety of coffee and tea at the ready, the torturous news often delivered within these four walls erased all the benefits the hospital tried so hard to provide. They'd even used a muted green to paint the walls, which research suggested provided a calming effect.

In Harper's experience, this had never been the case.

She faced the couple and grasped Claire's hand, unsure where to start. Code Blue didn't always mean death. That feeling in the pit of her stomach guided her from there.

I should have better prepared them for the possibility of losing him.

Roger spoke first, catching her off guard. "Harper, we want to thank you for allowing us to take him home last week."

Claire nodded in agreement. "Yes, it's the greatest gift you could have given us. We should have known this was coming, based on how he acted. We shared a milkshake and told funny stories outside by a bonfire. He tried to count the stars and said he couldn't wait to see them in person one day. Wallace said all his prayers had been answered."

Roger pulled his wife close. "It was the best weekend. Thank you."

On the third floor, Harper stared out the window of the vacant room that mere hours ago held Wallace Higgins. She could barely breathe. Even the cancer specialists were at a loss on why they'd lost Wallace so quickly. In the simplest terms, his vulnerable little body simply hadn't been able to fight off the pneumonia and fever.

Wallace had been in the hospital off and on since his second birthday. He'd arrived rosy-cheeked and full of life. Crazy curls bouncing as he scuttled through the hallways of the pediatric wing with a cape tied around his neck like he was a superhero.

For the past two years, he'd been that hero. Strong and stubborn, defiant and determined. A kid who beat the odds.

Until today.

How could the Higgins family possibly thank me? I completely blew it on this case.

The moon rose above the bustling streets of Savannah— headlights and taillights zooming past as if nothing had changed. Daylight clung to one corner of the sky, refusing to give in to the power of darkness.

Harper's stomach rumbled, but she couldn't even think about eating. She sent Presley a quick message to let her know she'd be late.

Today was supposed to be the day she focused on Grandpa Doe, but she hadn't checked on him since early that afternoon.

I'm about to lose him as well.

Harper wanted nothing more than to curl up in a ball and cry.

She made a quick escape to the nearest stairwell, scurrying to reach the first floor. There, she broke into a run until she reached the quiet respite of the chapel. Thankfully, she found herself alone and dropped into the last pew in a row of six.

She noticed the box of tissues strategically placed at the end of the bench and an oversized Bible that glowed from the beam of the overhead lights at the front of the room. The book lay open on a pedestal, inviting her to search through those pages for comfort. The back half of the room remained dimly lit, allowing for privacy and quiet meditation.

Harper wanted none of those things.

What she needed most was to throw something through the perfectly chiseled stained-glass windows that adorned the side walls. Or beat her fists against the bench until it ripped apart. She wanted to make something hurt as bad as her heart did in this moment.

Instead, she let the tears flow freely. Her sobs burst forth louder and more intense than she expected, releasing the deep pain she rarely had time to acknowledge. The sound ricocheted off the walls to the point anyone passing by was certain to hear her.

I can't do it anymore. Caring hurts too much.

She folded her hands to pray, but no words came. Harper closed her eyes and leaned over until her head rested on the bench in front of her.

Then she allowed the sea of exhaustion to take over.

Please God. Let me wake up to find out this entire day was one big, disastrous nightmare.

CHAPTER NINETEEN

Raphael waited outside the hospital until well past visiting hours as the parking lot cleared. Disguising his voice, he had called earlier to confirm the room number of the old man they described on the news.

The man he almost killed.

I need to see him for myself.

Through the windows of the rear entrance, he noticed a janitor gathering trash from the waiting room. Raphael moved closer, ready to make his move. He crouched behind a row of bushes, avoiding the sightlines of stationary security cameras. When the janitor propped open a door to lug heavy bags of garbage outside, Raphael raced through the open door and disappeared into the first stairwell he could find.

They rarely install security cameras in stairwells.

He made his way to the eighth floor, pausing to catch his breath at the halfway point.

What am I going to do when I see him?

He charged up the stairs, following his deep instinct to visit his victim. He'd figure out the next steps when he arrived. The room was vacant when he peered through the window. Raphael took that as a good sign.

His stomach churned as he stepped inside the room.

The man's face remained bloated and bruised. The only signs of life were the spurring and beeping of machines. Tubes ran from every visible opening, including one attached to the top of his head.

This is all my fault!

He lowered his head to look directly into the stranger's face.

"Hey, old man, my name's Raphael Henry. What were you doing in the middle of the road? I tried to stop. Honest to God." Raphael dropped to one knee and wiped away tears with the back of his hand. "I almost called 911 myself but was too much of a coward to admit to what I'd done. Not that it matters. I'm either headed to jail or Mexico. Either way, I lose my family."

A few sobs escaped before he could move on. "It should be me lying here. Not you. I'm the one who deserves to die. I have to make this right."

Raphael rocketed to an upright position when he heard footsteps in the hall, holding his breath until the person moved past. Then he noticed the cards on the wall. After reading a few, he ripped out a sheet of paper from a notebook on a table and scribbled a quick note of his own.

I'm sorry. Please forgive me.

He hid his note behind a larger one and moved to the door to make his escape.

Raphael glanced both ways before exiting the room. He maintained a quick pace and slithered through the door to the hidden confines of the stairwell. Once he reached the bottom floor, he poked his head out to check for activity. Straight in front of him was a sign that pointed toward the hospital chapel.

That's exactly where I need to be.

Harper jolted out of a deep sleep and squinted as she tried to identify her surroundings. She touched her face and discovered a trail of dried drool that ran from the crease of her mouth to the hard bench beneath her. Her eyes felt puffy from crying as she checked the time.

It's almost midnight! I've got to call Presley!

She reached for the phone in her pocket. Dead.

Something stirred near the front of the room. Harper peeked above the seat and saw a young man—Hispanic, handsome, and distraught—pacing.

Does he know I'm here?

The man dropped to his knees, sobbing.

No, he does not.

"Dear God, why are you doing this to me?" he cried out.

Should I do something to help him?

"I never meant to hurt him. Please don't punish me by taking my family away."

Did this man hurt his family?

Her skin prickled. Trapped and frozen in place, she had no choice but to let the stranger release his guilt. Harper peered over the bench with one eye and wracked her brain as she attempted to recall any recent child abuse cases, but none came to mind.

The stranger moved to the Bible, flipped a few pages, and read to himself in Spanish.

Without warning, he turned to exit the chapel. Harper dropped to the floor and crawled under the bench, now proving to be more of a stalker than a highly skilled social worker.

Whatever brought him to the chapel suddenly felt like none of her business.

You can't save everyone, Harper. Meanwhile, your own daughter is home alone.

She sighed and pushed herself up from the bench. Time to head home. She could deal with everything better once she'd had some sleep.

As she turned the key in her car's ignition, she felt the pull of her warm bed. The streets were deserted at this late hour, and she made it home in record time. Brewster barely stirred from his spot at the foot of the sofa as Harper tiptoed in through the garage entrance. She peeked in on Presley, who had left her a note on a dry erase board on her bedroom door.

I called but your phone was dead. Again. You need a new phone. Can I get one too?

Harper grinned and shook her head, drawing a frowny face and a heart in response.

"No, your phone works just fine," she wrote.

Harper flopped across her bed without changing out of her hospital attire. She expected to sleep like a rock.

A series of closed doors met Harper as she tiptoed down a long hallway. A beam of light shone underneath each door beckoning her closer. But she knew each room contained a haunting trial from her past. No matter how hard she tried to erase those memories, they remained persistent, dredging themselves up at random times as if she still had a lesson to learn.

She braced herself and opened the first door. The goodbye note her mother had left behind when Harper was fifteen lay on the kitchen counter, next to a box of their favorite peanut-butter cookies. Harper unfolded the piece of paper and began to read her mother's overly medicated penmanship.

DEAR Harper,

I can't do this anymore. I may never find happiness, but I know it isn't here.

You'll be fine. You're a beautiful girl, much prettier than I ever was. That handsome boyfriend will take care of you. Never let him go.

I love you,

MOM

P.S. Please show this to your father.

Harper squeezed the note to her chest as she paced the floor.

Her father hated surprises.

Harper slammed that door shut and slogged to the next.

She next approached the door with the brightest light shining beneath it. A shadow moved across the light every few seconds. Harper sensed waves of darkness, but flung the door open anyway. She deserved whatever waited for her there.

Inside, she stood on Solomon's porch showing off her new cheerleading uniform. She swirled around, filling her old friend in on the details of her first football game as a cheerleader.

But then, out of the corner of her eye, she glimpsed Julian peering out from an old oak tree.

"Julian! This is my friend Solomon. I want you to meet him."

Julian stood with his arms folded and remained silent as if he never heard her. His eyes were hidden beneath the brim of his ball cap and she felt a wave of scorn.

"I'd better go, Solly. Will you come to our first game this Friday?"

Solomon patted her on the back on her way down the steps. "Wouldn't miss it for the world. I'm glad you're so happy, Harper. Thanks for stopping by."

Harper pulled away from him. "I'll come back soon. I've been swamped with practice and homework. Maybe after football season?"

Solomon nodded as if he understood.

She'd made it to the bottom step when he called her name. "Harper?"

"Yes, Solly." She turned to face him, shielding her eyes from the evening sun.

"Always remember to guard your heart. Everything you do flows from it."

Harper smiled. "Of course, Solly." She offered a quick wave and scurried to Julian, ignoring the sick feeling in her stomach.

"What did that old geezer say to you?" Julian asked, loud enough for Solomon to hear.

She steered Julian in the opposite direction. "Oh, nothing. Solomon always offers advice, but I don't know what he means half the time."

Julian grabbed her by the shoulders. "Listen to me. You need to stay away from that old man. He's probably a pervert, wearing those old-timey outfits, and spending all his time with kids. That's not normal."

Harper cringed at the coldness of his words. She jumped to Solomon's defense. "Julian, leave him alone. He's the kindest man I've ever met. He's been my best friend since I moved to Ginger Ridge."

She held her breath and waited for a response. She'd never stood up to Julian and had no idea what might happen next.

He said nothing and took off at a fast pace. Harper struggled to keep up with him, wishing she'd kept her mouth shut.

After a few minutes, he calmed down and draped his arm around her shoulder. They moved in step with one another, and she leaned into him, enjoying her rightful place in the world. He kissed her on top of the head and a smile spread across her face.

"Want to go to the diner?"

"Sure," she whispered, not the least bit hungry, but grateful everything had returned to normal so quickly.

In their favorite booth, she sat across from him while he ordered the usual—a double bacon cheeseburger with loaded fries. She doodled on a napkin, scrawling their initials and "Go Eagles" in block letters.

"Harper?"

She lifted her eyes and smiled, but then she noticed his cold look once more.

"Let me be clear. No girlfriend of mine is going to hang out with that old man."

Harper felt herself nodding as if she agreed with him.

She backed away from the room as she studied Julian's sneer and remembered how she'd visited Solomon less after that night.

The choice should have been easy, but she'd wanted so badly to be loved by Julian.

In the next room, an adult version of Harper tiptoed up Solomon's front steps to apologize to him.

Solomon's porch. The safest and most loving place she'd ever known.

What she wouldn't give to return once again. To rest in his swing, drink a frosty glass of lemonade and wait for him to point her in the right direction.

CHAPTER TWENTY

Since sunrise, Raphael had meandered through the back streets of Madison, delaying the inevitable. With one final stop to fill the gas tank, he backed his shiny Mustang into a parking spot at a furniture store. He'd gone a shade or two darker on the color and had her looking brand new. A complete overhaul—new windshield and hood. And of course, a new back seat.

That Mustang had been his first purchase when he'd arrived in America. He'd socked away a few paychecks and paid cash. That old car gave him a sense of pride and responsibility. From that moment, Raphael and his car had become inseparable—loyal companions, exploring the world and finding life's greatest treasures.

Raphael opened the hood and lifted his chin, preparing to say goodbye. The first of many goodbyes, and this one would prove to be the easiest.

Another car pulled up. Raphael recognized the driver from their brief encounter months earlier and reached to shake his hand. The guy handed Raphael the keys to his car, a brand-new BMW, and he and his adult son took off for a test drive in the Mustang.

When they returned, Raphael ripped off the bandage by signing over the title and the other man handed him an envelope that held $8,000 in crisp hundred-dollar bills.

He asked the new owner to drop him off at a used car dealer down the road, which gave him one last hoorah in the Mustang. He bit his lip as he took in the smell of the new leather seat. No turning back now.

Raphael had already scoped out the dealership in advance and knew exactly which vehicle he wanted. Within an hour, he made a hefty down payment on a late-model, maroon SUV with a third-row seat and low mileage. The best feature was the DVD player in the rear for the kids.

This SUV will be perfect for Isabella once the baby arrives.

Raphael settled in and adjusted the seat and mirrors. He lowered his sunglasses from the top of his head to cover his eyes—an attempt to look as cool as he once did in his Mustang.

Not a chance.

Raphael put the family-mobile into gear and exited the lot. A few minutes later, he careened into the parking lot of Rapid Realty for his next appointment. He'd already sent over several pictures of their home.

He clicked the lock with a remote and trudged toward the realtor's office as if forced down a gang plank on a pirate ship.

A feisty lady with spiky blond hair in a business suit almost bowled him over as he opened the front door.

"Good morning! I'm Heidi Hightower. Very nice to meet you." She thrust her hand forward to greet him. "I checked the photos you sent, and I'm thrilled to handle the sale of your gorgeous home."

Her grip was firm. Raphael saw this as a good sign.

She scares me a little.

The woman handed him a folder full of information he wasn't ready to absorb.

"As soon as you sign the dotted line, your home will be officially on the market. We should have an offer within hours."

Raphael gulped as his stomach roiled. Isabella had yet to hear of his plan, and he needed time for her to come around. He'd reveal it one step at a time, but this was too much, too soon, even for him. The spiky-haired woman rattled on in animated ways. Her hair was shellacked in place by some kind of shiny substance and never moved.

"Your place is perfect for a young and growing family with that creek in the back yard and all those trees to climb. Your hardwood floors are a realtor's dream. I'm sure it's difficult to sell a house you built with your own hands."

Her words kicked him in the gut and his voice cracked when he spoke. "It's been a perfect place to raise my family, but our needs recently changed."

"I understand completely," she said, brushing him off. The heels of her shoes clicked across the floor like a countdown as she escorted him to the door.

There's no way this exuberant, American citizen can understand.

He turned to face her. "Listen, I need time. My wife and I have many decisions to make. She's seven months pregnant, so I can't throw too much at her at once. I'll let you know when we sign the papers."

The woman paused as if unsure what to do with a client who failed to match her level of excitement and energy. He could tell his cautious approach annoyed her.

"Fine." She thrust the wooden handle of a yard sign in his hand. "After you drop off the papers, put this sign in your yard. Close to the road." She waved goodbye and shut the door while answering her cell phone.

Raphael gave a thumbs-up through the frosted glass of the door. As much as it gutted him, he had to consider every aspect of his situation. If they stayed, Isabella wouldn't be able to handle the yard work or the mortgage payment. His goal was to find a home that allowed the kids to walk to school, so Isabella could focus on the baby and avoid spending hours in school pickup lines. He thought he had the perfect spot in mind, though he no longer trusted his instincts. At this point, every choice felt wrong. He dropped his shoulders and tossed the cheesy yellow and red sign that showed a close-up of the perky blonde with an expression that dared anyone to turn her down into the back seat.

Say yes to the ad-dress!

Cute.

She reminded him of a cartoon character from a show his kids watched. He wondered if she might transform into a killer robot within a moment's notice. But he felt she'd come through on her promises.

Now, I've just got to get Isabella to consent to my plans.

Brock signaled the driver of the delivery truck to a spot where he could drop the dumpster in place as close to the church building as possible. After the pipe burst, he thought it best to dispose of anything that had showed signs of mold. He'd circled off an area on the flattest part of the church lawn with stones to hold a bonfire to burn the larger items, putting only small things in the dumpster. That way, it wouldn't get full too fast.

He paid the driver and checked his watch, setting his alarm with a reminder to meet Deacon.

Brock sent a group message from his phone to his church members asking for help to clear the building. A daunting task, but much easier accomplished with more hands on deck. While he waited for a response, he took a lap around the building, praying for the town like he did every morning.

Rumor had it the high school was scheduled for demolition within the next month. Same as the church, it was in such a state of disrepair it was no longer safe. After an emergency declaration from the mayor, a man Brock had yet to meet, the high school students had relocated to a wing of the middle school. With under fifty students in their last graduating class, Brock wondered if they might close the doors altogether in the coming years.

On the back side of the church building, a house with crumbling front steps caught his attention.

On the porch, a wooden swing splintered through and one side drug the ground. To his left, a busted railing leaned outward as if someone had fallen into it. Shattered glass from bottles littered the corners, and an old bookcase with a plastic cover leaned sideways beside the door. The storm door creaked an ominous warning as he pushed it aside.

Brock knocked on the door, shocked to find it standing open a few inches.

"Hello? Anyone home?" he called out.

No answer.

He scratched his head underneath the ball cap he wore turned backward and looked down at his clothes splattered with paint from past projects. Maybe he'd call back at another time when better dressed. He stood with his hands on his hips and considered his next move. Experience and his military training told him to wait for back up.

Never put yourself in a position to be accused of anything, Timberland. What if this house belongs to a drug dealer, and he accuses you of stealing drugs or money?

Despite his concerns, his curiosity got the best of him as he nudged the door open with his elbow. His feet carried him inside before the worst-case scenarios took over in his mind. A wave of heat knocked him backward. The stench of mildew, urine, and rotting trash hung in the air. Brock whipped out a bandana from his back pocket and held it over his nose and mouth as his eyes watered.

He left a trail of footprints across a heavy layer of dust that covered dark wooden floors. Recent shoe prints scattered in each direction.

A swarm of flies buzzed past his head.

He flipped on a light switch. Nothing.

Brock stopped and turned back toward the door.

What if I find a dead body in here? Do I notify the police? Does this town have a functioning police and fire department?

He did a quick internet search and located the Ginger Ridge Police Department number. He dialed, but the call rolled to a recording. Brock hung up in frustration.

Through one of the grime-encrusted windows, he noticed a couple of cars pulling into the church parking lot. With one last glance around the house, he exited to the porch, closed the door behind him, and scurried across the street to greet those who'd answered his cry for help.

I'll check this out later.

CHAPTER TWENTY-ONE

Raphael steered up the long gravel driveway leading home.

I hope Isabella isn't looking out the window.

He hid the new SUV in the garage, taking the time to arrange the car seats in a way that made the most sense. Zander could climb into his booster seat by himself in the third row. Xavier still needed help, so he strapped his in the middle, leaving room for an infant car seat next to him.

Raphael did a full turnaround on his property allowing flashbacks of great memories to roll over him. Building the treehouse. Pillow fights that stretched the entire length of the front porch. Flashlight wars and nighttime giggles when he'd camped out with his boys in the back yard.

A wave of honeysuckle wafted over from a patch at the edge of the woods making the moment even sweeter.

And more bitter.

Raphael couldn't repress the pendulum swing of feelings no matter how hard he tried.

Stay strong, dude. You've got to lead Isabella through this.

As if on cue, Isabella staggered to the front porch with sleepy eyes. Her hair swung in a loose ponytail. Other than her very pregnant belly, she still resembled a teenager.

"You're home. Wonderful!" She bent from the top step to kiss him and lost her balance.

Raphael caught her, planting a kiss on her lips.

She looked up through her lashes. "I forget how top-heavy I am. If I could see my own feet, that would help."

"Let's go for a ride and stop for lunch before the boys get out of school. I've got a surprise for my girl."

Her eyebrows furrowed. "A good one, I hope."

"Yes, I think this will be a great one."

Isabella glowed in anticipation and waddled off to find her shoes. When she returned, he led her to the garage where he made her pause and turn toward him.

"Close your eyes."

"Raphael, please. I can't see my feet as it is. Closing my eyes is just asking for trouble."

He took her hands in his. "Trust me. Just a few more steps. Okay, you can look now!"

Isabella popped her eyes open and then clapped her hands and jumped up and down the best she could.

"Oh my. That's beautiful. Where in the world is your Mustang?"

Raphael's grin was wide and genuine. "I sold it to buy this for you and the kids. Your new car, large enough to hold a family of five."

Or four. I may not get the chance to ride with them.

Isabella threw open the passenger door to check inside. "This is incredible! It's huge."

Raphael's eyes bulged as he remembered the real estate sign he'd tossed in the back.

"Here. Why don't you sit on the driver's side? He held the door open for her as she followed his lead.

Isabella wiggled herself into the driver's seat. She punched at the buttons on the dashboard. Loud country music blared from the speakers, and she turned the air conditioner on full blast while rolling her window up and down repeatedly.

Raphael used her distraction time to carefully slide the sign from the car and stashed it behind some shelves in the back of the garage.

"Wow, we've never had power windows before. What does this button do?" she asked, never realizing he'd stepped away. Isabella fiddled with something on the side of the steering wheel and turned her head to catch the rear window wiper blade in action.

"Whoa, calm down, m'lady. One gadget at a time." He couldn't help but laugh. Her reaction was better than he hoped.

"This car is so perfect, Raphael. This feels like Christmas morning. I won't drive it until after the baby is born. I can't see the foot petals, and I'd hate to mess up our car."

Raphael's shoulders tensed.

I won't be around to teach you how to drive it after the baby is born.

He cleared his throat and tried to shake off anything that might ruin the special day he had in store for them. "Okay, I'll drive. I've got a big day planned for us."

Good news first, followed by horrible, shocking news. She asked for a plan, and this is the best I can do.

Pulling into the hospital parking lot, Cam stifled a yawn. His hands trembled as he returned Harper's phone call.

Day fourteen without a cigarette, and one day closer to victory. Replacing one habit with a better one, he filtered through a bag of bubble gum and choose a couple pieces. He gripped the bag in his hand as an unexpected smile spread across his face.

This is the same kind Daddy used to bring home as a treat from the airport.

The beep sounded in his ear as he shook off the unexpected memory.

"Hello, Miss Phillips. I'm wrapping up an overnight shift and bringing our victim's belongings to you. These items must remain sealed in case we need the evidence for court at a later date. Don't open or remove anything from the bags. Talk soon."

Cam caught his expression in the mirror, surprised by how pleasant he sounded on the phone. He lifted his sunglasses to check his eyes. Still accented by decades of frown lines, but they appeared brighter, more hopeful.

I'm not sure what is happening to you, Detective, but keep it up.

He dialed a number he hadn't called in months. He was greeted with a recording and a beep there as well.

"Hi, Braxton, it's Dad. I know you're in school and can't answer, but I've been missing you. Give your old dad a call sometime and let me know how football is going. I'd love to come watch you play if your mom will allow it. Oh, and I quit smoking, just like I promised I'd do one day. I'm on day fourteen without a cigarette and there's no turning back. I love you, Son. Don't ever forget."

Cam hung up the phone and then dabbed at his eyes with a coffee-stained napkin from his passenger's seat.

I probably won't hear back from him, but at least he'll know how I feel.

He regained his composure and forged his way into the hospital entrance doors. Cam stopped at the front desk and placed the carton of evidence on the counter.

"Good morning, Rosie."

"Hello, Detective Sterling. Any news on our patient? We'd be thrilled if you marched in here with all the answers. Harper will never forgive herself if she doesn't resolve this before it's too late."

He shook his head. "No. Nothing yet. Speaking of Miss Phillips, is she available? She requested I bring these by."

"No. She's running late this morning. But I can lock the box in her office and let her know it's here."

"Thank you. Please be sure no one tampers with it. Since I'm here, I thought I'd visit our victim to see if there's anything he needs to tell me."

Rosie shrugged, already moving toward the escalator with the box in tow. "If only it were that easy," she called over her shoulder.

Cam added to his wad of bubblegum while he waited for the elevator. On the eighth floor, he made the right turn toward his victim's room. Once inside, he was moved by the number of cards and letters displayed on the wall.

"For someone with an unknown identity, you sure are a popular fella." He walked over to the bed. "All right, sir. I'm going to treat you like I would anyone else. Let's start at the beginning." He whipped out his notebook. "Who are you? What were you doing out at night? Why hasn't anyone reported you missing? When did this happen exactly? And where are you from?"

Cam lowered his voice. "Give me something to work with here. You're making me look bad, Mr. Doe."

Harper slouched into the lobby, looking even worse than she felt—eyes bloodshot and hair still wet. She tried to stifle a series of yawns. Her work pants, still wrinkled and damp, proved she'd taken them out of the dryer too soon.

"Whoa," Rosie exclaimed when their eyes met.

"I know. Rough day and night. I hardly slept enough to call it Tuesday. I hate running late. Feels like middle school all over again." She rolled her eyes. "Please tell me Grandpa Doe is still with us?"

Rosie's pause lasted longer than necessary.

"No, Rosie. Don't tell me we've lost him!"

"No, not yet, but it won't be long."

Harper's head dropped with the weight of Rosie's words. "We're running out of time. Any leads on his identity?"

Rosie shook her head. "Not that I'm aware of, but Detective Sterling was here first thing this morning to drop off a box for you. It's on your desk."

Harper pursed her lips. "Great. That box holds our only clues to this case. I'll be in Grandpa Doe's room if you need me."

DECEMBER 1977

Solomon rustled around the kitchen preparing meatloaf and mashed potatoes for dinner. Sadie Beth's favorite.

Tap. Tap. Tap.

He lifted his head to confirm the knock on the door.

That's odd. We don't get many visitors.

He checked the watch Sadie Beth gave him when he'd dropped her off at Perkins University a few short months ago.

His daughter was due home within an hour. Solomon planned to surprise her at the Bluegrass Bus Station. When they last spoke, she'd called from the wall phone in the crowded hallway of her dorm, and proudly announced she'd aced all her exams. The two of them had grown accustomed to catching up during five-minute phone calls. He hated to hang up but the line of chatterbox girls waiting behind Sadie Beth made it difficult to hear.

"Three days. I can't wait to sleep in my bed for an entire month," she'd said. "I love you. See you soon."

Even as she'd hung up the phone, he sensed something bothered her. Perhaps it was a touch of homesickness or exhaustion. Daddies know these things, and he couldn't wait to see her in person to make it all better.

In the corner of the living room, he'd set up their silver Christmas tree, which came with a color wheel that illuminated the tree as it spun in slow motion. As a child, Sadie Beth had adored that tree and had often slept on the sofa to watch the ever-changing colors before dozing off.

I hope she falls asleep on the sofa for old time's sake.

He looked around once more at the spotless house. Sadie Beth's presents were wrapped and stacked neatly under the tree. Their stockings hung side-by-side on the oversized mantel. He'd even donned his *Perkins University Dad* sweatshirt.

He'd counted the hours until her scheduled arrival and his heart raced now with anticipation as he strode toward the door. Getting through these past four months was one of the most difficult things he'd ever done.

He hated being alone, the daunting task of admitting his fears and vulnerabilities, and coming to terms with the fact he could never control such things. For Sadie Beth's entire life, Solomon had been a nervous wreck. So afraid something might happen to her and terrified of letting Winnie down. His entire existence had depended on protecting his daughter.

He'd worked hard to be at peace, which he hoped would ease Sadie Beth's mind at as well. Would she notice the difference in him?

A second knock at the door rattled him out of his thoughts. This one, much louder. Unnerving.

Solomon removed his handkerchief from his pocket and clutched it in his hand as he opened the door.

"Mr. Thomas, I'm Chaplain Westerman from the Ginger Ridge Police Department. We've confirmed some disturbing information from the Campus Police at Perkins University in South Carolina regarding your daughter ..."

CHAPTER TWENTY-TWO

After a long, sweaty morning, Brock released the four volunteers who had helped him clear the church building. Before they took off, he shot them a question.

"Do any of you know the history of this town? Specifically, who lives in that house?" He pointed to the house he'd explored earlier.

"I'm new to the area," one of the volunteers responded. "Came here for the low cost in real estate."

The others nodded in agreement.

Brock sent them away with a wave and checked Main Street for any signs of life. A maroon SUV steered into a parallel parking space in front of the old bakery.

Welcome to Ginger Ridge, but I'm afraid you'll be disappointed. That bakery's been closed for years.

He stood with his hands in his pockets and sauntered to the bell tower that he'd blocked off with yellow caution tape. Their first day in town, Deacon scurried underneath the bell and yanked on the dangling rope inside the tower. Once Brock caught up to his son, he realized the heavy iron dome of the bell leaned to one side—a death trap for anyone who dared to step beneath it. His heartbeat raced at the memory of that day.

One problem at a time. Maybe we should start with this old bell tower.

Brock nibbled on half a bag of chips from his truck and chugged down a warm bottle of water while plotting his next move.

With his bandana, Brock wiped the sweat from his forehead and jogged toward the abandoned porch he'd visited earlier. A series of dying, tangled rosebushes blocked the view of the house.

Attached to the wall beside the front door was an old-style rusty mailbox which Brock failed to notice earlier. He lifted the lid to check for any mail.

A swarm of wasps charged him. Brock ducked through the front door, slamming it to seal himself inside.

He caught his breath and decided to notify the police before he got in over his head.

What should I say? "Hi, this is Brock Timberland, the new minister in town, and I let myself into someone's house ..."

Brock shook his head and dialed the number again for the local police. After waiting through the same recording he'd heard earlier, he left a message at the beep.

"Hello, this is Brock Timberland, the new minister at the Ginger Ridge Church. I found a door open on a house, and I'm concerned about whoever lives here. Address is 17 Ruby Road. Can you send someone to meet me here?" He hung up and looked around.

I'm already inside. Might as well check things out.

A long sofa faced a spotless fireplace where black and white framed photos decorated a dusty mantel. A series of notes dotted the walls with reminders scribbled across them. Some had dates written at the top in standard military format—day followed by month. Day-to-day tasks, with no years specified.

11 APR Go to bank
31 JUL Pay electric bill
11 SEP Buy flowers / Visit cemetery
26 MAR Get new glasses
12 JUN Bring Sadie Beth home

Brock moved past the living room, a formal dining room, and into the kitchen. He opened the refrigerator and regretted it as the stench of rotten food shot across the room. He thrust his bandana over his mouth and nose.

Yep, the electricity has been off for quite a while.

At the foot of the stairwell along the left side of the house, the railing dangled from the wall. He cupped his hands to his mouth.

"Hello! Anybody home?"

No answer.

He tiptoed up the stairs, careful to avoid the series of footprints left in the dust. A wave of guilt washed over him at such an intrusion of privacy.

I'd hate for anyone to rummage through my house like this, but I need to make sure no one is injured. Or worse.

The hall contained four dark wooden doors. Pink flowered wallpaper adorned the walls in sharp contrast. The disgusting odor from downstairs didn't seem as prominent on the upper level, freeing Brock to use his bandana to open each doorknob without leaving fingerprints.

Attached to the first door was a plaque with SILAS written in blue, block letters. Brock opened the door an inch at a time. As his eyes adjusted to the darkness of the room, he discovered a nursery with gray walls and a fuzzy blanket draped over the side of a white crib. A matching rocking chair sat in the corner with a stuffed elephant in the seat. In the closet, Brock found a row of newborn baby clothes hanging with tags still attached. An arrangement of white picture frames adorned the walls.

The room looked like it had never been used.

So, what happened to Silas?

Brock gulped and backed into the hall as a heavy sense of sorrow overtook him. Leaning his head against the doorframe, he offered a quick prayer.

For Silas.

A bulletin board hung on the next door with graduation photos of a beautiful blonde. In the pictures, she displayed a diploma and opened her graduation gown to reveal a Perkins University t-shirt.

Underneath the photo, it read: Ginger Ridge High School, Class of 1977

In the center of the photo display was a handwritten note.

Thank you, Daddy, for helping all my dreams
come true. You will be with me every step while
I'm away at college. See you at Christmas! I love
you, Lightning Bug

A musty replica of a teenager's bedroom from the
seventies lay inside the door. The blinds had been left
partially open to allow in natural light and a poster of a
young Elvis hung on the wall. With curled lip and movie-
star hair, the guy had more than his share of talent.

The world still needs that guy.

Index cards with Scripture references written in an
assortment of colors adorned the edge of a mirror above
a dresser. Right on top in the center was a prayer request
written in childish script: *Please help Daddy want to go to
church with me!*

The opposite wall held an array of bookshelves from
floor to ceiling. On the nightstand sat a diary with a
matching pen and a framed photo of a woman with a little
girl in her lap riding in a horse-drawn carriage in the snow.

The bed, covered with a patchwork quilt and a slew of
decorative pillows, sat wedged into a corner where the
ceiling slanted. Brock wondered how anyone had slept in the
bed. On the incline of the ceiling, the name Sadie Beth was
spelled out in a series of photos pinned with thumbtacks.

The photos depicted more scenic nature shots than
people. A tombstone with the last name of Thomas
caught Brock's attention. The sun reflecting off a creek. A
mountaintop with a dollop of snow. A tree covered trail. A
close-up of a curious owl. A rose in bloom with droplets of
morning dew on each petal. A silhouette of a man wearing
golf cap and knickers photographed from behind while
standing on a cliff.

*Is that the same man from the photos I found at church?
The one who drove a carriage and presented the bunny at
Easter?*

Brock checked the closet which was mostly empty
except for a few sealed cardboard boxes with the name
Thomas written across the top.

Brock's heart pounded with a powerful urge to run out the front door to escape the sense of sadness that hung in the air.

No, Timberland. That's not what ministers do.

He wiped clammy hands on his shorts and adjusted the ball cap on his head. Brock clinched the bandana in his fist and forged on to the next room.

This room stood spotless and in perfect order without a speck of dust. The bed was covered with a vintage white bedspread that hung to the floor. No fluff. Only two pillows pin-tucked under the bedspread.

Whoa! This is not what I expected.

On the dresser a wallet, a pocket flashlight, and a pair of glasses sat ready and waiting as if their owner would return any second. A thick scrapbook lay in the center of the dresser, open to a picture of the blonde teenager Brock now recognized as Sadie Beth. At the foot of a chair stood a shoeshine stand with a fresh rag and a can of black shoe polish. An open Bible lay on the nightstand. On the opposite side, an old black and white wedding photo drew Brock in. The bride, a lovely blonde with curly hair, wore a shoulder-length veil with a simple white dress that fell to her knees. Her smile glowed as much as the twinkle in her eyes as she gazed up at the handsome man in an army uniform standing next to her.

Brock opened the frame of the wedding photo to check for a date.

Our wedding day—Solomon and Winnifred Thomas. 12 JUN 55

Despite their hopeful expressions of happily ever after, Brock sensed a deep sense of tragedy had occurred in this home.

He returned the wedding photo to its polished silver frame. In the closet, he tugged at the pull chain.

No electricity. Right.

A row of identical dress clothes—knickers, white shirts, bow ties and suspenders—hung in perfect order. Seven sets, enough for each day of the week. The maroon, hooded sweatshirt with *Perkins University Dad* on the front stood out in stark contrast to the other clothes. A row of worn-out black loafers, arranged in a perfect line, stood ready for use on the floor. He lifted a pair of shoes to the light from the window. The sole separated from the shoe.

Knickers. This has to be the same gentleman from the church photos. Is he still alive, this Solomon Thomas?

On the dresser, he flipped to the front of the scrapbook to find pages and pages of photos of the same old man with knickers and bow tie with his arm around different children on his front porch. Kids of all ages, size, and race. Some held American flags, books, a glass of lemonade, or a stuffed animal. There was also a great photo of a young blonde holding a baby girl, though Brock didn't recognize the porch in that particular picture.

"Solomon Thomas ... Where are you? Are you still alive? Why is your house unlocked and your wallet still here?"

He lifted his phone to notify the police a second time when, through white curtains, he noticed a patrol car slowing to a stop in front of the house. Brock bolted down the stairs and out the front door to greet the officer.

An older gentleman in uniform propped the car door open and took a long while to get out of the car.

Brock grew impatient and moved in closer. "Good afternoon. I'm Brock Timberland, the new minister here at the church. Thank you for responding so quickly. Do you know anything about the man who lives here?"

"That's Solomon's house. He wanders off from time to time, and we have to bring him home. How long has he been gone this time?"

"I'm not sure. I found the door open and took a look around. His wallet is still on his dresser, so he wasn't planning to be gone for long."

"We'll keep an eye out for him. He's probably over at the cemetery."

"Okay, thanks. I wanted to let someone know. Also, his electricity has been disconnected. Do you know who I can contact to pay that bill?"

"Call Hazel at the co-op."

Brock couldn't help but smile. "Thanks. I'll look her up. By the way, what's your name?"

"Sergeant Beauregard. Folks around here call me Bo."

The alarm sounded on Brock's watch.

"Listen, I've got to run. I'll call tomorrow to make sure Solomon is all right."

"Sounds good."

Brock broke into a sprint toward the elementary school. *I'm coming, Son. I promised I'd always show up.*

MAY 1978

Solomon thrashed around on his made-up bed. Every time he closed his eyes he heard his daughter scream for help, but he could never find her, no matter how hard he tried. He bolted upright and lunged off the bed to gaze out the window. The moon rose above the church steeple, casting a peaceful glow across Ginger Ridge.

Eventually, Solomon stopped trying to sleep. It wasn't worth the effort, and all the scenarios he envisioned when he closed his eyes proved to be way too painful.

"Please watch over her, wherever she is. If you can hear me, bring my girl home to me," he prayed aloud every night when sleep bypassed him, but he suspected God no longer heard his prayers after missing church for so many years.

Five months had passed since Sadie Beth had been reported missing by her dorm supervisor at Perkins University. They first thought she'd left early for Christmas break. When she failed to check out, they surveyed her room and found her belongings packed and ready to go. By that point, it had been three days since anyone had seen her in person.

In those early days right after Christmas, a detective from the Wingate police department updated Solomon often on their search efforts. As time passed with nothing to report, the calls soon dwindled.

Still, Solomon clung to a last sliver of hope that she'd walk through his front door. Battling the daily torture that came from not knowing what had happened to her took most of his energy. If Sadie Beth had died, he had to know. He knew how to handle death. Solomon had become a master at visiting the cemetery.

But this? He could neither grieve nor stop himself from imagining the worst. Solomon forced himself to go downstairs for a change of scenery. He shuffled to the kitchen in his bathrobe. His stomach rumbled, so he peeled open a banana he found on the counter. He bit into it and stared out the back window. The trees had fully bloomed. Last he checked, those branches had been empty.

Tap. Tap. Tap.

Solomon jumped.

Sadie Beth? Maybe she lost her key.

Solomon's ankles crackled as he rushed to fling open the door. "Lightning Bug? Is it you?"

A young man in uniform stood in front of him. Solomon squinted through his glasses to read the patch on his shirt.

Perkins University Security.

"Hello, Mr. Thomas. I called a few times but got no answer. I don't know if you remember me, but I met you on move-in day last fall. I'm Officer Spencer Patton with the Perkins University Campus Police." His voice cracked as he leaned in closer. "I brought Sadie Beth's belongings from the university. Rather than have them delivered, I thought I'd go for a long Sunday drive and bring them to you myself."

Tears filled Solomon's eyes as he groped for a response. His first thought was to insist he didn't want them—that Sadie Beth would need those items when she returned to campus.

The man spoke again. "I'm sorry, Mr. Thomas. Clearly, I've caught you off guard. I considered Sadie Beth a friend and wanted to make sure her belongings were well taken care of. I thought you might need assistance bringing these boxes inside."

"Please, come in." Solomon lifted a handkerchief from his pocket and led the officer to stand in front of the mantel. Before either of them could speak, Solomon turned toward Officer Patton, collapsed into his strong arms, and openly sobbed.

After a few moments, Solomon gathered himself and they settled onto the sofa. Solomon wiped his face with his hanky. "I'm sorry, Officer Patton. I've held it in for so long." He took a deep breath. "You don't think she's ever coming back, do you?"

Officer Patton cleared his throat and looked straight into his eyes. "Please, call me Spencer. Sir, I sure hope she will return. Like I said, I think very highly of your daughter. I sometimes blame myself for whatever happened to her. I cautioned her about running those trails alone. That girl just loved to run."

Solomon lifted his chin. "My Sadie Beth? Loved to run? Are you sure?"

The officer nodded. "Let me get you a drink of water, and we can talk for a bit. I'm in no hurry."

Solomon sipped on the glass of water while Spencer brought in five sealed cartons with the name Thomas written across the top. "Where would you like me to put these?"

"In her closet, so they'll be ready for her when she comes home. It's the second bedroom at the top of the stairs."

Solomon gathered his thoughts while he waited for Spencer to return. So many questions.

"Mr. Thomas, can I get you anything else? Do you need me to go to the grocery while I'm in town? I sense you've been in this house alone for quite some time."

Solomon shook his head. "You have great manners. Do you come from a military family?"

"Yes. My father was a career Marine."

"Your father must be proud. Thank you for taking the time to do this. Can I ask you a few questions?"

Officer Patton paused and then his voice softened. "Of course."

"What can you tell me about Sadie Beth? Start at the beginning. Tell me about all run-ins you had with my daughter."

Spencer brushed his knuckles across his chin and smiled. "Sadie Beth was always pleasant, though we often had to kick her out of the library at closing time. I think she read every book owned by the university."

Solomon rubbed his hand across his whiskered face to cup his chin. "That's definitely my girl. Did she have any friends? Or any boys that hung around too often?"

Spencer shrugged. "That didn't seem to be her priority. Many kids are there for social reasons—sometimes we wonder if they ever go to class. But Sadie Beth's priority was clearly her education. I did catch her at the first football game. She stopped to say hello on her way out at halftime. I'll never forget what she told me. 'If my dad asks, now I can say I attended a football game.'"

Solomon moaned. Hearing details of his daughter in action at college took his breath away. Their conversations on the hallway phone had been so brief and segmented. "A football game, huh? She never mentioned it. Is there anything else you remember?"

"Like I told you, she loved to run. If she wasn't in the library, she was jogging laps around campus. I'd often spot her on the trails leading into the woods behind her dorm with headphones in her ears. It was tricky to get her attention sometimes."

Solomon shook his head in confusion. "That doesn't sound anything like her. Are you sure?"

"Yes, sir. She said she did her best thinking while running. Around Thanksgiving, she admitted to being homesick and threatened to run all the way home."

Tears rolled down Solomon's cheeks. His voice cracked with his next words. "Thank you so much for stopping by. You've given me quite a gift. Can I call you if I have any more questions?"

Spencer handed him a business card. "Yes, sir. Call me anytime. I'm going to touch base with the church across the street and have them keep a close eye on you. Do you know anyone there?"

Solomon shook his head. "Not anymore. Winnie used to drag me to church, but it never felt right to go without her. Sadie Beth used to go all the time without me."

Spencer patted him on the back. "You did a wonderful job raising Sadie Beth. I've never met anyone like her. It turns out she and I had a lot in common. I will keep praying that she comes home safe and sound, Mr. Thomas."

Solomon stood to escort his new friend to the door. A wave of dizziness passed through him, but he didn't let on.

He waved goodbye and locked the door. Standing in front of the mantel, he picked up a framed picture of Winnie and Sadie Beth, hugging it to his chest.

"Oh Winnie ... I'm afraid I lost our daughter. I'm sorry. I tried so hard to keep her safe."

CHAPTER TWENTY-THREE

Isabella remained too enthralled with their new car to notice how long they'd been on the road. Giggling like a schoolgirl, she fiddled with the buttons and raised the seat until she rested a good six inches higher than her husband.

They rounded a bend on a country road with hills on either side of them. To the right, a massive water tower read:

**Welcome to Ginger Ridge—Home of the Eagles
Georgia State Football Champions 1997–1999**

Isabella shot up from a reclining position.

"Where are we? I've seen that water tower before."

"About thirty minutes from Madison."

Isabella returned her chair to a sitting position. "Where are we headed?"

"You'll find out soon enough." He gave her a wink.

Isabella scrunched her shoulders in anticipation. "You said this day would be filled with surprises. I can't wait!"

That's one way to put it. Surprise. Shock. Despair. I'm not sure how any of this will go, but I'm running out of time.

Raphael tapered his concerns and followed the faded signs to Ginger Ridge. The listing price of real estate drew him to this town, but as he took a sharp left onto Main Street, he better understood why rental rates had been so low. There were no immediate signs of life as they cruised through the abandoned town.

Plywood covered each storefront, creating the perfect canvas for a sea of offensive graffiti to welcome them. Broken glass scattered across sidewalks. Raphael squinted to read the faded sign of what had once been an ice cream shoppe and an old drugstore. A classic red, white, and blue barber pole clung for life beside a narrow store. A few rusty parking meters remained on one side of the street.

Up ahead, a cracked digital time and temperature sign rose like a flag of surrender in the parking lot of a bank. Webb and Fletcher Community Bank commanded half a block at Florence and Main, directly across from a modest building that housed the Webb and Fletcher Funeral Home.

Raphael suspected both Mr. Webb and Mr. Fletcher were long gone. The feeling in the pit of his stomach warned him to whip up a backup plan. Ginger Ridge had been his only hope.

Reminder. It's not wise to select real estate online.

Raphael was ready to concede his idea, but then he spotted it. The bakery, past the bank on the corner of Main and Evelyn.

He grinned and took that as the first positive sign since their arrival.

Evelyn. The name means light and life. A perfect name for our daughter. And maybe the perfect place for my family to start over?

He maneuvered the SUV into the last parallel parking place. The street narrowed to what had once been a residential section of town, but the houses appeared to be empty and boarded up like everything else.

"Isabella, let's get out for a minute."

She turned her head from side to side. "Why? It looks awfully dangerous."

"I think we're safe. We're in broad daylight, and I want to check something." He gave her a quick kiss on the cheek for reassurance, though he agreed with her instincts.

Raphael helped Isabella wiggle out of the vehicle. She gripped his arm until her footing was stable. She pointed to the street sign.

"Look, Raphael. This street is named Evelyn."

He nodded. "I know. What are the chances?"

Her attention was drawn elsewhere, and Raphael wondered how long it might take her to notice the corner bakery.

"I remember now. Ginger Ridge. We lived in this town until my fourth birthday. I've been to that church on the hill, and we used to have picnics underneath that bell tower. We attended Christmas Eve service, and had our picture taken on a buggy ride afterward."

She pointed to the shop. "This used to be a bakery, right next to a diner. My parents allowed me to walk here with an older girl from church, though I think they followed from a distance. We bought a fried chocolate pie and shared a glass of milk with two straws." Isabella beamed. "You could smell this place all the way from our house."

Raphael allowed her to continue her march through time while he snuck to the side of the building and estimated the square footage.

He knew from the real estate listing that a four-bedroom, two-bath residence sat above the bakery. Behind the residence stood a double garage with access to the house.

The building ran deep behind the boarded-up storefront. The upper portion of the window on the Evelyn Street side remained intact and uncovered, allowing Raphael to jump on the ledge to peek inside.

Next to the display cases of the bakery, Raphael discovered enough open space for ten tables and chairs, plus a few booths in the corner. He guessed the bakery must have been one of the last businesses to shut its doors as it appeared in much better condition than the surrounding area with little vandalism or neglect.

Raphael dialed the phone number from the sign posted in the window and requested an immediate showing of the interior of the property.

I need to see it for myself.

The agent agreed to meet him within thirty minutes. Raphael joined Isabella in the street. No car had passed since their arrival.

"Isabella, do you feel like taking a walk?"

"Sure."

Raphael took his wife's hand, and they moved toward the church.

"Looks like they're doing some demolition work over there. They've brought in an industrial sized dumpster. Let's avoid that hill."

Isabella didn't appear to be listening as she picked up her pace and dragged him down the street. "Raphael, I remember. That's my street on the right. We used to sit on the curb and watch parades go by. We're near Fort Bryce, right?"

"Yes, Fort Bryce is directly behind us, about five minutes. They closed the base ten years ago. And please slow down. You're going to walk that baby right out."

She gave him a playful grin over her shoulder. "When I was little, the entire town gathered for a parade every time the soldiers completed a deployment. We'd all jump up and down as they marched by in formation. We were so thankful to have them home, and we'd follow the soldiers to the end where they scattered to join their families. Then later that night, the church held a square dance under the stars. It all seems like a fairy-tale. A perfect childhood."

Raphael had a tough time picturing her idyllic scene with the town in such shambles around them.

How could I have known she'd lived here as a child? Is this a sign my family belongs here too?

She let go of his hand to rush forward. "Come on. Let me show you my old house."

Isabella took off, but soon jolted to a halt causing Raphael to almost run her over.

"Raphael, see that brick house over there, behind the church?"

He gave her a nod.

"I've been there before. On that porch."

"Really?" Raphael couldn't describe the look he saw in his wife's eyes. She'd grown up as a military kid, moving every two to four years. He'd never seen her tear up with memories or connections to a specific place.

This town must have been a special place in its heyday. "There was an older gentleman who read stories to us on that porch. He gave us lemonade, and a piece of candy as an after-dinner treat. Our babysitter took Sergio and me there to meet him."

Isabella smiled and then moved on. As they walked up to a simple one-story brick structure with an attached carport, she paused. She held out her arms as if making a presentation on a game show.

"There it is. Our house. These memories are so vivid now. When helicopters from Fort Bryce flew by in formation, we'd lay on a blanket in the yard to watch."

Raphael moved in front of her to get her attention. "Sounds like great memories. Do you remember how to get to the elementary school? I'd like to estimate walking distance to the school."

"From where?"

"The bakery."

"Sure. Our house was a couple streets down. I'd skip beside Mama to meet Sergio after school. When Daddy got home from work, he'd grill the best food I've ever tasted out on our deck."

Isabella led the way, rubbing her belly with each step but never slowing down. "There it is. The school, exactly as I remember it."

Raphael surveyed the area. Nothing fancy, but a quiet and comfortable school building. An amphitheater had been overtaken by brush and weeds to the left side, but it wouldn't take much to make it operational. Stripes in the parking lot had been repainted recently, which proved a level of ongoing maintenance.

"There are kids on the playground, so there must be a few families still in the area." Raphael moved closer to get a better look. "I'll be right back."

He took in the dilapidated playground equipment. Swings hung from broken chains and the metal slide had a hole rusted through in the center.

"We could organize a bake sale with some of your goodies to raise money for new playground equipment,"

Raphael called over his shoulder. He turned to catch Isabella's response, but caught his breath as she approached a police car that pulled up to the curb behind her.

His heart stopped beating.

Are they here to take me into custody? Could they have followed me this far?

Isabella leaned in to speak to the officer, but Raphael couldn't hear their conversation. He held his breath and kept his distance. His phone zapped with a notification from the realtor, causing him to jump.

Finally, the officer pulled away and Isabella waved him over.

"What did that officer want?"

"They're trying to track down an old man who gets lost easily. They asked if we'd seen him, but I told him we haven't seen anyone since we got here. Raphael, I'm starving. You promised me a lunch date."

"Okay. Soon. But first, there's someone we need to meet at the bakery."

CHAPTER TWENTY-FOUR

Cameron Sterling reached for an antacid tablet from the open container wedged in his center console. He grimaced as he chewed and then flushed the chalky residue down with a swig of lukewarm black coffee. Grabbing the steering wheel once more, he maneuvered his departmental SUV up the quiet, winding road that led to the Gruff Bluff.

Outside his jurisdiction by twenty miles, the overlook had been given its title by his first street supervisor with the Madison Police Department. Lieutenant Dexter often gave wise guidance Cam pretended not to need at the time. Their most memorable conversations took place before shift changes at this exact spot. Always worth the trip, Cam couldn't remember the last time he'd ventured this far.

"This is where I go when I'm frustrated or need answers. Best viewpoint in the entire county. You can see for at least fifty miles," Lieutenant Dexter had once said. "I've solved many cases up here by letting it simmer and creating a little distance. Citizens depend on our experience and ability to not get rattled. Over time, this becomes the greatest skill we can offer. Frequenting a place like this to clear my head sure makes me look good."

Dexter had been right. He'd often come here to let a situation simmer.

Last Cam heard, his favorite lieutenant puttered around in a golf cart in a senior living complex in Florida.

Good thing. I'd hate for him to see me now.

Cam parked his SUV and retrieved his phone which had dropped under the seat at the last hairpin turn. He brushed across the unmistakable rustle of plastic on a pack of cigarettes. His heart pounded at the unexpected crossroad.

You've almost made it fifteen days. It takes thirty days to create a new habit. You're halfway there. Don't give up now.

He jumped out of his vehicle and paced with his hands on his hips, plotting his next move as if on the prowl on the football field.

The all-knowing Atlanta skyline taunted him in the distance.

I used to do my best thinking while smoking.

Cam reached under his seat and grabbed the half-empty pack of cigarettes. In his pants pocket, he fingered the lighter he still carried around with him out of habit.

I told Braxton I already quit.

Cam shook his head and slammed the door shut. Lunging a few steps to gain traction, he hurled the pack of temptation off the cliff and tossed the lighter as an afterthought.

A smile spread across his face.

Now, let's get down to business.

He mulled over the facts of the John Doe case, taking in the panoramic view as if the answers might fall from the sky.

Keep the big picture in mind. Perspective and experience. That's where you excel.

Cam decided to take the opposite approach. Offense, rather than defense.

What does my experience tell me?

He began ticking off the things he knew about the case.

The victim had been dumped in Madison, but if it happened in town, there should be a witness to the accident.

Dropping him off at the fire station shows remorse. Besides, who would run over an old man on purpose?

Whoever dumped him was most likely male. Most females couldn't carry his body weight, even in his frail state.

Why hadn't anyone reported him missing? Maybe the old man had been sick or previously injured. What if he'd sought help in the street, causing him to get hit?

Wherever the accident happened, we should find evidence left behind. Skid marks. Broken vehicle parts or an item belonging to our victim.

Detective Sterling scurried to his SUV with a renewed sense of purpose.

I've got to find the scene of the crime before this becomes a vehicular homicide and they transfer it to the Cold Case Squad.

Gruff Bluff had done its job once again.

I definitely need to visit more often.

Harper leaned against her office door, making sure it closed completely. On her desk sat the evidence carton from the Madison Police Department with a note taped on top.

This goes to forensics on Wednesday. Guard it with your life, and don't open any of the plastic bags. Nothing jumped out at me. I wish you better luck. Sterling.

Harper dropped into her chair and rolled to the window for better lighting. She wound her hair into a bun and patted her cheeks to wake up. Lifting her paper coffee cup to her lips, she realized it was empty and tossed it in the trash can in disgust.

As she pried the top off the box, the pager buzzed on her hip.

LAZURUS: Young girl in labor in the ER. Alone. You asked to be notified on such cases, right? Sorry.

Harper sighed.

Harper: Yes. Always. Be right down.

She made sure the door locked behind her and took the back stairwell to the emergency room floor.

I'll never be too busy to respond to this type of call. It hits too close to home.

MAY 2000

Harper and Julian entered arm-in-arm for their senior prom. Julian looked so handsome in his black tuxedo. Harper had opted for a white gown with enough red trim to contrast him perfectly.

Since they met on that first day of school four years earlier, Harper's heart remained in a constant flutter. She had no doubt his face would one day appear on billboards—the epitome of all-American boy perfection. His hair hung to his shoulders and curled on the ends as the day wore on. Harper loved that about him, as she did everything else. His confidence, drive, eyelashes, biceps … his deep voice. The fact that he shaved every morning before school. The shadow of a mustache formed above his upper lip.

By this point, Julian had the world eating out of his hand. After leading the Eagles to their third straight football championship, he'd been offered numerous scholarships. He'd held out for a full ride at the University of Alabama—a dream come true, and a huge steppingstone to his plan to one day star in the NFL.

With the extra notoriety, Harper could feel him slipping away. Once he'd signed the official letter of intent back in February, everything had started to change between them. He rarely had time for her, and she suspected he'd hooked up with a few girls at the university on his frequent weekend visits to campus. He was already a legend and had yet to arrive on campus in Tuscaloosa as a student.

Still, she never fully understood why he'd chosen her in the first place. How had she gotten so lucky? From the start, she'd vowed to do whatever it took to not mess this up—to do whatever it took to hang onto him, just like her mother wrote in her goodbye letter.

Harper tried not to think about that as she forged ahead with plans of her own. Accepted to the University of Florida, she didn't care what happened after that. She was ready for something bigger, wherever that took her. She found Ginger Ridge suffocating after all these years.

With the two of them headed in separate directions, a break-up seemed inevitable, but she couldn't bring herself to do it. She trusted him to handle their relationship status when he decided the time was right. Until then, she planned to celebrate being his girl and to enjoy their last prom together.

They posed momentarily for their photo and then Julian snuck outside to partake of the kegs of alcohol behind the stadium with other football players. She chided herself for not making him dance with her before he'd made his escape. When—and if—he returned, he'd barely be able to stand up straight.

Harper moved from girl to girl, raving about how pretty everyone looked and then found a spot in the back corner and sipped her punch. Too soon, the class president vaulted on stage.

"I'm proud to announce your Class of 2000 Prom King and Queen—Julian Alexander and Harper Phillips!"

Harper's eyes grew wide, and she rushed out the back doors to grab Julian. She found him with his back against the wall, shirt untucked. A beer in one hand and a girl in the crook of each arm.

"Julian, come here! We're needed on stage."

He shoved the girls away and handed off his beer. "Coming," he said with a roll of his eyes.

Harper straightened his tie while he tucked in his shirt as they scurried to the stage to accept their crowns and sashes. The band played the opening notes to their favorite song, and they danced in the spotlight while people clapped. Harper vowed to remember this moment forever.

She gazed up at him and stood on tiptoe to kiss his cheek. Someone snapped a photo.

Prom King and Queen for the Year 2000. Big news for such a small town.

As the evening drew to a close, like a scene from a movie, Julian lifted Harper to place her in the passenger's seat of a yellow corvette convertible his parents had rented for them. Harper pinned her hair up to keep it from blowing and then bent her head back and closed her eyes. She loved that feeling of freedom, riding down the highway next to the most handsome man she'd ever met. She snuggled beside him and hoped the world would never change even as she sensed it slipping through her hands with every passing second.

They ended up at a gorgeous overlook a few minutes outside of town. The city of Atlanta lit up like a Christmas tree in the distance, and the moon shone brighter than usual. Julian turned off the engine, flipped on the radio, laid his seat back, and pulled her to him.

Harper took in a deep breath. She'd warned him she wasn't ready to take the next step, though she couldn't explain why. Of course, tonight would be the night he'd refuse to take no for an answer. At the very least, she should have prepared herself. She pushed against his chest.

"Come on, Harper. You know I can have any girl I want. After four years together, if you aren't ready now, you won't ever be."

"I feel weird doing this outside, out in the open. Like God is watching us."

Julian swatted away her resistance with a clumsy hand. Heavily buzzed by this point, he stunned her with his next comment.

"That's okay. I was meant for the spotlight!"

As he began nibbling her ear, Harper didn't have the will to push him away.

As if resisting were even possible.

Julian was too drunk, too strong, and too persistent. He rolled on top of her, and she squeezed her eyes shut.

A song she once learned at Bible school popped into her head and she sang it to herself, over and over.

This little light of mine, I'm gonna let it shine ...

When he'd finished, Julian quickly fell asleep in the back seat and Harper snuggled under a blanket in the passenger's seat to wait out the night. Their parents weren't expecting them until morning, believing they were at a senior class party.

Harper sighed. That experience was nothing like it showed on television and the movies.

I feel nothing. This can't be all there is. I probably didn't do it right.

"God, if you're listening, I know you're angry with me, but if it helps, I really didn't enjoy it."

The moon slid behind a cloud formation, casting angry shadows across the mountain. Harper shivered, folded her legs underneath her, and pulled the blanket to her chin. At least Julian had thought to bring a blanket.

He can be so kind and thoughtful sometimes.

Harper spent the rest of the night searching the sky for answers.

CHAPTER TWENTY-FIVE

Harper did her best to switch gears as she met the annoyed gaze of Lazarus. His eyes conveyed more than his sassy mouth at times.

"Hey, Laz. What is it this time?"

"See for yourself," he muttered, pulling back the curtain to reveal a young girl sitting cross-legged on the bed in street clothes as if sharing secrets at a slumber party. Her eyes remained glued to the screen of a cell phone in her hand.

The girl twirled a strand of long, dark hair with teal highlights through her fingers. A hospital gown draped across her lap while she popped bubble gum in her mouth.

"This is Jewel. She's sixteen years old and in advanced stage of labor, though it took a while to convince her of that fact. I'll leave the two of you to talk in private."

Harper saw no signs of pain in the girl's face. She also suspected Jewel had fudged her age at check-in.

This girl can't be as old as my daughter.

"Hi, Jewel. What's your last name?"

"Diamond. I don't have a driver's license, so I don't have any ID."

Harper extended her hand. "Nice to meet you, Jewel Diamond." The girl ignored the handshake and bit her fingernails instead.

Reviewing the girl's chart, Harper checked the monitor to confirm a steadily advancing pattern of contractions.

Jewel continued to stare at her phone.

"We need to move you to the fourth floor to labor and delivery. Is there someone I can call to be with you? A family member or friend? I hate for you to go through this alone."

Harper remembered that moment far too well—the hours of pain and pushing and then finally cradling Presley Rose against her chest, floating in a sea of equally terrifying and thrilling emotions. Harper had never been so proud of herself. Yet she still fought a sense of shame too.

She hoped Jewel Diamond wouldn't face that same trap.

Jewel had yet to respond to Harper's question.

"Anyone at church, even a best friend? You'll need all the support you can get once the baby is born."

Jewel shook her head. "No one knows. I'm not keeping the baby."

Harper bit her lip. "Okay. We can discuss those options later. Jewel, I'm proud of you for coming to the hospital so you and the baby get the proper care. That was a brave thing to do."

Jewel shrugged and continued to play a game on her phone.

"I need you to change into your gown while I arrange transport. I'll meet you on the fourth floor in a few minutes."

"Okay." Jewel licked her lips and picked up the gown.

Harper backed away to find Lazarus. She tracked him down at the front desk and pointed her finger in his face. "Spill it, mister. Tell me everything you know about our patient."

Lazarus shrugged. "I know nothing. Except she's lying. Her name, age, all of it. However, she is in labor. That much is true, and she came to the hospital. I give her credit for that."

"Clearly, she's under the influence of something. Have you ordered blood work?"

He shook his head. "Nope. She refused. That's when I paged you. If anyone can create a bond with her, it's you."

Harper looked back at the closed curtain. "At least she agreed to put on the gown. I wonder if she's trying to hide signs of abuse?"

"She's hiding something, for sure. She barely looks pregnant and has received no prenatal care."

Harper dropped her head and sighed. "Why do you do this to me?"

"As I recall, you made me promise. Said you wanted no babies delivered at Savannah Regional without full support for the mother. Like you are the Savior of the World or something. Newsflash—we already have one of those, remember?"

Harper scrunched her nose at him. She appreciated his teasing, which reminded her not to take herself so seriously.

Perfectionism. My best friend and worst enemy.

By the time she reached the fourth floor, the on-call doctor was examining Jewel who now donned a yellow polka-dot hospital gown.

Progress.

"Looks like we might have an hour before it's time to push," the doctor announced. "Your baby is in position, and it's too late for anesthesia, so it looks like we're having this baby naturally. You're sure handling it well. I'll be back soon."

Jewel's eyes fluttered in slow motion, but she didn't seem too concerned. Each of her reactions, if she had one, were noticeably delayed.

Harper waited until they were alone. "Jewel, are you in any pain?"

The girl shook her head.

"Okay, let me ask you this. We don't have any records on file for you, so we need to draw blood to confirm whether you and the baby have the same blood type. It can cause complications if we don't know ahead of time."

Jewel lifted her head and made eye contact. "Will it hurt?"

Harper shook her head. "If active labor isn't fazing you, a needle prick will have no effect. Trust me."

"Okay."

Harper relaxed and lowered her voice. "I'm required to ask a few questions. Has anyone hurt you to put you in this position?"

"No." Jewel shook her head in defiance.

"You mentioned you don't plan to keep your baby. Have you made adoption arrangements with an agency or private party?"

Jewel shook her head.

"Are you sure there's no one I can notify on your behalf?"

"No. I didn't realize I was pregnant until two months ago. I kept it hidden and never told a soul."

Harper lifted a business card from her pocket and scrawled her number on the back. "I know you feel there are no good options at this point. There are agencies in town that can help. Have you ever heard of Harbor House?"

"No." Jewel gnawed on her fingernails but appeared to be listening.

"I now serve on their board of directors, but I also was a client when I was about your age. They offer many services to young ladies like us. They'll even provide a place to live until you can get on your feet." Harper slid the card into Jewel's hand. "I wouldn't be here today if not for Harbor House."

The girl looked at the card and then set it aside.

Harper reached to pat her on the arm.

Jewel flinched.

Harper sighed. "I'll be back soon. Call me if you need anything. There are people who will step in to support and guide you if you give us a chance. You are a brave girl, and I'm proud of you."

Jewel offered a half-smile. "Thank you, Miss Harper. No one's ever told me that before."

Detective Sterling lifted his foot off the gas pedal to lower his speed around the steep curves that spiraled from the overlook. He'd seen too many accidents on this stretch of road, so he fought the common temptation of law enforcement officers to ignore posted speed limits.

A car burst around the next bend at least three feet into Cam's lane. He punched at the horn and stomped on the brakes to avoid a collision. The male driver of a silver sedan corrected his vehicle and mouthed the word sorry as he passed.

Cam flipped on his blue lights to flash a warning as the car shuttled up the hill. With no place to turn around, he let the infraction slide.

He caught his breath and continued to maneuver the treacherous twists and turns.

Around the next hook in the road, Cameron noticed a set of skid marks that led to a patch of tall grass in a ditch. The right two wheels of a car had recently plowed through the ditch, leading to another set of swerve marks on the road.

Cam pulled over as far as he could and studied his surroundings. To his right lay a steep embankment that had served as a landing pit to many speeding cars in the past. To his left, an old, overgrown cemetery that had seen better days.

He rolled down the window to check for the sound of any approaching cars. Hearing nothing, he carefully inched out of his SUV and shut the door, hoping his blue lights served as a signal to slow oncoming vehicles from either direction.

Cam stood with his palm against his forehead and followed the recent tire tracks.

If this wasn't an accident scene, it was a near miss, for sure.

He craned his neck to check sightlines from nearby homes but none were visible. Trotting up the hill to get a better viewpoint, he confirmed two sets of skid marks headed straight for each other. One swerved off the road into the weeds. Cam snapped photos with his phone and made audible notes on his recorder.

"Put in an official request with the county to get streetlights and guardrails installed on Old Serpentine Road."

His head jolted when tires squealed higher up the mountain. The sound drew closer with each second.

Cam sought a safe place to get out of the road and found himself in the defined rut in the shallow ditch that first caught his attention. Avoiding the fresh tire tracks, he glanced down, hoping there were no snakes curling around his feet.

Cam shuddered.

The sun reflected off a shiny object.

What is that?

The detective whipped out a handkerchief and carefully lifted a shattered lens from a set of eyeglasses. He scanned the area again with a more focused eye. Splintered pieces of a wooden cane lay scattered around a ten-foot area. Carved into the hook of the cane, still intact, was a name.

"Winnie."

Oncoming tires screamed the last warning as an old powder blue pickup spun out of control and barreled around the curve. Cam cringed at the sound as it crunched into his departmental SUV, sending it rolling into the abyss below.

CHAPTER TWENTY-SIX

Isabella remained abuzz with excitement after touring the bakery. Her girlhood memories of the town seemed to fuel her dreams of opening Bella's Best Bakery.

"I envision a blend of small-town bakery and modern coffee shop, where patrons spend quality time with each other. They can study, read, and drink coffee with my pastries."

Her response proved even better than Raphael had hoped.

Now for the hard part.

On their way home, he took Isabella to lunch at their favorite diner, choosing a booth in the back corner. The perfect place to present the facts of his looming deportation and a felony indictment for vehicular homicide. Once the old man died, Raphael expected to enter a plea bargain for involuntary manslaughter. Still a felony, but a lesser charge.

Raphael still aspired to find an attorney to represent him on both fronts.

But first, Isabella.

She gazed at him with trusting eyes while rattling on about the bakery. "We could undertake this project in a year when the baby is a little older. I need time to purchase supplies and obtain proper licenses. You could get a job in this area once we resolve your legal issues."

Raphael waved his hand to stop her. "Whoa there. You make it sound easy. I have no reason to believe my predicament will resolve itself anytime soon."

"What do you mean?" She cocked her head and fiddled with her ponytail.

Raphael launched into the gut-wrenching update he'd practiced in his mind a hundred times. Calmly. Gently. Truthfully.

"I can't describe how poorly my visit with the lawyer went yesterday." He ruffled his fingers through his hair. "It was brutal, but I asked for honest advice, and that's exactly what he gave me."

Isabella frowned. "What did he say?"

"That you and the kids must prepare to live without me for at least a year. I have to appear in court on Friday morning, but he offered no way to fight it. Worst-case scenario—I return to Mexico, banned from reentering this country for ten years."

Isabella's eyes grew wide. "Ten years? That's impossible. We'll never survive without you. Should we get a new attorney?"

"Wilburn refused to represent me. Instead, he encouraged me to invest our money into my family. To prepare you for what's coming."

Isabella jerked backward as she received a swift kick from the baby. She shifted in her seat to get more comfortable. "The baby does not like what you are saying any more than I do. What are we supposed to do? Move in with my parents? We can't give up."

He shook his head and took her hands in his. "No, Isabella. I've got a better plan. That's why we visited Ginger Ridge earlier today. I realize this brings many changes at once, but I must know you and the kids are all right while I fight my legal battles."

A nearby server studied them out of the corner of her eye. Raphael waited for her to pass before he continued.

Isabella said nothing but rubbed her belly in a circular motion as if trying to comfort the baby.

"Isabella, we have to speed up the plan. We don't have a year to get ready. I already bought the SUV so you would have a reliable vehicle with enough room for three car seats. Also, I contacted a realtor so we can sell the house."

She gasped. "Raphael, no! You built that home for us with your own hands."

"I know. I can build another house. The real estate market is hot, and we need the money to cover your expenses while I'm away. How about this? We purchase the bakery and you and the kids live in the residence above it. I'll make all the repairs, but we're running out of time. After you recover from having the baby, you can open for business in the spring. You'll need the income. The kids could walk to school. My hope is Bella's Best will inspire the revitalization of Ginger Ridge."

He couldn't read her expression as she picked at her food.

Raphael checked his watch.

It's almost time to pick the boys up from school.

He launched his next bombshell without warning. "Isabella, there's more. I've gotten myself into quite a quagmire."

"Raphael, I don't even know what that means. What is a quagmire?"

He struggled to recall where he learned that phrase. "I heard it on the radio. I think it means a complex situation."

Isabella tilted her chin at him. "Then I agree. I'd call this a big quagmire. How could it possibly get worse?"

"It can. Trust me. You remember the day I lost my job?"

She raised her eyebrows. "Of course, I remember."

"On the way home, I stopped at an overlook outside of Madison. I was upset and trying to figure out how to tell you, which is why I didn't answer my phone."

"Yes, how could I forget? That seems like a month ago. Was it only last week?"

Raphael leaned in close to whisper. "Isabella, I had a terrible accident on my way home."

Isabella gasped and leaned away from the table. Her hands rested on Baby Evelyn's bump.

"Oh no! Why didn't you tell me, Raphael? Is that why you sold your Mustang?"

He shook his head. "No. Never mind the car. It's the least of my problems."

"There's more?"

He cringed. "Much more. Come closer. I don't want anyone to hear me."

Isabella winced. "I can't get any closer. Why don't you come over here?"

He moved around the table to scoot in beside his wife.

Raphael whispered in her ear. "Isabella, I hit an old man and almost killed him. You probably heard it on the news. He's listed as a John Doe at the hospital in Savannah, in critical condition."

Tears welled up in her eyes. "I can't believe you're the one who did that."

"Me neither. I shouldn't have been driving. I was crying too hard to see the road. This old man limped into the middle of the road and it was too late. I swerved to miss an oncoming car and bowled him over. He flew through the air and landed in my back seat."

Isabella's hand flew to her mouth as she gasped. Tears rolled down her cheeks, but she said nothing.

He should have handled this part of their discussion in the car, away from prying eyes.

Too late.

He kept on. "I dropped him at the old fire station where I knew someone would find him. I figured he wouldn't make it through the night. He was already so fragile, it's probably good that he's in a coma. The pain would be unbearable."

He knew Isabella processed things at her own pace, and he knew better than to force her to swallow multiple levels of shocking news at one time. Still, he had to get it out. Every crushing detail.

"He's still hanging on. I stopped in to see him late last night. They call him Grandpa Doe, and people have left notes for him all over his room. I wrote one as well. I apologized and asked for forgiveness."

Isabella raised her head and stared him down. The look in her eyes burned a hole through his soul. Raphael sucked in a deep breath and wondered if it might be his last.

"I need to get out," she whispered.

"What?"

"Move."

She bumped him out of the seat and headed straight for the restrooms.

What's she going to do? Walk home?

Raphael paid their bill and headed to the car to cool off and wait for his wife's angry arrival. He deserved whatever she tossed his way.

Finally, she burst through the restaurant doors and came straight for him, clutching her phone against her ear.

Who is she talking to? The police? Her father? Her brother and his angry friends?

Raphael reached across the seat to open the door and detected a sense of panic in her face.

"I understand. I'll keep you posted. Thank you, Dr. Greenfield." She finished her conversation and hung up as she climbed into the passenger's seat and slammed the door.

"Isabella, what is it?"

She pierced him with the dagger of her eyes.

"We need to get to the hospital in Savannah. Now."

CHAPTER TWENTY-SEVEN

Harper rested her head against the door to her office, thankful to be away from prying eyes. As much as she loved to help people, she'd had her fill of them.

She peeked into Detective Sterling's evidence carton. On top was an inventory list, straight and to the point.

INVENTORY LIST
TAYLOR HALL FIRE STATION (CLOSED TO PUBLIC)

1. Gold band wedding ring
2. Black suspenders (attached to pants with buttons)
3. White long-sleeved dress shirt with collar
4. Black trousers
5. Gray socks with black patterned squares
6. Black dress shoes, Size 10
7. Gray golf-style cap
8. Gray bow tie

Harper set the list aside and pulled out each bag to inspect the items. The first she noticed was the white, formal dress shirt spattered with bloodstains around the collar and chest.

Oh, you poor man. I'm sorry this happened to you.

Next, she examined the black and gray argyle dress socks and the worn black loafers with holes in the bottom.

You need new shoes. Do people in caskets wear shoes? Wait. What's this?

She flipped a bag over to find black dress pants with buttons at the waistline where the suspenders would be attached and a matching set on the cuffs of each pant leg.

Knickers. I've only seen one person in my entire lifetime wear knickers.

And finally, she picked up the last bag.

Suspenders? Bow tie? Solomon!

She sent Detective Sterling a message.

"It's Harper Phillips. Call me. I think I've identified our victim!"

Cameron Sterling paced in a circle with his hands folded on top of his head. He mumbled a few choice words and reminded himself to breathe in and exhale slowly before he blew an internal gasket.

The driver of the blue pickup truck remained inside the vehicle, flitting around, proving he was conscious.

It's best for both of us if you remain in your vehicle, dude. I might hurt you if you get out right now.

The other car was an older model powder blue Chevrolet. One of a kind.

He made eye contact with the driver and pointed a warning at him, unable to find the words to address him directly. A white male. Country boy. Late thirties, missing a front tooth and, from the vacant look in his eyes, possibly missing a few brain cells possibly because of a past drug addiction.

All too common in the poorer parts of the state.

Cam wondered how the guy's rusty pickup had made it this far up the mountain. Even more, how the beat-up truck was still on the road while Cam's brand-new SUV lay in what he was certain was a pancake formation in the ravine.

Cam refused to look down the hill to confirm his worst fears.

Too soon. Life isn't fair.

He knew this to be true. Proving it repeatedly was not his favorite pastime.

His hand rested on his stomach. "Where are my antacids?" he blurted out to the angry universe.

In my vehicle. At the bottom of the hill.

The only departmental gear he had on him was his cell phone, handcuffs attached to his belt loop, and a police revolver in a holster near his right ankle. He wisely had left his gun in its rightful place.

Cam held his face in his hands and played through the explanation he would put in writing for the looming incident report. Suddenly, he remembered why he was in that location to begin with.

The evidence!

The cane. The glasses. And possibly, his saving grace.

I've got to solve this case before the county suspends me. The commissioner will launch an investigation, so that buys me a few days.

Cam forced himself toward the pickup and motioned for the driver to roll down his window. The window made a popping sound as the driver opened it with a hand crank.

Hand crank—a late seventies model.

"Sir, are you okay?"

The driver nodded. "I'm fine. Sorry about your car. I saw the blue lights but couldn't stop in time. These brakes are out of whack."

Cam took in a quick breath. "Okay, sir. I think it's best that you stop talking. I've got to notify my supervisor and investigating officers will soon crawl all over this hill. Save your details for the report."

The driver pretended to button his lips. Cam noted a childish air about him. Maybe it wasn't drugs after all. Perhaps an emotional or mental condition? Or both?

Cam continued. "I've got to check out the damage to my departmental vehicle and gather my belongings. You can't stay in your truck. It's too dangerous, but I can't turn you loose either. What's your name?"

"Bubba."

"Okay, Bubba. Have you been drinking today?"

"No. Not yet. How'd you know I was coming back from the liquor store?"

Cam cringed. "I'm a detective, I just know things. All right, fella. Come with me. I need to find a safe place for you to wait while I investigate. Would it be okay if I put handcuffs on you for a few minutes? They won't hurt, but I must keep you from leaving the scene."

Bubba's eyes lit up. "That would be cool. Could you take a picture of me with them on? I wanna show my brother. He's at work."

Cam shrugged. "Sure. Sure. Whatever makes this more pleasant for you."

Bubba's truck had folded into itself on the front end like an accordion, blocking the driver's side door from opening. Cam jerked the passenger's side door open to the sound of crunching metal and reached out a hand to help Bubba get out. He led him across the street to the shallow ditch that provided the only safe space to wait.

"I need you to stay in the shade of this tree. You can stand or sit, but you have to promise not to run away."

Bubba jerked his head toward Cam. "Am I under arrest, officer?"

"No, not at this time." He snapped the handcuffs off his belt. "Bubba, I'm placing these handcuffs on you, allowing you to keep your hands in front of your body, so you'll be more comfortable. Got it?"

Bubba held out his hands and clasped them together.

Cam loosely clicked the cuffs in place.

"How's that feel? Are they too tight?"

Bubba shook his head. "No, Your Honor."

A chuckle escaped Cam's lips, though nothing about this situation was humorous. Cam had to admit this citizen lightened the mood, entering the scene like a set-up on one of those candid camera shows.

I wish this was a cruel prank gone too far. If only.

"All right, Bubba. I'll be back shortly. Don't move. Don't touch anything. Don't eat anything. Don't sniff anything. Stay out of the road. Don't do anything to get me in more trouble than I already am. Okay?"

"Yes, sir. I'm going to need you to give me a note. My brother's gonna kill me when he gets home. That's his truck, and I don't have my license."

Cam dropped his head and elected not to respond.

Bubba dropped into a sitting position, where he launched into an exuberant version of "I've Been Working on the Railroad."

Cam snapped a few pictures of the original evidence field—the pieces of a cane and glasses in the ditch a few yards down from Bubba. He used the recorder on his phone to document what he found.

"Fragments of what appears to be a wooden cane scattered among a shallow ditch in a ten by six area. We're in the five hundred block of Old Serpentine Road. No houses visible from this location."

Bubba interrupted. "Officer, help! My nose itches."

"Come on, Bubba. Your hands are in front of you. You can still use them."

Bubba let out a huge laugh. "Oh yeah. I forgot. But they're so heavy."

Cam popped over to check Bubba's puffy and bloodshot eyes. "One more thing. What's your last name?"

"Wilson. Just like my mama's. May she rest in peace."

Cam made notes on the palm of his hand. "And your date of birth. When were you born?"

"December 25, 1980. I'm a Christmas baby." He grinned. "Fa la la la la ..."

Cam winced. "Okay. I'm sure Bubba is a nickname. What's your proper name?"

"No, Bubba's my real name. But my first name is Willie. William, if you want to get fancy."

Cam bent down on one knee. "You're doing great. I'm heading down this hill, but I want you to keep singing as loud as possible."

"Sure. Whatcha wanna hear?"

"Since you're a Christmas baby, how about some Christmas songs?"

"Goody. I love Christmas songs." Bubba flopped his hands together like he was trying to clap despite the handcuffs. He laughed longer than necessary in a childish way, but at least Cam could hear him as he inched down the hill.

"Dashing through the snow, in a one-horse open sleigh ..."

Cam caught sight of his SUV, which somehow had landed in an upright position. Most of the windows were shattered and the driver's side door had completely caved in.

If I'd been in that driver's seat, they'd be planning my funeral right now.

Cam counted his blessings as he shook off the wave of worst-case scenarios that flooded his mind. He snapped a few photos of the damage to send to his commanding officer, then punched in the number for his sergeant and moved to the top of the embankment to find a stronger signal and monitor his prisoner.

He left a message at the beep. "Hey, Sarge. This is Sterling. I need you to call me back ASAP. Meet me on Serpentine Road. I'll be unavailable until further notice."

Cam knew to keep any details of the accident off the police radio so media wouldn't pick it up from the police scanners.

He drew in a deep breath and retreated down the hill to the passenger's side of his car. He wedged the door open and found the bottle of antacids scattered over the floor. Without hesitation, he popped a couple in his mouth and grabbed his clipboard, an empty evidence bag, and his walkie talkie.

He attached the radio to his belt and strapped the microphone to his shoulder. After grabbing a pair of latex gloves, he sidestepped his way back up the steep incline. Progress was much slower as he stopped periodically to gather the debris he'd discovered at the side of the road.

Bubba blended the lyrics of whatever songs came to his curious mind. "Rockin' around the Christmas tree ... had a very shiny nose ... and when they placed it on his head ..."

Cam couldn't help but smile.

What are the chances I'd get to spend such a terrific day with this special fella?

Cam leaned over the ditch and began placing evidence markers at each piece of debris. An earpiece to the glasses remained intact. One lens was shattered but remained whole. There were no pieces of the cane larger than three inches long, but the hook with the name Winnie was sure to provide his best breakthrough.

If I find this person named Winnie, I can find the owner of this cane. Surely, this belongs to that tiny shell of a man lying on his death bed in Savannah.

Bubba stopped singing and launched into a conversation with himself. "Never in a million years did I think I'd get the chance to wear handcuffs. Aren't you the stuff now, Bubba Wilson?"

Cam's phone rang. He drew in a deep breath and stepped away from Bubba's ramblings.

"Hey, Sarge. You want the good news or the bad?"

Sergeant Lewis forced a chuckle on the other end of the line. "Coming from you? Neither."

"I'll tell you one thing. Someone's gonna get killed on these old roads one of these days if they don't straighten out these curves."

"What's that noise?" Sergeant Lewis asked.

"That's Bubba Wilson. He's the genius who totaled my departmental vehicle. A white male, possibly deranged or mentally delayed, unlicensed, and uninsured. You're gonna love him."

"Can't wait."

Cam filled his supervisor in on the details. He confirmed the location and cautioned the sergeant to go slow.

"The only positive is I think I've found evidence from the hit-and-run from last week. That's the reason I stopped on this stretch of road."

Sergeant Lewis assessed the situation as only a law enforcement officer would do. "Gotta look at the bright side. You're alive. If you're doing your job, these things happen. I hope the city council understands that fact."

Cam appreciated the attitude of his supervisor. Hopefully, the powers-that-be up the chain of command would offer that same sense of leniency.

"Thanks, Sarge. See you in a few. When we're done here, I need a ride to Savannah Regional to meet with the caseworker there."

"I'll be glad to take you. I'd like to meet our victim before we lose him."

Cam disconnected and slipped his phone in his pocket. He crouched to gather shreds of evidence into the bag. In the distance, Bubba escalated his tirade.

"Cars come whizzing through here like the Road Runner on that cartoon with the coyote. It's a wonder all of us on this mountain haven't been run over like that old man last week."

Cam shot upright and ran like going in for an open tackle.

"I'm sorry, Bubba. What did you just say?"

CHAPTER TWENTY-EIGHT

Isabella breathed in quick rhythm like they'd practiced during birthing class. She leaned back in the passenger's seat, covering her face with one hand.

Raphael hit a curb as he pulled into the hospital parking lot and Isabella moaned.

"Sorry. I'm still getting used to our new car." He tried to lighten the mood. "I'd like to thank you for not giving birth in it."

No response.

In between contractions, Isabella used her phone to arrange for her brother Sergio to pick up Xavier and Zander from school. Then, she'd alerted Savannah Regional they were on the way. This was not their usual hospital, but their first two babies hadn't arrived six weeks early either.

"How's Evelyn?" Raphael asked as he pummeled another curb.

"She's coming. Quickly. Please stay on the road."

A fair request, I'd say.

"They're waiting at the emergency entrance. At the hospital for women. Not the main entrance."

"Okay. We're here. This place is hopping. I'll drop you off."

He stomped on the brakes, threw the vehicle into park, and hurried to Isabella's side of the car. She got out without making eye contact. Raphael touched her elbow to escort her inside, but she jerked it away. She left a wet trail on the ground with each step.

Not a good sign.

"Help. My wife is in labor, and it's too soon," he called to the lady at the registration desk as they entered.

"What's the last name?"

"Henry. Isabella Henry."

"Got it. We've been expecting you. Dr. Greenfield is on the way."

The double doors popped open, and someone appeared with a wheelchair. "We're taking her to labor and delivery on the fourth floor."

"Okay. I'll be there in a minute." Raphael kissed his wife on the cheek and squeezed her hand.

A tear rolled down her face as she lifted her eyes to meet his. A wave of pain and betrayal flashed across her face.

I wish she hadn't looked at me.

Isabella deserved better, especially on the day she would give birth to their daughter.

This thought rattled Raphael, but a sense of peace soon followed when he realized they were experiencing it together. Even in the midst of her anger.

I get to be with my wife when our daughter is born. That's all that matters right now.

Raphael circled the parking lot until he found a tight spot in a back corner. The larger vehicle was difficult to park and left him little room to get out. He locked the car and took off to find his wife.

Two police cars were parked near the main entrance, facing opposite directions so the officers could talk to each other. The engines were running, and the officers inside appeared to be in an intense conversation.

I hope they aren't here for me.

Raphael tucked his chin and picked up his pace. His heart beat so loudly he was certain the officers might hear as he passed. If their intention was to take him into custody, they'd have to wait.

First, I get to meet our daughter.

Detective Sterling clutched a metal clipboard against his chest and thought through his next words. The one he now knew as Bubba Wilson, minus the handcuffs, rested in the back of a black departmental SUV with the hatch door open above his head. Bubba sipped on a can of Dr. Pepper in between eating cashews out of a can, both provided by a uniformed officer of the Madison Police Department to keep their star witness on track.

"You know something? This car looks a lot like your vehicle did before it tumbled off the mountain," Bubba announced. "It's nice. Very nice."

"Thank you. Let's go over this one more time. I need to jot down your answers, so bear with me, okay?"

Bubba nodded. "You want to ask about how I slammed into your car, right?"

Cam shook his head. "No. Another officer will record your statement on our accident. I'm here to obtain information on what you witnessed last week. Let's start at the beginning. You said you saw an old man get hit, correct?"

Bubba nodded and wiped his hands against his faded jeans.

"That's right. Flipped into the air like a beach ball. That had to have hurt."

"Where did this happen?"

Bubba looked in each direction. "Right about here, where we're standing. That red car and mine were headed straight toward each other. He veered into that ditch over yonder and then swerved back. The reason I was in his lane was because there was an old guy walking all crazy-like in the middle of the road. I barely missed hitting both. But that red car wasn't as lucky."

Cam's heart rate picked up as he made a few notes.

"I'm not one to brag, but that's not bad driving for a guy with no license. Am I right?"

Cam shook his head and forged through his investigative questions. "How fast were you going?"

He shrugged. "Fast enough to get up the hill, which ain't easy in my brother's old truck."

"Fair enough. What time of day was this? What happened when you rounded the curve?"

"That's too many questions."

Cam patted him on the shoulder. "Duly noted. One at a time. Time of day?"

"Right there when the afternoon becomes nighttime. When it's too shadowy and you can't see really well. My headlights were on, but they didn't help much."

"Got it. So, you rounded the curve, and then what happened?"

"I swerved to miss the old man, but the headlights of the red car got me in the eyes. My brother's horn don't work, so I couldn't honk. I don't know how I missed hitting that guy myself. Me and the red car went toward each other, with the old man in the middle, but I turned away in time. Guess the other guy didn't."

Cam couldn't write fast enough to keep up.

Sergeant Lewis sauntered over, but Cam gave him a hand signal to stay back to avoid any further distractions. His superior stepped aside out of Bubba's line of vision to wait.

Cam looked Bubba in the eye. "What did you notice about the other driver?"

"He was one of them Hispanics, I think. Darker skin. Great hair down to his shoulders, and a mustache and short beard like those guys on the front of romance novels like Mama used to read."

"Handsome, maybe? Is that how you'd describe him?"

Bubba pointed his finger in Cam's face. "No, sir. I definitely would not say he's handsome. I'm not like that, if you know what I mean. But I bet the girls at the corner diner would give him a wink and a discount without him having to ask. That's all I'm saying."

Sergeant Lewis had to step away to keep from chuckling.

Cam continued. "All right, Bubba. You saw a red car hit the man. What kind of car?"

"One of those topless ones, with no roof. That driver's hair flopped around in the wind."

"Do you know the make or model? Was it old or new? Two-door or four-door? Anything like that?"

"Two doors. An old car, but real shiny like a new one."

Cam ducked under the open hatch door to perch himself beside Bubba.

"Bubba Wilson, I can't tell you how glad I am that we met today."

"Even though I hit your car?" Bubba grinned and finished his Dr. Pepper.

"That's right. Do you ever watch the evening news? Because you're about to be on it."

Bubba shook his head. "Nope. Too depressing. Besides, we ain't got cable, and service stinks around here. I do like to watch *Andy Griffith* every night though. That Barney is hilarious."

"Yes, he is, Bubba. Yes, he is." Cam stood and surveyed the accident scene. There were at least ten officers or detectives working the area. He estimated they'd be a couple more hours, at least. He motioned another officer to come over.

"Bubba, I'm turning you over to Officer Shelton here. He'll get your statement on our accident, and then he'll take you home when you're done."

Bubba touched Cam on the arm. "Where are you going? You don't have a car no more."

Cam cringed. "True. My sergeant is taking me to the hospital. I'll be in touch. We've got a sketch artist on the way to create a drawing of that Hispanic guy you saw driving the red car."

"Okay, but I don't know how to draw."

Cam gritted his teeth.

I need more antacids.

He continued. "That's fine. We've got someone who will draw him for you. We need you to say when the picture looks like the guy you saw the other night."

"Yeah. I seen that kind of thing on TV."

Cam stepped away and heard the police radio chatter and beeping of the tow truck as it inched toward the ravine in reverse.

He dialed a number and held the phone up to his ear.

"Miss Phillips, this is Sterling. We finally caught a break in our Grandpa Doe case. I'm on my way to Savannah Regional. See you soon."

CHAPTER TWENTY-NINE

Dr. Greenfield stepped into the room. Balding, stocky, with a soft voice that didn't match his stature, he was a large and comforting presence to Isabella, but Raphael's instincts always urged him to leave when the doctor entered. He hated the intense feeling of helplessness as he watched his wife go through the most invasive inspection he'd ever witnessed.

"Mr. Henry, we need you to exit while we give her an epidural." The doctor's stern voice left little room for argument. "Grab a cup of coffee and come back in twenty minutes. Long night ahead. Isabella's blood pressure is elevated. We're watching your wife and the baby closely."

Raphael focused on the baby's heart monitor, which raced along showing 170 beats per minute. Typical for a female, they said. He shifted his eyes to the blood pressure screen—178/97. Too high for Isabella.

"It's okay. We'll be right here with her. The baby's oxygen is good and Isabella's blood pressure has lowered since she arrived."

"It's too early. Baby Evelyn isn't due for thirty-five days," Raphael told him.

The doctor nodded. "We'll be ready for any outcome."

Raphael interpreted the doctor's guarded response to mean they could make no promises. He hid his concern and bent to kiss his wife. She squeezed his hand. There was much she wanted to say, but they both knew this wasn't the time.

"Doctor's orders," Raphael said with a shrug. "Twenty minutes, tops."

Isabella smiled a weary approval.

Raphael slunk into the bright lights of the hallway, feeling more like a weasel than a celebratory father-to-be. He checked his phone to confirm the time. Four fifteen. He approached an older lady with a silver bun on top of her head at the nurse's station. She beamed a wide smile at him.

"Excuse me, ma'am."

"The name's Virginia. What can I do for you, honey?"

"Hello, Virginia. I'm Raphael Henry, husband of Isabella Henry in room 448. I'm going to be upstairs for a few minutes. There's something I've got to take care of. How do you say it? Stat?"

The lady's eyes widened. "Something more important than your new baby?" Her hand flew to cover her mouth, too late to keep her words at bay.

Raphael pressed the button for the elevator. "Thank you, Miss Virginia. This is what my wife would want me to do. I'll be right back. I promise."

The woman smiled and waved, fanning herself with a green folder.

Tired of waiting, Raphael broke left for the stairs, but not before he heard Virginia's voice above several others.

"My, my, I could listen to that gorgeous man say my name with that accent all night long. This old gal hasn't blushed like that in a long time."

Raphael stifled a smile as the stairwell door closed behind him.

I hope I'm not too late.

Harper exited the elevator on the labor and delivery floor.

"Hey, Virginia. Just checking on Jewel Diamond. How's she progressing?"

The silver-haired nurse fanned herself with a folder and shrugged her shoulders. "I think she's ready to roll any minute now. Dr. Greenfield is on call, and he's got another patient in labor as well. Said he'd be back in thirty minutes to deliver Jewel's baby."

"Has anyone shown up to join her?"

Virginia shook her head. "Not that I'm aware of, but it doesn't seem to bother her."

"Exactly. Nothing bothers that girl. I sure hate to have her lying there by herself on one of the most important days of her life."

"My guess is she won't remember any of it," Virginia said. "The toxicology report isn't back yet, but I'm certain she was under the influence."

Harper tapped her fingernails against the counter. "I suspect you're right. I'll be here when her baby is born. I'm waiting to confirm dental records on another case, and I've got to schedule a press conference. I'll be back soon."

JUNE 2000

Harper pulled the bathroom door shut and cinched the belt on her bathrobe tighter. She tried to run a hand through her muffed-up hair, still stiff from too much hairspray from graduation the day before. She zipped across the hallway to her bedroom and locked the door, hoping her father wouldn't react to her footsteps. He typically rose at dawn, so she knew he was on patrol in or around their house. Soon, the whir of the weed eater confirmed his location as he edged the corners of their perfectly manicured lawn.

She breathed a sigh of relief. The neighbors had gotten used to him being such an early riser over the years.

Harper checked the time, and then lifted her graduation gown off the chair to return it to its hanger, looping the strap of the cap and the Class of 2000 tassel around the hook to hang them on the closet door. The gown looked good as new, pressed and starched to the point no wrinkle would dare invade the satiny royal blue fabric.

She twisted her mouth as she replayed the events from graduation day. She'd looked forward to it for so long, and it had been over in a flash.

Not once had her dad mentioned he was proud of her even after a day full of festivities, posing for photos on the church steps, the picnic, or when he presented her with a new computer. He simply stood at the edge of the crowd with no expression. The only compliment he could muster had to do with her graduation gown.

"Not a wrinkle in sight. That skill will serve you well in life."

Harper doubted that to be true, but his comment caused her to wonder what skills she might possess that could launch a successful career one day. Nothing came to mind. She found her future existence to be overwhelming.

Now here she was, one day past graduation. Life as she knew it no longer existed, and it felt like a free-for-all.

Harper flopped on the bed and checked her phone to see if Julian had called, though she didn't expect as much. He should be in Miami by now, waiting to set sail on a one-week cruise to Barbados—one of his many graduation presents from his influential family.

She picked up a frame that held their prom picture from a few weeks ago. Ginger Ridge High School, the reigning Prom King and Queen. Her eyes still lit up when she gazed at him.

Harper wondered if he remembered any of that evening. She would never forget it, no matter how hard she tried.

Her stomach rumbled and her hand automatically dropped to rub it. She took in a swig of flat soda from her bedside table and nibbled on crackers. She stared out the window in a daze, checking her watch every few seconds.

Time.

Harper was running out of it.

She scuttled to the bathroom and locked the door. She hated the image that peered back at her reflection in the mirror—exhaustion, smeared mascara, and swollen eyes.

She took in a deep breath and exhaled slowly. Part of a verse from the Bible she once learned on a youth retreat in middle school popped into her mind.

"He will never leave nor forsake me. Joshua one verse five." She repeated the verse to herself a few times. "God loves me. No matter what."

It had been a long time since she recalled any Scripture, but there it was, hidden in her heart to use when she needed it most.

Harper tied her hair in a loose bun on top of her head. Her mother hated it when she wore her hair like that. She often said it showed laziness and proved she didn't care about her appearance.

Mama was right, but she was also gone.

Probably a good thing on a day like today.

Harper opened the cabinet door to reveal the test strip and cup of urine she'd concealed exactly fifteen minutes prior. She placed them on the counter and covered her eyes with one hand.

She lifted the test strip and forced one eye open to peer between her fingers.

A plus sign.

Positive.

She dropped to the floor in a heap.

"How can this be happening?"

After what seemed like only a few seconds, she detected a faint knock on the door.

Her father cleared his throat. "You okay? You've been in there awhile. How about blueberry pancakes for breakfast? You loved them when you were little."

Harper adjusted to a sitting position and leaned against the wall. She masked the pain in her voice.

"Sure, Daddy. That sounds delicious. I need to take a quick shower. I'll meet you downstairs in thirty minutes."

She couldn't remember the last time they'd eaten

breakfast together, but Harper never rejected a show of kindness from her father.

"Okay. I'll see you forthwith."

Harper shook her head at his formal military terminology. He was the only one she'd ever heard use that phrase, yet she remembered practicing that word to make the *th* sound in speech therapy sessions during the first grade. At the time, she assumed she'd use that particular word every day of her life.

Oh, to return to those days when life was simple and carefree.

Harper stepped into the shower and allowed the steamy water to swallow her like a cocoon. She dropped to her knees to let the stream roll off her back. She pretended the past fifteen minutes hadn't happened.

I've got one week until Julian comes home. He should be the first to know.

CHAPTER THIRTY

Harper flopped into the chair at her desk and held her breath while she listened through a string of voice messages.

"Hey, Brock Timberland from Ginger Ridge. I found some old photos at the church, and hoped they'd remind you of happier times in your hometown. I'm on the way to visit Grandpa Doe. See you soon."

Harper drew in a deep breath and made notes on her desk calendar. "No time today, Rev. Sorry."

The next one played through. "Hello, this is Wanda From Creation to Cremation. I wondered if a decision has been made on your mystery patient. Please call back if we can assist."

Harper tapped her pen against the desk. "No, thank you. I will give Solomon Thomas a proper burial even if I'm forced to pay for it myself."

She stood as the next message launched.

"Detective Sterling here again. Disregard my last message. I'm thrilled you identified Grandpa Doe. I had a breakthrough as well. We located the actual crime scene and stumbled upon a witness. I'm on my way with a composite drawing of our suspect. Alert the media and we'll get this on the evening news. See you soon."

Finally, she reached the last message. "Hello, Miss Phillips. This is Arthur McCoy with the forensic lab. We've got a match on your John Doe. He is none other than Solomon Thomas. I've faxed over the report."

Harper retrieved the report from her fax machine and rushed past Rosie in a flash.

"Rosie, we've almost solved the case. I'm scheduling another press conference, so send any media teams to the conference room. I'll be in Solomon's room if you need me!"

Rosie answered, "Wait! Who's Solomon?"

"Watch the news. Grandpa Doe. He'll be famous!" Harper called over her shoulder.

She rounded the corner to poke every up button she could find to summon an elevator quicker than usual.

Oh Solomon, how did I not figure this out sooner? I thought you died years ago. You were there for me when I had nowhere else to turn. I can't wait to hug your neck.

That horrible day—the one where her father kicked her out of their house—burned into her memory.

It had been the last time she'd seen Julian Alexander face-to-face.

Still, she'd found Solomon waiting on his porch.

JUNE 2000

A couple of days after Julian returned from the cruise, Harper asked him to meet her at the park. She'd prepared a mental script to cover various outcomes.

Best-case scenario? He'd take her in his arms and assure her they'd get through this. Together.

Worst case?

There were many horrible ways this could go. The park seemed as good a place as any to drop the bomb. At least they'd be out in the open.

As usual, butterflies took off in her stomach as he sauntered toward her. With sun-kissed strands of gold in his hair, a razor stubble beard, and a fresh tan, he'd reached a heightened level of heartthrob status.

Oh, my stars. His baby will be gorgeous!

Her hands dropped to her stomach as she tried to contain the sense of awe bubbling up inside of her. Until that moment, she'd only considered the baby as a predicament, not a person.

Julian's eyes avoided hers as he approached. She reached to hug him and gave him a quick peck on the cheek.

"Julian, you look terrific! I've missed you."

He kept his arms crossed and didn't directly respond. He ripped a leaf off a tree and fidgeted with it. "Listen, Harper. I've done a lot of thinking on the cruise. You know we're headed in separate directions. No long-distance relationship ever works out, and you know I've got to focus on football. I can't have you or any girl weighing me down, if you know what I mean."

Harper turned away, stunned at the cold slap of words that shot out of his mustached mouth. She shouldn't have been surprised. He'd avoided her since prom night.

"Harper, are you going to answer me? Do you understand what I'm saying? We are officially breaking it off."

He looked at her as if it were a question. As if her response mattered. It didn't, and she knew it.

He'd already moved on.

Still, he deserved to know the truth.

She took his hands in hers and flashed a brave face, determined not to be pitiful. Not this time.

"Julian, I want you to know how much I love you. I'm sure I always will. No matter what happens between us."

He bit his lip. "Harper, you're not getting it. We're finished. If it's meant to be, it'll work itself out one day. Don't you think?"

Harper felt herself nodding as if she agreed.

Stop that, Harper.

"I doubt this will change anything, but I wrote you a letter. You don't have to read it here."

Julian pulled away. "Harper, I've already told you what I want. We need to break up. Now."

"Just read it. Later. I'll be home all day tomorrow so we can talk."

She pressed the letter against his chest. Her note folded into its own envelope like one of those *Do you like me—yes or no?* letters from elementary school.

Rather childish for such an intense moment, Harper now realized.

She kissed his hand and turned to walk away. She heard the rustling page as he opened the letter. Not the way she'd planned it. It wouldn't take long for him to reach the second paragraph. She picked up her pace.

She didn't want an immediate response. He deserved time and space to adjust to the news in private.

What she hoped for was his next-day response. After he had time to memorize her loving words. After he'd studied their photos on the bulletin board she'd given him as a graduation present. After he'd clutched their Prom Queen and King picture to his chest and remembered how much he loved her. They'd been through so much together. Mostly wonderful, coming-of-age moments. Harper hoped he'd focus on those.

She turned the corner and followed a trail leading into the woods to slide out of sight.

He needed time. Distance. Space.

She sped to a jog, thankful for the respite of the surrounding woods to help hide her secret.

Is running good for the baby?

She heard him shouting her name.

"Harper!"

It was her secret no longer. He knew.

She took off in a sprint, doing her best to avoid tree roots along the path.

Too late.

His footsteps pounded the path behind her. She turned to catch sight of his long, determined strides. A quarterback scrambling for the end zone. A man on a mission.

She chided herself for not staying out in the open.

Too soon, he grabbed her arm and jerked her around to face him.

She winced to brace herself for whatever might come next. Would he get violent? Shove her to the ground? Slap her across the face?

Anything seemed possible, but there was no way she could have prepared herself for what he said next.

"Harper, if you ever want to speak to me again, you will get this taken care of immediately. I'll pay for it, and we can drive to Atlanta first thing tomorrow morning. No one knows us there. You're eighteen now. An adult and old enough to sign off on an abortion."

Harper's heart stopped beating for a full minute. She felt herself floating away from her body as if watching the two of them from above.

With no warning, his eyes grew cold and angry, unfeeling and hardened. Had he always been so self-absorbed? Had she ever mattered to him?

Now, it was clear she was simply someone he needed to get out of his way.

And so was their baby.

Something snapped inside of her. So strong and suddenly, Harper didn't have time to rein it in.

She backed away while he spoke with outstretched arms trying to persuade her. His voice sounded more like a growl by this point, but he laced it with kindness.

"Listen to me, my beautiful girl." He laid his hands on her shoulders and tried to pull her close, but she stood her ground and forced him to look her in the eye. "This will ruin both of our lives if you don't take care of it ASAP. You know how much I love you. You can't do this to us. It'll destroy our entire relationship. You've got to get an abortion. Now."

Abortion. He tossed the word around like a football. Harper cringed. She never explored how she felt about that choice until this moment. She hated the idea.

Julian moved behind her to wrap his arms around her waist. He kissed her hair. His voice softened as he whispered in her ear.

"You know we've got my football career to consider. That must be our only priority until after college. When

I make it to the NFL, anything is possible. We can get married and have a house full of kids. I promise."

Harper caught her breath as her stomach curdled. This was the first time Julian had ever mentioned their future together.

Her heart melted, along with her resistance.

Julian cleared his throat and tossed out a concise list of instructions.

"I'll swing by to pick you up at nine in the morning and have you home by afternoon. No harm and no pain. By the day after, we can pretend none of this ever happened."

Harper unwrapped his arms and faced him. She shook her head.

"Julian, I'm not sure I can do it. None of this is the baby's fault."

Anger flashed across his face. "Come on, Harper. Don't be so emotional. You know it's not a baby yet. You can't turn this into one of your romantic dreams where we ride off into the sunset. The timing's all wrong. What are you going to do? Raise a baby by yourself in the dorm in Florida?"

That idea sounded ridiculous even to Harper in her fragile state of mind.

She shrugged. "I don't know. I'm not sure what to do, but an abortion doesn't feel right either."

Julian stuck his finger in her face. "Harper, it's not open for discussion." His tone softened once again. "Listen, baby. I'll pick you up first thing tomorrow. I'll take you to lunch somewhere nice while we're in Atlanta. We'll make a day out of it. Okay?"

Harper dropped her head. Her knees felt weak. A tear escaped, though she'd promised herself she wouldn't cry.

Julian wrapped his arm around her waist and led her out of the woods. "That's my girl. I'll walk you home. Get some rest, and I'll pick you up in the morning. I'll whip by the bank for cash on our way out of town."

Julian sounded so practical. He thought of everything. She appreciated his tenderness and the way he protected her. She leaned her head against his shoulder and followed his lead.

"Harper, we're going to be fine. We'll be back to normal when this is over. You're just overthinking it right now."

Back to normal?

Maybe there was a brighter side to this entire debacle.

She and Julian were finally back to normal. This experience had drawn them closer.

And the best part? She wouldn't have to tell her father.

There'd be nothing to tell him after tomorrow.

CHAPTER THIRTY-ONE

In the stairwell, Raphael tucked his hands in his pockets and raised the hood of his sweatshirt to cover his face. Exiting on the top floor, his gait was quick and determined. He circled past room 815 until it cleared.

He tiptoed to the window to peek inside. There he was, same as before. Broken, but still hanging on.

Raphael tiptoed in to position himself beside the old man.

"Hey, it's me again. I'm here to make a deal with you. My wife is in labor on the fourth floor. It's too early for the baby to come, and Isabella is having blood pressure problems. I wonder if God might take them away from me, as a punishment for what I've done to you. Is this how he works?"

The old man's machines whirred in response.

Raphael wiped away a tear.

"I'm going to make you a promise. If everything goes well with Isabella and Baby Evelyn, I'll turn myself in to the police. It's the only way to make this right."

Harper heard the ding of the elevator doors at the far end of the bay.

"Wait. Hold those doors." She dashed at them before they left.

An arm bolted out from inside the elevator to force the doors open.

"Thank you so much," Harper said as she ducked inside, catching her breath. "I would have taken the stairs if you left me." She pressed the button for the eighth floor and leaned her head back to think through the looming press conference.

"Harper, I was hoping I'd run into you."

She turned her head to catch the kind gaze of Brock Timberland. She expected his presence to annoy her on such a busy day. Instead, he brought the opposite effect. She found it comforting he'd driven all the way from Ginger Ridge to visit a stranger. Her special stranger.

She realized his only reason for being here was to visit Solomon.

"Let others help carry your load, Harper. You can't do this alone."

Solomon Thomas once gave me that advice. That rascal.

"I've only got a few minutes. I dragged my son here with me. I set him up with a milkshake in the cafeteria. He's drawing a picture for Grandpa Doe."

Harper grinned.

Brock continued, "I know you're busy, but I discovered these old photos at the church. I hoped you might fill in some blanks about the history." He lifted a framed picture out of the box to show her. "No rush. I'm blown away by what an amazing church this once was. I'd love to renew that spirit."

Harper accepted the photo from him and a smile spread across her face. "Wow. This is one of our hayrides for the Fall Harvest Festival. I'm in this picture. Here, in the bottom corner with my mother. There she is in her flowered dress and fancy hat. Back then, the entire community revolved around your church."

"What do you know about the houses near the church building? Yesterday, I found a door open and went inside to see if anyone needed help. Someone still lives there."

Harper shrugged. "I left Ginger Ridge after I turned eighteen and never looked back. I'm sure everyone I know has moved away since then."

"I understand, but what can you tell me about an old man named Solomon Thomas?"

Harper's mouth dropped as she stared at Brock, unable to speak. The elevator doors squeaked open, but she couldn't move.

She laid her hand across her chest and swallowed hard, forcing the words rattling around in her head into the open. "No way. Solomon Thomas? He still lives there? With the huge wooden mantel in the living room, the rose bushes out front, and the swing on his porch?"

Brock took off his glasses. "Yes. From what I could tell, he still lives there."

"Yes, of course he does. Solomon hated change." Harper stepped off the elevator. "Rev, he's our Grandpa Doe! We matched dental records this afternoon. Follow me!" She took off and Brock followed close at her heels. She spoke over her shoulder. "I've got a press conference scheduled in half an hour to release Solomon's identity. The detective working the case is on his way. He's got a lead on the suspect. I'm telling you, once word gets out Solomon is our guy, his story will spread across the country. Everyone loves this man, and I hope they show up in droves to prove it."

The two of them burst into Solomon's room and stopped in their tracks. Before them stood a man wearing jeans and a gray sweatshirt with the hood pulled over his head. He leaned over Solomon as if he was praying. He snapped his head away from them.

"We're sorry to interrupt. Are you a friend of this man?" Harper asked.

No answer.

"Should we leave the room? We can give you a few minutes of privacy."

The man pivoted on one foot and dropped his head to brush past them.

"No hablo inglés. No hablo inglés," he muttered as he rushed out the door.

Harper and Brock gawked at the man until he rounded the corner.

"That guy sure looked familiar," Harper whispered.

"Odd, but you said even strangers came by to visit," said Brock.

"True, but if he can't speak English, how could he know of Grandpa Doe?"

Brock shrugged and settled the box of photos in the corner, then moved to Solomon's bedside. "It's him. The old guy from the pictures. Now that we know where he's from, why don't I hold a candlelight vigil tonight at his house?"

Harper's eyes widened and she snapped her fingers. "A fantastic idea. Do you have a few minutes to give details during our press conference?"

"Sure. What about my son, Deacon?"

"Bring him. He can be on TV with you. Won't that be cool? Meet me on the first floor at the main desk in twenty minutes."

Brock disappeared and Harper couldn't keep from smiling. She leaned her head against Solomon's arm.

"Solly, I owe you the biggest apology. How could I not know it was you? Presley Rose got her name because of the Elvis music always playing at your house and those gorgeous roses that surrounded your porch—two of my favorite memories combined into one name." Harper wiped away a tear. "You were right. That girl is the best gift you and God could have ever given me."

JUNE 2000

Julian escorted Harper home from the park.

Like they'd done a thousand times, Harper stood on the bottom step in front of her house to kiss him goodbye.

Julian winked. "See you in the morning. You'll always be my girl, sweetheart."

Those same words. That same kiss. Like they'd done a thousand times.

He sped into a jog, tossing his hair about his shoulders like a slow-motion shampoo commercial. She'd watched him go, feeling the same feelings of love she'd always felt. Back to normal.

Harper wandered to her back yard and tiptoed along the bank of the creek. Then the thought of aborting her baby came to the forefront of her mind, and her surroundings spun, causing her head to swim. She felt herself being jerked in all directions like when the current used to pull her under in the creek after a heavy rain. She pictured herself trying to stretch her toes to reach the bank to pull herself to safety.

Her heart fluttered at the thought of Julian as she repeated his last words. "You'll always be my girl, sweetheart."

She hated it when he called her sweetheart. It felt like more of a reprimand than a term of endearment.

Same as when her mother used to call her sweetie.

Soon, her heart caught fire and burned from within. Her stomach rolled. Harper raced to the front door and scuttled up the stairs, barely noticing her father in his recliner reading the paper.

"Harper, are you all right?" he called after her.

She didn't have time to answer before rushing to the toilet to toss the peanut butter toast she'd nibbled on for breakfast. She whipped on the bathtub faucet so her father couldn't hear the multiple gags coming from the depths of her soul.

When the episode was over, she splashed water on her face and dabbed at it with a towel. She moved to the top of the stairs.

"Sorry, Daddy. I'm not feeling well. I'm gonna take a quick bath and a nap. I should be fine after that."

"Okay. Let me know if you need anything. Will you be home for dinner?"

Harper appreciated the tenderness of his voice. "Yes, sir."

Maybe the reality of her graduation had gotten to him, or maybe he was relieved his mission was nearly complete. All he had left to do was to deliver her safely to the University of Florida by August 17, and he could mark her off his list.

As it turned out, it wouldn't take that long.

Harper threw in her favorite bubble bath and filled the tub to her chin, staying in until the water turned cool and the bubbles dissipated. She held her hands against her flat but angry stomach.

How will it feel tomorrow? Will the procedure be bloody? Painful?

Her stomach gurgled in response. Her heart raced, and she felt the need to flee as if she was in serious danger.

Harper stepped out of the tub and dried off, shivering as if it was the dead of winter. She wrapped herself in a robe and tiptoed across the hall to scoot in under the covers of her unmade bed. The mid-day sun warmed her through the window, but still didn't take away the chill that shook her from deep within. She squeezed her eyes shut and let the tears fall until she drifted off to sleep.

Julian loves me. He said we're going to be okay.

She repeated his final, reassuring words until she believed them. Almost.

Deep down, she knew it was a lie, no matter how hard she tried to convince herself.

Harper jolted out of a deep sleep. Her heart climbed out of her chest, racing for an unknown finish line. Leaning her head against the tufted gray cloth of her headboard, her entire body bounced to the rhythm of her rapid heartbeat.

What is wrong with me? Should I go to the hospital?

The sun had slipped to the western side of the house. Late afternoon. The scent of meat cooking in the kitchen directly beneath her room teased her nostrils. Roast, potatoes, and carrots—her father's one and only slow cooker specialty.

Too soon, he knocked on her door.

"Harper, are you feeling better? You've slept for hours. I've made your favorite dinner."

She should have made an excuse and remained in her room for the rest of the night.

But she didn't.

Maybe her heart pounded so hard it shook the wiring loose in her brain. Perhaps his display of kindness lulled her into a false sense of relationship between the two of them.

Most likely, she earnestly craved his guidance.

In the years that followed, whenever Harper analyzed this one, catastrophic evening, she never fully understood why she chose this moment to tell him.

But she did.

Harper drew in a deep breath and opened the bedroom door a few inches to reveal the outline of his body against the light in the hallway.

"Daddy, there's something I need to tell you."

And with that, a bomb exploded. One of those military bombs they often tested at Fort Bryce, shaking every house within a ten-mile radius.

What happened next was a complete blur.

The sound that came from his mouth was the cry of an animal. He folded his hands on his head and paced in formation along the railing to the stairs. He repeated a phrase Harper didn't recognize—probably some type of battle cry.

He retreated down the steps.

Harper knew better, but she followed. By the time she reached the kitchen, he'd jerked the slow cooker off the counter without unplugging it and slammed it against the opposite wall. She thought the entire kitchen might tumble down around them. Carrots landed on his perfectly polished shoes. Potatoes splattered the ceiling.

His hands trembled as they covered his face. He kept his back to her.

She'd never seen this side of him.

Major Garrett Phillips III had no room in his life for failure.

Yet Harper had just handed him a humiliating defeat.

The exemplary soldier, her father considered any unforeseen circumstance to be an attack. Each threat must be crushed—annihilated at the point of origin, so it could no longer present any danger.

He handled Harper and her announcement with those same tactics.

The military brass up the chain of command would be proud.

Major Garrett Phillips III had no room in his heart for a daughter, especially one who tarnished his stellar reputation.

A dish crashed against the wall.

"Get out. Now! Don't you ever set foot in this house again. I won't pay for college and I'll delete you from my will. I'm done with you, Harper Gail."

She hated the way he screamed her name—loud and angry, like a curse word.

Harper bolted up the stairs. In her bedroom, she threw a few items of summer clothing into the largest suitcase she could find—a pink and blue-flowered set her mother had given to her before church camp when she turned twelve.

She surveyed the room. The only items that jumped out at her were school yearbooks and Ginger the Bunny. She squeezed them in the suitcase and zipped it.

Harper marched down the stairs and straight out the front door without looking back. She left it all behind. Photos of her high school years that covered her bedroom wall. Her cheerleading uniforms. Her graduation gown. Her new computer, and her acceptance packet from the University of Florida.

Most of all, she left behind the constant fear of setting her father off and the shame of causing her mother to leave.

With that, came a strange sense of relief.

After tomorrow, there won't be a baby to deal with, Harper reminded herself.

She still hated the thought of an abortion, but it seemed the only logical choice now that she had no place to live. In a week's time, she had become the problem no one wanted to deal with. By default, the plan Julian suggested was her only option.

I'll call Julian and ask him to meet me in the church parking lot.

Harper regretted packing the school yearbooks. Their weight slowed her progress, causing the suitcase to rub a bruise against Harper's leg as she rounded the corner by the church. The sun stretched out its fingers between the clouds as if reaching toward the steeple—a powerful sight that brought a sense of peace.

Harper turned her head to catch Solomon sitting in his swing as if he'd been waiting where she left him all those years ago.

"Well, if it isn't Miss Harper Phillips. I'm just out here capturing this brilliant sunset before we lose it. No two are ever the same, you know. Remember when we used to watch them together?"

"I sure do."

Solomon stood to greet her. "I saw you from a distance at graduation last week but couldn't reach you through the crowd. I'm proud of you!"

Harper forced a smile, but Solomon saw right through it. He reached to take the suitcase.

"Where are you headed, m'dear?"

Harper shook her head. "I don't know, Solly. I need help and don't have anywhere else to turn."

"Come on. Tell me all about it. Can I get you some lemonade?"

He hobbled up his steps and led her to the porch.

The safest place she'd ever known.

"Yes, please. I'd love a glass of lemonade."

CHAPTER THIRTY-TWO

In the passenger's seat of his sergeant's vehicle, Detective Sterling drew in a deep breath and stifled the desire to suggest they'd would've already reached their destination if he had been driving. His therapist listed this as proof of one of many control issues.

Keep your mouth shut, Sterling. Remember, you're currently under investigation for an on-duty accident.

As it stood, the sergeant was the only one in Cam's corner, and he appreciated the vote of confidence.

He patted the sergeant on the shoulder. "Thank you for giving me a chance to solve this case. I knew you'd be furious since my vehicle is totaled."

Sergeant Lewis grinned. "The investigators will ask why you parked on a road with no shoulder. Let's make sure we give them a good reason for it."

"Thanks, Sarge. I can count on one hand the number of people who've backed me up like this."

OCTOBER 1980

Mama laid out their navy-blue Easter suits on each one of their beds, and Cameron and Grayson did their best to wiggle into them. The sleeves were now too short and pinched hard on their upper arms, but this was no time to be buying new suits.

"It's important we look our best to give your father a proper goodbye," Mama said, tightening Cameron's tie around his neck.

Cam couldn't breathe, but the necktie wasn't to blame. He'd been holding his breath since those military officers left their front porch a week earlier.

Daddy's body had arrived from overseas a few days after the officer's visit. American flags flew at half-staff all over town, and the sky had remained gloomy as if on command. The boys missed school for several days, and their teachers brought books and assignments to them in person. Strangers had showed up at their door to deliver casseroles and cakes.

Daddy loved casseroles and cakes, but no one left in their house was hungry.

"You and your brother will have to become the men of the house now that your daddy is gone. I need all the help I can get from the two of you," Mama said on the night Daddy's body came home.

Cam didn't want to be the man of the house.

He took a minute to look deep into his mother's tired and puffy eyes. She hadn't put on her makeup yet, but he thought she was beautiful. Still, the spark she'd once had was gone. That weird delight she found in simply being their mama, fixing their food, and making sure they got where they needed to go on time ... gone.

The ideal military wife—being in charge when she needed to be, stepping aside to let Daddy shine when he returned home—had not been an easy balance, but she'd lived it to perfection.

Now, the entire universe had fallen out of balance. Cam felt vulnerable and unprotected, trying hard not to resent everyone else who went on with their lives.

Mama asked the boys to wait on the couch, and they did as they were told. Cam glanced at his brother and turned away. Neither of them knew how to handle the pain in the other's eyes.

They took turns crying in different rooms so the other wouldn't see. Grayson spent most of his time holding his mother's hand, making sure she didn't grow lonely. Cam could do nothing more than hold his father's photo against his chest and stare out the window.

They should have turned to each other, faced it together, arm in arm and brother to brother, but that's not how it went down.

Mama sniffled as she inched down the stairs, wearing a black dress Cam had never seen. Her hair looked pretty, tucked beneath a matching hat with a piece of see-through netting that covered her eyes. She'd remembered to put on lipstick. She rolled a handkerchief through her fingers.

The clock ticked a countdown that never stopped from the mantel.

Tick. Tock. Tick. Tock.

The room seemed too silent. Cam wanted to scream, to wake up from this nightmare.

There was a knock on the door, but no one moved.

Tap. Tap. Tap.

Tick. Tock. Tick. Tock.

Tap. Tap. Tap.

Mama heard it this time. She moved to the door, set her shoulders, and forced the door open a few inches.

Cam heard an older man's gentle voice.

"Good morning, Mrs. Sterling. My name is Solomon Thomas. We met last night at the funeral home. I'm here to walk you and your boys to the church, so you won't have to go alone."

Mama fell into the arms of this stranger and wept. The man hugged her until her tears abated, and she could once again stand upright. He dressed funny, wearing short pants and a bow tie with suspenders. The kind of outfit Mama liked to make Cameron and Grayson wear when they were too small to voice their opinion.

Cam felt like he'd seen him before but couldn't remember where. One thing he knew for certain, the old man felt safe, and Mama needed him. Mama leaned against his shoulder, and he wrapped one arm around her.

Grayson held her hand and leaned into her. Cam followed along the best he could.

The old man turned over his shoulder and held out a hand. Cam grabbed it and held on for dear life as they followed the sidewalk that led to the church. His shoes squeaked against the pavement. The smell of flowers drifted through the air.

Everyone in town showed up for the funeral, but Cam never felt so alone.

Except for his new friend, Solomon, who took the time to notice them.

"See that church steeple up there?"

Cam nodded.

"Like your daddy, it always points to heaven. Remember that when life gets hard, okay?"

Cam didn't understand what he meant, but he liked the way it sounded. That old man had a way of making sense, just like Daddy.

From that moment on, Solomon appeared at every football game. He sat beside Mama with his short pants and bow tie and acted like he loved football. Every single birthday party, he brought bags of groceries and books. He took the car for repairs, installed a new lock on the door, and reattached the shutters to the house after a severe storm. Anytime Mama needed someone to do man-type things around the house, Solomon was the one who showed up.

Cam never remembered thanking him until he followed that same dreaded path to the darkened funeral home to say goodbye to Mama twenty years later. There he was, wearing those same short pants, suspenders, and a bow tie. Cam took one look into his kind eyes and allowed himself to fall into those gentle arms for comfort.

Like he did for Daddy's, Solomon escorted both men to the church for Mama's funeral. They dwarfed that tiny man, yet he squeezed in between them so they wouldn't have to walk alone.

"Thank you, Mr. Thomas. You must understand what grief feels like to show up like this."

"It all points to heaven, like that church steeple. Remember?"

Detective Sterling strode to a bay of microphones bundled together at the podium. "Good afternoon. We're thrilled to announce crucial updates to the unsolved case involving our elderly hit-and-run victim known as Grandpa Doe. We have located an eyewitness and believe whatever happened last Thursday evening was a genuine accident. We beg the driver of the vehicle to come forward."

Harper waited with Brock Timberland and Deacon outside the range of cameras. Deacon whispered questions to Brock about everything going on around them. Harper fidgeted with the buttons on her sweater while waiting her turn to speak. She was pleased with the turnout. All four local television stations and one from CNN were present.

Detective Sterling held up the drawing of the suspect. The cameras blocked Harper's view, but she'd perused the old newspaper article she found that depicted a younger version of Solomon.

Her old friend Aaron Foster waved from across the room. Harper lifted her chin and threw a smile his way, her cheeks burning at his presence. She closed her eyes and began reviewing her upcoming remarks in her head.

Detective Sterling repeated the description of their suspect vehicle. "To the driver, it is imperative that we speak to you in person to determine exactly what happened. If you choose to cooperate before we lose this victim, we might plea down to a lower charge."

The detective gave out a phone number and motioned Harper to the microphones.

"I now turn this over to Harper Phillips, who is Grandpa Doe's case manager here at Savannah Regional."

Harper lifted her head and eased into the bright lights.

"Thank you for joining us today. I have some incredible news to share. Because of the intensity of the injuries our victim sustained at the time of the accident, it's been difficult to make a positive ID on him until early this afternoon. This gentleman was a dear friend of mine from my childhood."

Harper bit her lip to hold back tears.

"Our beloved Grandpa Doe is none other than Solomon Thomas. To my knowledge, he has no remaining family. But that never stopped him from becoming like family to anyone who crossed his path. In our military town of Ginger Ridge, about an hour from here, people moved in and out of the area. Solomon welcomed us all to his porch to drink a frosty glass of lemonade or read a story. On Solomon's porch, we found a safe place to land when our world spun out of control."

Harper could feel the warmth of Solomon's smile as she continued. "A veteran himself, he understood how difficult it was to grow up in a military family. Solomon referred to us as soldiers and told us supporting our parents was our mission." Harper studied the ceiling as she chose her next words. "There was no greater patriot. He served as the grand marshal in town parades. The first one in the door at every funeral, be it military or otherwise. He placed flags at each tombstone at the veteran's cemetery on holidays."

Harper shook her head to stop herself. She could go on for hours.

She displayed the old newspaper article from the *Ginger Ridge Gazette* which showed Solomon as the grand marshal of the annual Christmas parade. Video cameras zoomed in for close-ups and flashes went off in a wave across the conference room.

"Solomon Thomas is my hero. A skilled listener who gave the best hugs. He drastically altered the outcome of my life, and there are many others who will say the same." Harper spoke quicker and louder, like a preacher getting her final point across. "I have no doubt there will soon be a parade in heaven, and my dear friend Solomon Thomas will once again be the grand marshal who leads it."

Harper closed her eyes to enjoy the image dancing across her mind. "It will be my honor to escort him to those pearly gates."

She wiped a tear and introduced Brock Timberland. With Deacon in his arms, he gave details of a candlelight vigil set to begin at 8:00 p.m. in front of Solomon's house.

Harper detected sniffles throughout the room as she journeyed to room 815.

As Miss Phillips began her interview, Cam Sterling used a handkerchief to wipe his forehead. His stomach gnawed at him for not eating since sunrise. Cam popped a mint in his mouth and crossed his arms over his chest to listen.

Harper handled the press like a pro. "This gentleman, formerly referred to as Grandpa Doe ... Solomon Thomas ... has no remaining family ... Ginger Ridge ..."

Cam's heart dropped.

Our victim is Solomon Thomas? From Ginger Ridge?

When the minister finished speaking, cameras surrounded both Cam and Sergeant Lewis, blinding him as he did his best to answer follow-up questions. He scanned the room but saw no signs of Miss Phillips.

One thought crossed his mind—more shocking than any other stunning developments that had taken place on this eventful day.

I need to call my brother.

CHAPTER THIRTY-THREE

"The baby's heart rate is dropping," Dr. Greenfield uttered to the nurse. "We need to deliver now." He perched on a rolling stool at the foot of Isabella's bed.

Raphael wiped his wife's forehead with a washcloth.

"Okay, it's time to push. Let's meet your baby girl. I'd rather get her here naturally than wheel you down for surgery," said Dr. Greenfield.

Isabella squeezed her husband's hand during an extended contraction. "Raphael, tell me she'll be all right."

"She'll be fine. Our bebé is strong, like her mother."

Isabella's fluttering eyelashes indicated a softening heart.

Has she forgiven me?

Raphael moved in to prop her up from behind. He kept silent, learning long ago not to speak during these moments. Anything that came out of his mouth sounded ridiculous, even to him.

Who am I to advise the strongest woman I've ever known on how to bring a human into the world?

Besides, it was all he could do to keep from passing out. He had to remind himself to inhale and exhale, keeping rhythm with Isabella's patterned breaths.

Don't you dare pass out. You can't miss this, dude!

Dr. Greenfield kicked his stool away. "Here she comes! Dad, do you want to come to this end to witness everything?"

Raphael lifted his head, only to realize his teeth were chomped down on the corner of one of Isabella's pillows, as if he was the one shoving a baby through his body.

He lowered his voice to make it sound more masculine. "No thanks. I don't care to see all of that. I'm fine staying at this end."

On the elevator, Harper texted Presley a quick update.

HARPER: Won't be home tonight. Can you spend the night at Sidney's? I will call her mother.

PRESLEY: Sure. At her house now. You OK?

Harper clutched her phone to her chest.

HARPER: It's Grandpa Doe. He's my old friend Solomon. Watch the news!

Presley sent a smiley face.

PRESLEY: No way! I'm so glad you two found each other again.

Harper punched the number eight again as if it might speed up the elevator. The doors whirred open, only to reveal a team of nurses rushing a crash cart toward his room.

"CODE BLUE. ROOM 815. CODE BLUE."

Harper gasped.

"Dear God, no! Please don't take him yet," she called into the open vestibule.

She burst through his door to find two doctors bent over Solomon working feverishly. They shoved the crash cart next to his bed, and soon his body thrust into the air like a bouncing football.

Harper's hand flew to her mouth.

"What happened? Please tell me he's still with us."

The heart monitor picked up a faint rhythm.

A man she knew as Dr. Davis turned over his shoulder to answer her question. "He coded, but with no DNR papers on file, we had to revive him. We brought him back this time, but it's only a matter of hours. He can't undergo any more shock treatments. And we're going to break the rest of his ribs if we do CPR again. Any luck contacting his family?"

Harper couldn't speak over the lump that formed in her throat. A million visions of Solomon flashed through her mind, a constant presence through every phase of her childhood years.

"Yes. I'm his family."

JUNE 2000

On the swing, Harper leaned against Solomon's shoulder and poured it all out for him. Prom night. Telling Julian. Her father's vicious attack with the pot roast. And more damaging than that, the words that flew from his mouth.

Harper would never forget what Solomon did next.

For the first time in her life, he invited her into his house.

No one was ever allowed in his house. Kids or adults— it didn't matter. All were welcomed to his porch, but never any further.

Harper asked about it often, and he gave the same response. "As a young lady, never put yourself in a position you can't get yourself out of."

She never knew what he meant. Until tonight.

As he listened to her story, darkness settled around them. Solomon must have decided the safest place for Harper was inside his house. There, in his living room, he motioned for her to sit on a massive sofa, a maroon velvet monstrosity with shiny gold striping at the edges.

She sensed her presence made him uncomfortable. Solomon paced in front of her, his perfectly polished loafers echoing a tap with each step. He mumbled under his breath.

A strong sense of intrusion hung in the air, as if she had violated him by being in his personal space.

Harper grabbed a pillow and held it to her stomach. She gazed around the room but remained quiet, giving him the time he needed to adjust. Solomon hated change, and this was a big one. No matter how much he loved her.

His home was immaculate, as Harper expected, and resembled a museum with the same sort of reverence, echoes, and period decorations. The floors were formed from the same dark wood that paneled the bottom portion of the walls. Flowered wallpaper adorned the walls, with candle sconces spaced out every few feet.

The mantel itself was gorgeous, taking up most of one wall. The massive fireplace remained spotless, as if it had never been used. Framed black and white photos lined the mantel.

Underneath the window was an old record player with a matching wood cabinet filled with Elvis records.

"My Sadie Beth was a huge fan of Elvis Presley," he often explained, recognizing he didn't come across as the Elvis type.

On the back of the front door was a framed letter with Sadie Beth's name scrolled at the bottom. In the hundreds of conversations they'd shared, Solomon always deflected questions about his daughter. Instead, he'd steered Harper back to God and her own family. Eventually, Harper quit prying about his.

"Pray for your parents. Most adults do the best we can with the lot God gives us. You only get one family, and they are meant to be cherished. Even when it's difficult."

Wise advice for those with a normal family. On this night, even Solomon appeared at a loss on to how to calm her.

She had yet to tell him the worst part.

Solomon screeched to an abrupt halt. A pained look flashed across his face.

"I'm sorry, Harper. I can't let you sleep in her room. Would you mind using the couch?"

Harper stood and patted him on the shoulder. "Of course, Solly. It's fine. Is that what's gotten you so upset? That couch is plenty big for me, don't you think? I brought Ginger along, so she can keep me company. You remember that old bunny I won at church on my first Easter Sunday?"

Solomon nodded and heaved a sigh of relief.

Harper chuckled to lighten the mood. "Something told me to grab Ginger on my way out the door. I think I'm going to need her, like when I was a kid."

Solomon shook his head. "Thank you for understanding. I don't mean to be rude, I'm just not ready."

Harper led him by the elbow to the couch. "It's fine, Solly. I completely understand. Come sit with me. I didn't finish my story. Julian is so smart—he came up with a solution for our predicament."

Solomon cocked his head. "A solution? What do you mean?"

Harper rattled off the plan as it had been presented to her. "He's taking me in the morning to Atlanta for an abortion. He says now is not the time for us to become parents, and he's right. Julian has his football career to consider, and it wouldn't be fair for me to ruin it for him."

Solomon dropped his head. "But Harper, is this what you want?"

"What I don't want is to inconvenience everyone. Like Julian said, we'll take care of this problem, once and for all. I must do what's best for everyone. I can't be selfish at a time like this."

Solomon's face froze and tears filled his eyes. As if in a trance, he took off his cap and glasses and lifted a handkerchief from his pocket. Harper expected him to dab at his eyes, regain his composure, and say something to comfort her. To praise her for making such a tough decision.

Instead, he dropped his face into the handkerchief and sobbed. Openly, as if he'd been holding in a lifetime of pain and chose that moment to release it into one hanky.

Harper threw her arms around him and cried too, unsure if he was crying for her or himself. She tossed out a string of apologies to comfort him.

"Solomon, I'm sorry I let you down. I'm sorry I had sex with Julian." She forced out jagged words between tears. "I'm sorry you aren't ready to let anyone sleep in Sadie Beth's room. I'm sorry I didn't visit during my high school years."

His tears soon dried to a trickle, and he took her hand in his. "Oh, sweet girl. Don't you understand? I'm not crying for me. I'm crying for you and your baby."

Harper pulled away in confusion.

"The baby? *My* baby?"

Solomon wrapped an arm around her. "It's not fair that the two most important men in your life caused you to feel this way. As if this is something you did to them. It may seem like there are no good options, but please listen to me."

He stood and wiggled his glasses into place. "Are you hungry?"

She rubbed her hands together. "Starved."

Solomon limped toward the kitchen. "Come on. I'm going to make you a sandwich, and tell you a story about Silas."

Harper rose to follow him. "Who's Silas?"

Solomon flipped on the light and turned over his shoulder to answer with a strong and defiant voice. "Silas was my son."

The next morning at the crack of dawn, without ever notifying Julian, Solomon and Harper waited in line at the Bluegrass Bus Station. She nibbled on a sausage biscuit he bought from a drive thru. In her hands, she held a bag with six more, in case she grew hungry on their trip.

Harper tapped Solomon on the shoulder. "Solomon, I need you to know something. You remember what you said last night, about the two most important men in my life being my father and Julian?"

He nodded and nudged them forward in line.

"You were wrong. Solly, you are the most important man in my life." Harper leaned her head against his shoulder. "I can never thank you enough."

Solomon stroked her hair. "My Winnie used to say we were made for each other."

Harper smiled. As per usual, she was unsure where his train of thought might take them.

Solomon continued, "I feel the same way about you. You and I, we each need a family right now. Maybe we were made for each other as well."

A tear rolled down her face. "I'm really going to miss you, Solly."

He squeezed her shoulder. "I'll miss you too, but you need a fresh start. You know I'll do anything for you and your baby. Call me any time."

"I know, Solly. I know."

"Next." A lady with a baritone voice motioned them to the window.

Solomon wrangled Harper's suitcase between his legs. "Two tickets to Savannah," he announced, slapping a hundred-dollar bill in the tray.

"One-way or round trip?" she asked through a three-inch hole with a microphone.

Solomon thought for a minute and gave Harper a wink. "One of each. One of us will stay for a few months."

CHAPTER THIRTY-FOUR

Solomon's monitor showed a silent pattern of a faint heartbeat—slow but determined.

Harper kissed his forehead. "Solly, thanks for sticking with me. We need to get you gussied up for your guests."

From a hospital toiletry kit, she dug out a razor to shave his stubble and raised the head of his bed until he was in more of a reclining position. He already looked more like himself—wise and peaceful.

"Hmmm. Something's still missing."

Harper made a series of phone calls. Soon, maintenance delivered a love seat and comfortable chairs so Solomon's guests might feel at home. The cafeteria sent pitchers of lemonade and a plate of cookies. From the pediatric library, Harper borrowed a few classic chapter books.

Harper patted Solomon's hand. "I want it to feel like we're visiting on your porch, like the good old days."

She displayed the old photos from Brock on the window ledge. In most photos, Solomon stood front and center, with a confident grin and a permanent twinkle in his eye.

She remembered that people had often asked him, "How do you keep such a remarkable sense of joy?"

"I've already read this story, and I know how it ends," he'd explain.

The last photo Harper found was from Easter Sunday 1988.

"Whoa, Solomon, this is the day we first met." Harper held it up as if he could see it. "You remember? I found the golden egg, and you presented the Easter basket to me with that loveable old bunny inside. I swear I dragged Ginger everywhere for the next fifteen years."

Laz bounced through the door. "Special delivery for one Harper Phillips." He presented a shopping bag stuffed with goodies.

"Thank you, Laz. Did you have any trouble finding these items?"

"Don't you realize who you're talking to? Failure is never an option." He switched to his John Wayne voice. "You can't ask a boy to do a man's job, Pilgrim."

Harper chuckled. "Whatever you had to do to pull this off, I appreciate it."

She opened the bag to reveal a bow tie, a pair of reading glasses, a few bags of candy, and a gray golf cap. Setting the cap on Solomon's head to cover his bandages and tubes, she loosely fastened the bow tie around his neck and eased the glasses into place.

"He looks great. I think he needs a pipe," Laz commented.

Harper laughed at the mental picture. "Heavens, no. Solomon would never smoke a pipe."

Detective Sterling burst into the room and pointed to his watch. "I hate to interrupt, Miss Phillips, but it's almost six o'clock."

Harper gasped. "Thank you, Detective."

She used the remote attached to the railing on Solomon's bed to switch television channels.

"It's showtime, Solly. The world will soon learn your story." She clasped his hand.

The familiar theme music from WTVQ Channel 7 faded as the anchors launched into their headlines.

"Tonight, we bring you three important updates on the heartbreaking story of Grandpa Doe, the elderly victim of a violent hit-and-run that occurred five days ago."

They showed the picture of Solomon as a younger man with Harper's statement dubbed over it. She described what a giant of a man he proved to be. The video feed cut to footage of Harper during the earlier press conference.

"I have no doubt there will soon be a parade in heaven, and my dear friend Solomon Thomas will once again be the grand marshal who leads it."

From that point, the anchorman shifted focus. "In addition to learning the identity of this unsung hero, detectives from the Madison Police Department released a composite sketch of the suspect who was driving the vehicle that hit Solomon Thomas."

The sketch flashed across the screen, along with a description of the vehicle Cam provided.

Harper gasped and folded her hands over her mouth. "Oh, my stars! I've seen that guy before. The suspect! He was in Solomon's room. Today, right before the press conference."

Cam spent the next hour in the hospital security office reviewing activity on the eighth floor from every camera angle. He took notes on a borrowed clipboard and went over the details with Chief Turner.

He checked his notes. "At approximately 4:41 p.m., the suspect appeared from the corner stairwell, keeping his distance until staff cleared the room. He entered the room at 4:44 p.m. and Harper Phillips walked in on him at 4:50 p.m. The suspect remained in the room with the patient for approximately six minutes, then escaped into that same stairwell. But where did he go from there? Why can't we find him entering or exiting the building?"

Chief Turner shrugged. "I haven't been able to figure that out. I've searched all entrances an hour before and after this incident and see no record of him leaving. Even if he changed clothes, there is no one matching his description either coming or going during this time frame."

"Listen, my phone is going crazy with calls about this case, and I'm running out of time to visit Grandpa Doe.

I feel like we're missing something. Could you check the emergency room entrance? Could the suspect be a patient here? Or at least pretending to be one?"

Chief Turner handed him a business card. "Sure. Jot down your phone number and I'll let you know if I come up with anything. Go see your friend. He sounds like quite the hero."

Cam nodded. "He was. He's the one who showed up for our family after our father died. I never appreciated the way he took care of us until now. I was so caught up in my grief, I blocked many childhood memories."

"Why don't you go upstairs and tell him?"

"Thanks, Chief. I will." Cam patted the chief on the back and exited the security office.

With two armed guards stationed outside the door, Harper plugged in her phone as a message buzzed through from Rosie at the switchboard.

ROSIE: Calls coming in all over the country about Solomon. I'm staying late to answer them. Let me know if you need anything.

Harper grinned and sent a response.

HARPER: I can't imagine anyone I'd rather have serving as the ringleader of this circus. Thank you.

Harper placed her hand against Solomon's chest to feel the rise and fall of his breaths.

"Solomon Thomas, it's time to share the rest of your story. I know of Winnie and Silas, but whatever happened to Sadie Beth? Please tell me before you go. I'd like to share her story as well."

SEPTEMBER 1988

Harper scrambled to keep up with Solomon, wincing because her new boots were on the wrong feet. Solomon clutched a bouquet of flowers in one hand and his cane in the other.

"Wait up, Solly. I thought you said you had a bad leg. Why are we going so fast?"

Solomon slowed his pace to wait for her. "I apologize. I don't want to be late."

"How can we be late? It's a cemetery. Do they know what time it is?"

Solomon handed her the flowers. "Would you mind carrying these for me?"

She buried her nose in them as they entered through the metal gates. "Roses. They smell so pretty. Can dead people smell flowers? Is that why there are flowers on the graves?"

Solly sighed. "Who knows? I'm taking Winnie some of her roses. She planted those bushes, and she needs to see her roses. You sure do ask a lot of questions."

"I'm sorry. I guess I need a lot of answers."

"Sometimes there aren't any answers, Harper. Not everything gets resolved this side of Heaven."

Harper bit her lip. She could tell by the look on his face she needed to quiet down. Not a simple task, but she'd do it for Solomon. He only agreed to bring her with him because he'd promised a trip to the bakery—a reward for making good grades on her first report card. Harper wasn't likely to forget a promise like that.

"Why don't you wait on this bench. I'll only be a few minutes, but I need to be alone for a bit."

Harper nodded. "I'm sorry, Solly. Daddy says I talk too much when I get nervous. I've never been in a cemetery before. Is this what nervous feels like?"

Solomon shrugged. "It's okay. I'll answer your questions when I return."

Harper crawled to the bench and kicked her legs back and forth. She studied Solomon as he knelt in front of two grave markers. He kept his head down as if he was praying. She heard his voice but couldn't understand what he said. He settled the roses in a vase attached to the larger grave.

It bothered her to be watching Solomon when he preferred to be alone. She decided not to pester him to bring her next time. This was his thing. She didn't belong.

Harper laid back on the bench to count branches on the tree above her head. The leaves were changing to bright shades of orange and yellow. She closed one eye at a time to catch the crazy shadows the sun created as it burst through the gaps in the leaves.

Solomon's face popped in her view, causing her to jump.

"Whoa, Solly. You scared me. I didn't hear you coming."

He smiled and reached for her hand. "Well, I could say the same thing about you. I find it unsettling when you get too quiet. Now, let's go get that cookie."

"Can I ask one more question? You said one of those graves belonged to Winnie. Is Sadie Beth in the other one?"

Solomon gripped her hand tighter and limped in silence long enough for Harper to regret asking the question.

"No. Sadie Beth isn't home yet," he whispered as his voice cracked.

CHAPTER THIRTY-FIVE

Brock Timberland updated the old church sign to alert passersby of the candlelight vigil scheduled for eight o'clock that evening. Using a couple beat-up spotlights, he ran electrical cords to focus one on the bell tower and the other toward the porch of Solomon's house.

Deacon followed in his father's footsteps. "What's a vigil, Daddy? What's gonna happen?"

Brock let out a sigh. "I have no idea, but my hope is people show up to pay their respects. If not, it may be just you and me, kid."

Deacon reached for his hand. "I'm ready. How do we pay respeck?"

Brock chuckled. "It's respect, with a T. We do it by lighting candles and staying quiet to focus on what a great man Solomon is. Sometimes people sing and pray, or they may bring gifts."

Deacon's eyes lit up. "I'll be right back. Is your truck open?"

Brock clicked the button to unlock the doors from the key in his pocket. "Yes. Be careful. Watch that car pulling into the parking lot."

Deacon climbed into the passenger's seat. Brock could only see his son's feet wiggle around while he searched for something important.

What is he doing?

After the oncoming vehicle veered into a nearby parking space, Brock made his way to greet the driver.

A tall, older gentleman stepped out sporting jeans and cowboy boots.

"Good Evening. I'm Brock Timberland, the pastor here at Ginger Ridge Church. How may I help you?"

The man offered his hand. "Yes, I've heard about you. I'm Lee Martin, Jr. Current mayor of Ginger Ridge."

"So this town has a mayor after all."

The man grinned. "For the time being. I plan to retire before the next election. I inherited this position from my father. We have the same name, so my guess is people thought they were still voting for my father. To be honest, we've had trouble finding a replacement."

Isn't it the mayor's job to make sure the town doesn't fall apart like this? Maybe we should turn it over to someone else.

Brock still hadn't quite figured out how to filter his thoughts and make them more holy.

Maybe that develops over time. I sure hope so.

Deacon called out to him.

"Daddy, can I cross the street? I want to give Solomon my truck. Will that be a good way to pay respects, like you said?"

Brock grinned. "What a great idea. Wait there. I'm coming."

He shook the hand of the mayor. "Excuse me. Nice to meet you, but I need to walk my son across the street."

"I'll head over with you," the mayor offered.

"Sure. I haven't been in Ginger Ridge for long but wondered about future plans for this old town. Do you think there's any chance of saving it?" Brock reached for Deacon's hand and proceeded to the front steps of Solomon's porch.

The mayor dug his hands into his pockets. "I sure hope so. The possibilities are endless if we find the a few investment dollars and the right people willing to stick around to make this a community once again. As for me and my family, we've relocated to a farm about an hour away. My retirement plan, though it's the hardest job I've ever had. I still keep a home here in Ginger Ridge and make it back here once a week."

"I see. How do your constituents get in touch with you?"

"My secretary works ten to two every day. That seems enough for today's issues. I pay her out of my pocket. Not much of a budget available for payroll these days."

Brock grabbed Deacon's hand and led him to Solomon's yard.

"Where should I put it, Daddy?"

Brock pointed to the porch. "There, on the top step. I think that'll be fine."

"What are you fellas doing here at Solomon's house? Is he home?"

"I guess you haven't seen the news, huh?"

Mayor Martin shook his head.

"Solomon is the victim of that hit-and-run accident last week near Madison. They finally identified him and released a sketch of the suspect who's still at large. Solomon's probably not going to make it through the night, so we're holding a candlelight vigil for him."

"Madison? I wonder how he got that far away. Solomon hasn't driven for years."

"There's a ton of unanswered questions, but at least we finally know who he is. From what I understand, he was quite the hero of Ginger Ridge."

The mayor watched the sun set behind the church steeple. "No one loved this town as much as Solomon did. Mind if I stay for the vigil?"

"That would be great. The media should be here soon if you'd like to give a quick interview."

The mayor shrugged. "Sure. Let me grab my cowboy hat, or no one will recognize me."

Brock toyed with a portable sound system until he had a stream of peaceful music playing. By the time he lifted his head, there were fifteen cars in the church parking lot, with more lined up behind them.

"Solomon Thomas, it looks like you may be the key to bringing this old town back to life, after all."

SOLOMON'S PORCH
JUNE 1978

Solomon perched at the edge of Sadie Beth's bed. Pillows stacked around him like the grief that threatened to suffocate him. At his feet were five cardboard boxes sealed with Sadie Beth's belongings from Perkins University.

Proof that she existed.

Solomon waffled between craving answers and remaining terrified of them. He sliced through the tape on the first container with his pocketknife. On top of a stack of textbooks was one of her personal journals—a black cover with gold metallic hearts. It was one of the high school graduation gifts he'd given her. She'd put it to good use—each page already filled to the end.

Tears clouded his view as he opened the front cover. Her handwriting. Her diary. Her heart ... spread out before him.

It opened with the day Elvis died.

> *August 16, 1977—He's gone. I can't believe we lost Elvis. What a gift he had. What a gift he was. I'm more heartbroken that he lost that sparkle in his eyes as he grew older. Such sadness. That's no way to live. I'm sorry we couldn't help you, Elvis. Rest in peace.—SB*

> *August 27—Daddy just pulled away in his old truck. Perkins University is as incredible as I hoped. Such energy and possibility in the air, I honestly can't wait to try new things. I hope Daddy will be okay. He lives such a guarded life. I wish he'd go back to church and find some friends. He's had too much heartache. I gave him a watch and a hooded sweatshirt before he left. I hope he wears both. I'm so thankful for him.—SB*

Solomon flipped ahead a few pages into September, October, and November.

> *September 5—It's Labor Day. In my quest for new experiences, I went to the opening football game on Saturday. I had fun jumping*

up and down, even if I barely understood the game. I spoke with my new friend Spencer at the gate. He's a security guard on campus. He's a few years older than me, but his eyes are kind, and he's always helpful. His mother also died when he was little. I sensed the pain of his story when we first met. I feel like we are kindred spirits—like I already knew him before I got here.

I don't know the rules on that sort of thing. Can employees date students? Would he be interested? Does he feel the same way? I have no idea, so for now, I'll pray for him. That's the most powerful gift I can offer, right?

You'll never believe this, but I tried jogging today. It was a holiday, so no classes. I put on my tennis shoes and jogged until I ran out of things to think about. I loved it. The fresh air, nature, the wind blowing through my hair.

Daddy would have a fit if he knew. He'd never turn me loose in such a way. He sensed danger around every corner, but I only see beauty and promise. The further I go, the more I believe I can accomplish. I've never felt this way in my life.

I'm already hooked, so I must figure out a way to tell Daddy about this new hobby of mine, when the time is right.—SB

Solomon read until the last page. By this time, the sun had set, and the room darkened around him. He turned on a lamp to capture her remaining words. Toward the end of the semester, Sadie Beth apparently spent more time running than journaling, so there were fewer details regarding her life. She touched on being homesick at Thanksgiving, getting anxious about exams, and the excitement of coming home for Christmas. She felt guilty for going a few days without thinking about Winnie and Silas.

October 27—I don't know how to explain it when people say I "lost" my mother and baby brother. That's simply not true. I never lost them. I know exactly where they are. I feel them when I run—as if they spur me on to go further. Of course, I haven't forgotten them. Instead, I can never separate myself from them. They are part of me. They are in heaven, and heaven is inside of me. Does that make sense? Am I crazy?—SB

November 23—It's the day before Thanksgiving, and I'd give anything to be home right now. Daddy and I have our own tradition. He cooks the turkey, and I make the dressing. We end up with too much food, so we donate the leftovers to the local soup kitchen. We circle the town and talk about our plans for Christmas. I wish he would find a way to go back to church. I begged him to go with me for years, but he'd just tear up and get that faraway look in his eyes. It's hard to talk to him sometimes. I can't figure out how to break through his grief. He's such a treasure. It's not fair to keep him all for myself. I wish he could see that and learn how to open himself up to the world.—SB

December 13—I just spoke to Daddy on the phone. I can't wait to see him and to sleep in my own bed. To eat his pancakes and swing on our porch while sipping his famous lemonade. We'll visit the cemetery and open Christmas presents by the fire. We'll share an apple fritter from the corner bakery and drink hot chocolate while we stroll through town.

Recapturing tidbits of my childhood with my precious father is all I want for Christmas.

I'm no longer the same person as when I left, but I wouldn't be me without those memories. I'm not sure my world will ever be that small, contained, and safe again, but it's definitely how I want to spend my time away from school. Sitting in the swing beside my daddy.—SB

Solomon fumbled through to the last page that held her handwriting. Her final entry.

December 15—Great news! Financial aid informed me I had money left after all expenses were covered for this semester. "Spend it however you want," they said. So, I did. I planned a quick little jaunt to a trail I've been wanting to run. Should I go alone? Probably not, but that's the beauty of it. Quality bonding time with nature, God and me. And I'm never alone. I already told you that. Be back soon.—SB.

Solomon closed the book and clutched it to his chest. He fell into the cascade of pillows and closed his eyes as they billowed on top of him.

Oh, Sadie Beth. Where did you go? What happened to my girl?

The sun's rays reached through the window to rouse Solomon. Visions of Sadie Beth, happy and animated, energetic and playful, filled his overnight dreams. A smile spread across his face as he drew in a deep breath. He placed the diary on his daughter's nightstand, next to her photo with Winnie in the horse-drawn carriage from church.

One thought bounced around in his mind. Sadie Beth, her own voice with her own words: "Such sadness. That's no way to live."

Solomon sighed. The new minister from the church across the street told him the same thing. The man introduced himself as Pastor David and had found a way to visit weekly since Officer Spencer Patton took it upon himself to make the church aware of Solomon's needs. Since then, various strangers had come to clean his house and drop off groceries on a regular basis.

Solomon grew to appreciate the interruption of his routine. He tried to explain he hadn't been able to go to church since he lost Winnie and Silas. Church was Winnie's thing, and he wasn't sure how to do it alone. Solomon was certain God no longer heard his prayers, but that didn't stop Pastor David and his pushy friends from stopping by.

But something changed when he read the words of his own daughter. Words she was too afraid to say to him in person.

It's hard to talk to him ... can't break through his grief ... He's such a treasure ... learn how to open himself up to the world.

Solomon knew what he had to do. He lifted his head and stood in front of the bathroom mirror to trim his bushy hair and shave. He stepped into the shower to wash away decades worth of sadness. When he was finished, he dressed himself completely in the outfit Sadie Beth loved most.

He opened the windows to welcome fresh air and ate breakfast on the porch while listening to Elvis tunes. He dug out his pruning shears and gloves and prepared his rosebushes for a sizzling summer.

For the first time in years, he entered the church building across the street. Pastor David greeted him with a hug, and Solomon shared a few ideas on how they might serve their military community. From there, he headed to the funeral home on Main Street to get a schedule of upcoming funerals. He delivered flowers to Winnie and Silas, picked up an apple fritter from the corner bakery, and sipped on hot chocolate while he strolled through town, gaining strength and purpose with each step.

In the shadow of the bell tower at the church, he caught the view of his porch across the street.

"Such sadness. That's no way to live," he repeated to himself.

Making a beeline for his front door, Solomon relocated a bookcase to his porch. He brought down a few of Sadie Beth's books from her younger years and settled into the swing to marvel at the comforting view of the sunset behind the church steeple.

"I still don't know what happened to you, Sadie Beth. But I know exactly where you are now, and you're always with me."

CHAPTER THIRTY-SIX

Harper breezed past Laz at a check point he'd set up at the entrance to Solomon's room with another plate of warm cookies from the cafeteria.

"For the record, chocolate chip is my favorite cookie," he teased when she passed him by.

"They're for guests. Sign the guest book," she quipped.

She arranged the cookies on a table and turned over her shoulder to catch the hefty build of Detective Sterling bending over to sign the guest book.

"Detective Sterling? You don't have to sign the book. And when did you change clothes?"

He stepped into the light with a look of confusion on his face.

He shook his head. "Oh, I'm not Detective Sterling. I'm his twin brother, Grayson, a fire chief from Serendipity, Alabama. It's a couple hours from here."

"Oh my. I guess it's good you don't live in the same town, or people would get you confused all the time. They'd have you solving crimes and Detective Sterling putting out fires." Harper chuckled.

She reached to shake his hand. "Nice to meet you, Chief Sterling. Tell me, do you remember Solomon as well? Your brother told me the two of you spent some time in Ginger Ridge, long before I arrived."

Chief Sterling placed his hand against his chin. "Definitely. Mr. Thomas was willing to sit in the stands with Mama to watch us play football every Friday night.

I doubt Mr. Thomas even liked football, but he always showed up. We won the championship our senior year in 1988. One of the best years of my life."

"That's right. I remember seeing the signs. Ginger Ridge won a championship in eighty-eight."

Grayson nodded. "Yes, it was an exceptional year. My brother was a big reason we made it that far. He was quite the tackle on defense. I hated going head-to-head with him. I always paid for it hard the next day."

Harper shrugged. "Interesting. I used to love watching football. Detective Sterling never mentioned it, but we only discovered we're from the same town today."

"He's a private guy. Sometimes I feel like I barely know him myself," Grayson admitted. "Excuse me just a minute. I'd like to pay my respects to Mr. Thomas."

"Of course." Harper stepped aside.

At that moment, Presley burst through the door. "Mom! I came as soon as I could." She ran into her mother's arms. "Is he still alive?"

Harper squeezed her daughter tight. They observed him from a distance, arm in arm.

"He looks so cute, the way you've got him fixed up. I'll bet he was precious back when you knew him."

Harper led her daughter toward the window where they settled into cozy chairs facing one another.

"He was delightful, Squirt. This man saved our lives. Yours and mine. I've got quite the story to tell you. I think it's time."

JUNE 2000

A couple of blocks from the bus station, Solomon flagged a cab in the downtown streets of Savannah. Harper had fallen asleep on the lengthy bus ride and had yet to get her bearings. She guessed they were hours away from Ginger Ridge, which she found both comforting and terrifying at the same time. Her stomach rumbled, reminding her it was time for lunch.

"We're looking for a place on the south side of town. Maybe a home on the grounds of a local church? It's called Harbor House." Solomon gave the driver the address while Harper stifled a yawn. She had a tough time keeping her eyes open these days.

While they drove, she peered through the window and admired the town. Old trees formed a tunnel over neighborhood roads. The salty smell of the ocean hung in the air. The downtown area appeared clean and safe, with railroad tracks running through the middle of the street.

Harper spotted a cozy coffee shop with books lining the wall and developed a sudden urge for coffee even though she hated the taste.

Solomon tapped on the glass and leaned forward to give another set of instructions to their driver. He pointed to a parking lot up ahead and asked that they stop.

"Meter's still running," the man responded in a thick Italian accent.

"I understand. We'll hurry."

Solomon nudged Harper. "We're stopping by the department store to get whatever you need for your room. Let's divide and conquer. I'll pick up a microwave, a television, and a mini refrigerator. You choose any snacks, bedding, towels, clothing, or personal items you may need. From what I understand, they offer transportation, but we need to buy enough to make you feel at home for the next nine months."

Harper's mouth dropped open. "Solomon, I can't think past the next nine minutes. Much less the next nine months."

An hour later, they turned into a long gravel driveway covered by a canopy of trees that made Harper feel hidden and safe. To the right was a lake, circled by a walking trail, picnic tables, and a row of bicycles. To the left, a gazebo with a porch swing.

"Look, Solly. A swing."

Harper's shoulders relaxed for the first time since they took her mother away in an ambulance almost ten years prior.

They found the office in a converted garage behind what Harper referred to as a mansion—a massive brick home with columns and countless windows. She never knew such a place existed. But then again, she'd never needed to know until now.

Solomon handed her a Harbor House pamphlet, an application, and a pen. He spoke to the director in hushed tones about financial responsibilities.

Harper filled in each blank, not fully understanding her dire circumstances until she read it in her own handwriting. Pregnant, alone, with no job or plan for the future.

"Why would anyone help a girl who got herself into this situation?"

At the bottom of the page, it asked a simple question.

What brought you to Harbor House?

Harper thought for a moment before writing these words.

> *I'm here because both God and Solomon Thomas are in my corner. Now, I also take pride in the fact I didn't choose to end this pregnancy. One day at a time, I will figure this out. Someone is depending on me, and I trust this baby to show me the way.*

CHAPTER THIRTY-SEVEN

Cam Sterling did his best to turn off his investigative mind on the way to the eighth floor. His stomach burned with the realization their suspect had been so close.

Why did he come to the hospital? As a show of remorse or to finish the job?

Cam stepped away for a few minutes. Cases had a way of solving themselves when left to simmer.

He shifted his thoughts to Solomon. He never felt sure how to say goodbye. No matter how many times he'd faced death, he'd never grown comfortable with the process—not since following his father's casket out those church doors to the veteran's cemetery when he was ten years old. He often chided himself with the reminder that, as a thirty-year veteran of the police department, he should be able to handle it by now.

If being a man means death doesn't crush me, I'm not interested.

Through the window, he caught sight of his brother standing guard over Solomon's bed.

His heart jumped at the sight of Grayson. Same shaved head. Same stance. Same confidence. He'd lost a few pounds since they'd last seen each other, but the way he held his head down, with hands folded in front of him, was the same as when they were ten years old.

Grayson lifted his head when Cam entered. "Well, if it isn't my long-lost big brother. Man, I've sure missed you."

Grayson fell into Cam's arms. Together, they sobbed like fully grown men are never allowed to do. Locked in an embrace, they released their pain while Solomon watched over them.

Cam recalled the words Solomon had uttered to them before the boys were teenagers. "Everything that made your father such a hero lives inside of each one of you. Allow those qualities to rise to the top. Make him proud. Guard your heart. Never let it become bitter because everything you do flows from it."

He'd sensed how much the boys struggled.

The bond that united the brothers—grief—had also proved to be what drove them apart.

Harper squeezed her daughter tight, glad she was here to see Solomon's last moments.

"Mom, what's that?"

She looked to where Presley pointed to a note that had fallen on the floor. She stooped to pick it up.

"'I'm sorry. Please forgive me.' I wonder who wrote it."

Presley shrugged as Harper noticed a woman walk through the door. She didn't recognize the short woman— if not for her hairstyle she'd barely be five foot tall.

"May I help you?" Harper asked, slipping the note into her pocket.

The lady extended her hand. "Good evening. Your name is Harper, correct? I saw you on the news and was hoping to meet you in person. I am Judge Lucinda Weatherly. You may call me Lucy. I came as soon as I wrapped up my cases."

Harper shook her hand. "Very nice to meet you. You were a friend of Solomon's?"

Lucy nodded. "Yes, he served as a mentor to me as well."

Harper escorted her to Solomon's bedside and scanned the room. Presley moved to man the door, and Detective Sterling and his brother took the sofa by the window, entrenched in deep conversation.

"Tell me how you know Solomon," Harper encouraged.

Lucy touched Solomon's arm. "Like you, my father served in the army. We spent three years at Fort Bryce when I hit those awkward teenage years." She cringed. "I was nothing but buck teeth and braces, gawky as all get out."

Harper chuckled. "I remember those feelings well."

"Always the shortest girl in our school, but the scrappiest basketball player on our team. I could steal the ball from anyone because I was so close to the court." She frowned. "But I was also clueless. Another man moved into our house while my father served overseas. I thought that guy had rented a room from us, but soon he was kissing all over my mother, and she filed for divorce. I rarely saw my father after that."

Tears rolled down her face. Harper offered her a tissue, and Lucy dabbed at her eyes. "Daddy assumed since my mother no longer wanted him, neither did I. Daddy was the one who taught me to play basketball, and I no longer enjoyed the game without him. I missed that sense of pride in his face—the way I could feel him beaming, even from the stands."

"That must have been tough," Harper said.

"It was. I had such a hard time figuring out who to trust, but then I met Solomon. He invited me to his porch. We'd debate everything from history, the latest political riffraff, and even the weather. He taught me to weigh every side of every argument. To take the time to stand in other people's shoes. Even my mother's."

"He did the same for me."

Lucy touched a finger to her chin. "Solomon was who first suggested I become an attorney. He told me people make mistakes, and when they do, they'd need someone like me in their corner. He's the one who taught me to be fair."

Harper smiled. "Solomon was right. I'm sure you're a wonderful judge. Pardon me, I'll be right back."

Harper grabbed two journals by the door, handing one to Lucy. "Would you mind writing your story to add to our wall? I'll read these to Solomon later tonight."

Lucy accepted the pen Harper offered and tapped it against her chin.

Harper moved to Detective Sterling and his brother. "Excuse me, Detective. Would you and Grayson jot down your stories about the way Solomon affected your lives?"

Detective Sterling accepted the notebook and pen from her. "Sure thing."

A look of relief spread across the detective's face. Harper realized it was the first time she'd seen him in a full smile. Out of the corner of her eye, she noticed Presley greeting an unknown visitor.

Her hand dropped into her pocket, toying with the note Presley had given her earlier.

"Oh, Detective Sterling, I almost forgot. We found this on the floor." She placed it in his outstretched hand. "I think it's an apology for Solomon. Most people wrote prayers or notes of encouragement. Could it have been written by your suspect?"

Detective Sterling took it from her and turned it over. "'I'm sorry. Please forgive me.' That doesn't prove it's related to the accident, but it's a strong possibility."

"Is there any way to get a fingerprint from it?"

Detective Sterling shook his head. "No. That only happens on television. That note has passed through several hands now. If it's from the suspect, it confirms our theory this was indeed an accident, though."

Harper snapped her fingers. "Wait a minute. What you said jogged my memory. That Hispanic man, our suspect? He was in the chapel with me the other night. I knew he looked familiar when I spotted him in Solomon's room today." She recounted the story from the chapel. "It took me a while to remember, but he's the same guy. I'm sure of it."

Detective Sterling lifted his phone to his ear. "What night did you say this happened? I'll ask Chief Turner to check footage of your parking lots."

Harper thought for a minute. "Monday night. The day we lost Wallace Higgins. I was heartbroken. That's what led me to the chapel." Harper took a swig of water and closed her eyes.

"Miss Phillips, are you all right?"

Her eyes popped open as she remembered the way the stranger cried out for forgiveness.

"I just realized we were in the chapel for the same reason. That man's heart was crushed, like mine. I feel certain this was an accident."

Detective Sterling hustled out of the room with Grayson at his heels while Harper continued to greet visitors. As she suspected, each person had a life-altering story about Solomon and his porch.

A tall gentleman in a dark blue uniform entered. Not law enforcement, but a patch adorned the upper pocket on his chest. His hands rested at his hips as he surveyed the room.

"Good evening. I'm Harper Phillips."

"Yes, ma'am. I saw you on the news. I'm Jake Easton, an Air Medic helicopter pilot. I transported Solomon last week and was shocked to learn he was still with us. Once I realized who he was, I came to pay my respects in person."

Jake stood with his legs spread out to equal the width of his shoulders and his hands folded in front of him. A black rubber wedding ring adorned his ring finger.

"Thank you for coming. Let me guess. You must have a military background."

Jake smiled. "That's affirmative, ma'am. A ten-year veteran, honorably discharged, and now working as a chopper pilot. What gave it away?"

"You are basically standing at attention, and you keep calling me ma'am. My father was a career army man as well. I recognize the signs." She smiled.

Like any good army man, his expression didn't change. "How did you know Solomon?"

"We lived in Ginger Ridge for a couple of years, my last two years of high school. My father did not serve in the military, but he was a long-term contractor. He'd been assigned to Fort Bryce for a brief stint. We lived near the base. The airplanes coming in mesmerized me. I enjoyed their flight patterns, and the pilots' ability to land and take off on a dime. I loved how you couldn't hear them until they were right above you. I'd study them for hours, sitting on the hillside by the church. That was the best seat in town, which is where I met Solomon."

"I'm not surprised. Solomon never met a stranger."

Jake grinned. "One day, he asked about my plans for after high school. I told him I wanted to marry my girlfriend Maggie and join the army. I was so cocky and determined. I thought I was invincible. But old Solomon knew how to handle me. He marched me straight to the recruitment office and introduced me to your father."

Harper's heart stopped beating. "Excuse me? Solomon did what with my father?"

"Oh, pardon me. I may have made an incorrect assumption. Wasn't your father Major Garrett Phillips III? The army recruiter in town? He mentioned his daughter and showed me your picture."

Harper's eyes bugged out in response.

Jake continued, "Solomon made me believe I had what it took to be a soldier. My mother took my picture with Solomon on his porch and with your father in front of the recruiting office the day I left for boot camp. Both men were very influential in launching my career."

Jake chattered on, oblivious to the sea of emotions Harper waded through to hear him.

"Your dad is the one who cautioned me about marrying so soon, before I entered boot camp. He warned I would come out a different man, so it would be wise to wait until I graduated before making any life-changing decisions. He said military families often suffer and helped me understand Maggie needed time to adjust to this lifestyle. He said I shouldn't ram it down her throat."

"Major Garrett Phillips III said this?"

"He sure did."

Harper couldn't breathe.

My father? The same man who couldn't give a hug if he had a gun pointed at his head? The one who disowned me. My dad offered family counseling to someone else?

Jake crossed his arms over his chest, misreading Harper's silence as an invitation to keep talking.

"Expert advice. He reiterated it was much easier to become a great soldier than a good husband and father. It required an opposite set of skills to be a family man, and few are the men who figure out how to be good at both."

Harper's mind rolled through every memory of her father etched into her brain. Nowhere could she find Major Garrett Phillips III to be a family man or the type of person who would have befriended Solomon Thomas. Her father had no friends. Only subordinates.

I feel so betrayed by them both. How could Solomon become friends with my father?

"Mr. Easton, what year was this? When did you enlist?"

"August 2003. One of the proudest days of my life."

Three years after I left Ginger Ridge? Is that when Solomon became buddies with my father? Or were they friends all along?

A wave of dizziness passed through Harper as she leaned against the wall. Presley appeared at her mother's side and spoke directly to Jake. "Please sign our guest book and take a minute to write your story." She handed him a piece of paper and a pen.

Harper felt the room spinning around her. She searched for an empty chair, but there were none. The room was full, as she hoped it would be.

Presley poked her head into her mother's line of vision and waved her hand in front of Harper's face. "Mom, are you okay?"

"I need to get some air."

"Excuse us for a minute." Presley led Harper toward the door. "Where can we go?"

"To the roof. There's a courtyard patio up there."

They exited the room in a rush, scurrying past two security guards stationed outside the door, who were locked in an ongoing conversation. Harper kept her head down and said nothing.

"They've put out an APB on the teenaged girl who went AWOL this afternoon. She was quick, I'll give her that," said the guard on the right.

The one on the left answered. "Yep, she was in and out so fast you'd never know she delivered a baby."

Harper lurched to a halt and turned to face them. "Wait. What did you just say? Are you referring to Jewel Diamond?"

The uniformed guards nodded before one of them spoke. "Yes, ma'am. If that is her actual name. She's gone. Changed clothes and snuck out an hour after she gave birth to a baby boy."

"Is the baby okay?"

"He's fine. The nurses are smothering him with attention in the nursery."

Harper shook her head as Presley grabbed her arm and inched her forward.

"Mom, you're scaring me. Your face is flushed."

Harper felt tears rolling down her face. "I should have been there."

CHAPTER THIRTY-EIGHT

Raphael held Baby Evelyn against his chest and breathed in rhythm with his newborn daughter. She was the spitting image of her mother and the most beautiful sight he'd ever seen.

Isabella's eyes closed above her oxygen mask. They'd given medication to lower her blood pressure, but rest was what she needed most.

He stroked the baby's cheek. She wore a pink striped cap with the biggest bow he'd ever seen. "Evie, I can't wait for you to meet your brothers. They're a handful, but they'll protect you and teach you to be brave." He kissed the top of her head. "And your mother? She's the strongest, most stunning woman in the world. She'll show you how to become even more beautiful on the inside than you are on the outside."

He snapped a photo with his phone. Tears of gratitude, fear, promise, and failure streamed down his face to land on her cap.

Raphael regained his composure and strolled to the nursery. He held Evelyn up to the window. "See? I told you so. You're the most beautiful little girl in this whole place."

Raphael wandered into a corner waiting room where the television broadcasted the evening news. He scrambled to turn up the volume when a news feature caught his eye. The news clip showed at least three hundred people with candles outside the church in Ginger Ridge.

"We have identified the elderly hit-and-run victim from last week as Solomon Thomas, a beloved gentleman from the town of Ginger Ridge. To honor him as he remains on his deathbed, hundreds have gathered in prayer outside his home. Mayor Lee Martin says no one loved this town more than Solomon. His hope is the legend of Solomon Thomas breathes new life into a community that's been hurting and neglected in recent years."

Raphael muted the television and closed his eyes, resting his head against his daughter while she slept.

"Evie, your daddy is going to teach you something as well. I'll show you how to do the right thing, even when it's the most difficult choice. I made a promise, and when your mommy wakes up, I'll keep it. Know that I'm only doing this because I love you."

Harper remained in a daze as she swiped her ID card for roof access, dragging Presley along with her.

"I love it here, especially at night. I like to pretend I'm invisible and no one can find me when my job gets to be too much to handle."

"You can see in every direction. I think it's gorgeous." Presley ran her hands along the railing at the edge. "We should do this on our roof at home."

Harper chuckled. "This is probably against the rules, bringing a minor here with me. But I'll plead insanity. I'm honestly about to lose my mind."

"I could tell. Something got to you in there, Mom. What happened?"

Harper dropped her head into her hands and let out a sigh. "Honestly, I'm already exhausted and can't think straight, so it threw me for a loop. That man I was talking to? His name is Jake, and he's the chopper pilot who brought Solomon in last week. Turns out, he's spent some time in Ginger Ridge as well."

Presley sat down beside her mother. "Small world. He seemed nice enough. Was he rude to you?"

"Oh, no. He was over-the-top nice, with his fairy-tale view of what a magical place Ginger Ridge was to live. I almost threw up all over him, but he probably would have turned it into fairy dust and enjoyed it."

Presley chuckled. "He couldn't have been that bad."

Harper shrugged. "No, but my life only works because I'm able to separate my past from my present. I've created a protective bubble through the years, and Chopper Pilot Jake smashed right through it."

Presley cut her eyes at her mother. "You must tell me what he said to set you off."

"He claimed that Solomon introduced him to my father at the recruiting office and they worked together to help Jake enlist in the army." Harper threw her hands into the air. "Presley, what if Solomon and my father were best buds?"

Presley shook her head and laughed. "Would that be so terrible?"

Harper searched the moon for answers as her eyes watered. "Now that I've said it out loud, it doesn't sound so tragic. But you must understand most of my conversations with Solomon concerned my dysfunctional parents. Not once did I wonder if he might side with them or tell them anything I shared."

"You have no reason to believe he did, right?"

"I don't know what I believe. I can't think straight."

Presley stood and started pacing like she often did when she was on the phone or studying for a test. "You never had contact with your father after the day you left, right?"

"Right. Not until his lawyer contacted me a few years ago when Dad died."

"What about Solomon? When's the last time you were in touch with him?"

Harper thought for a moment. "I sent him pictures for a few years after you were born. Solomon is the one who paid for me to stay at Harbor House here in Savannah.

He covered our hospital bills and sent money each month for groceries." Harper leaned her head against the stiff cushion of her chair. "I was determined to make it on my own, so I worked nights at the hospital. We scraped by and moved into our own apartment. I promised him we'd get on our feet and sent him a letter when we no longer needed donations from him. Eventually, Solomon stopped writing back. We lost touch, but it was never intentional. And honestly, when his mail was returned as undeliverable years ago, I assumed he had passed away. I was so busy raising you I let my relationship with him fall by the wayside."

"Oh sure. Blame me," Presley teased, but then her face grew serious. "I wonder how your father's lawyers knew where to find you after he died."

Harper could see the gears working in Presley's busy mind. "I don't know. I never asked. I simply sent an attorney to handle it. He brought back a sealed box of papers, which I shoved in my closet and never opened."

"Mom, that's not a coping skill. That's an avoidance skill."

"I can't help it, Squirt. I believe it's the only way we've made it this far."

"By shoving things in the closet?"

"For the most part, yes. That and escaping to the roof every chance I get."

Presley clicked her tongue. "Are you ready to go inside?"

"No." She stood up and embraced her daughter. "You should be a therapist. Do you know that? Not my therapist necessarily, but others would be lucky to have you in their corner."

Presley squeezed her back. "No thanks. I've got my hands full raising you. Tonight, I'll let you save the world. But tomorrow, we're going into your closet. We have questions. We need answers."

Harper's phone rang. She stuck out her tongue at Presley and quickly answered it. "Oh good. Saved by the bell. Hello?"

"Harper, this is Brock. How's it going at the hospital?"

"Hello, Rev. I stepped out for a few minutes to get some air, but Solomon's room was packed when I left. I'm looking forward to clearing it out soon so I can spend some time alone with him. How are things at Solomon's house?"

"You wouldn't believe it. We've got about four hundred people here, and most of them are planning to stay until Solomon passes. Some knew him personally, but others have fallen in love with his story. They keep coming. Watch the eleven o'clock news. This prayer vigil has become a story of its own."

"That's amazing. Solomon deserves nothing less."

"From what I've heard about him, I agree. I spoke with Mayor Martin earlier tonight and learned some interesting information."

"Mayor Martin is still the mayor? How is that possible? He should be a hundred and twenty years old by now."

Brock chuckled. "No, this is his son. Lee Martin, Jr. First of all, there are rumors Solomon suffered from dementia. He lived alone, so the police brought him home when they found him wandering about."

"That may explain why he was out so late in the evening."

"Right. And listen to this. Did you know Solomon's daughter was reported missing a long time ago? They never found her, so she was presumed dead. As far as I know, the case remains unsolved. She was attending college in South Carolina, and no one knows what happened."

Harper closed her eyes for a minute, trying recall anything Solomon ever said about Sadie Beth. Suddenly, she slapped her palm against her forehead.

"Oh, my goodness. That's what he kept muttering to himself in his living room when I was in his house!"

"Excuse me?"

"Brock, I've got to go. We're running out of time."

Detective Sterling's eyes began to cross from watching extensive security camera footage. They had yet to figure out how their suspect entered or exited the hospital after visiting Solomon's room. In his opinion, everyone coming and going were beginning to look alike. His stomach growled and he stood up to stretch.

Chief Turner moved to one side of the hospital's security office. His hands were full investigating an abandoned baby case.

Cam's phone buzzed. "Grayson, can you take over for a minute? I need to take this."

He stepped into the hallway.

"Detective Sterling here, how may I help you?"

There was a long moment of silence.

"Hello? Is anyone there?"

"Daddy, it's me. I saw you on the news tonight."

"Braxton? You sound all grown up. I'm so glad you called." Tears flooded his eyes as he kept the phone glued to his ear.

"Are you still at the hospital? I asked Mom if I could come see you. She's willing to drive me if you can wait. I know it's getting late, but I really miss you."

"Of course. I'll be here all night. Call me when you get close, and I'll meet you at the front entrance."

"Okay. I'll wear my new football jersey. I can't wait for you to see it."

"Sounds great! Thanks for calling, Son. I'll see you soon."

Cam couldn't stop smiling. He hadn't seen his son in three years. Miranda had married a fancy doctor who enrolled Braxton in a great private school. Braxton had trouble sleeping whenever he came for a visit, and Cam thought it best to fade into the background so his son wouldn't feel torn. He'd assumed his son was better off without him.

One of my greatest regrets.

His phone buzzed again.

"Hello, did you forget something?"

"Detective Sterling? It's Harper Phillips. Can you meet me on the roof?"

Chief Turner was the first to exit onto the rooftop. Cameron and Grayson Sterling sauntered behind him in slow motion as they absorbed the brilliant view.

Harper couldn't help but smile at the comforting sight of the three men.

"You look like a band of superheroes coming to my rescue."

Chief Turner was the first to speak. "They had no roof access without me, and we needed to break away from those screens for a while. What's going on?"

Harper crossed her arms over her chest. "Detective Sterling, I need your help in trying to solve a cold case from the late seventies. It's Solomon's daughter. Her name was Sadie Beth, and she attended college somewhere in South Carolina, but never came home after her first semester. She should have been eighteen or nineteen years old. I've ordered a DNA test on Solomon so we can match it if needed."

Detective Sterling whipped out a notebook and jotted down details. "What brought this to light?"

Harper cupped her chin. "It's been there all along. Brock Timberland, the minister from Ginger Ridge, discussed it with the mayor earlier. But honestly, I had all the information I needed swirling around in my crowded head the entire time. Tonight, it finally clicked."

"What do you mean?"

"Once, when I was little, I tagged along while Solomon visited the cemetery. There were only two gravestones that he paid attention to. This was long before I knew he had a son named Silas, so I asked if the second one belonged to Sadie Beth, and he mumbled that she hadn't come home yet."

"Wow." Detective Sterling shook his head.

"I was too young to realize what he meant at the time. Something else happened about ten years later. Out of all the time I've known Solomon, I've only been in his house once, right before I left Ginger Ridge. I was in a desperate situation, and he allowed me to spend the night."

"That sounds about right. We've never been inside his house either. Only on his porch," Grayson piped in.

Harper pointed at Chief Sterling. "Right. Solomon invited me in as a last resort but having me in his space upset him terribly. He tinkered with his wedding ring and paced pack and forth, muttering something under his breath. Finally, he admitted he wasn't ready to let anyone sleep in Sadie Beth's room, and asked if I would mind sleeping on his couch."

"Makes sense," said Detective Sterling. "I'd probably feel the same way."

"Sure. We all would. But it didn't hit me until tonight what he kept murmuring to himself. He said, 'What if she comes home? She only went for a run.' The thought of me sleeping in her bed would be a sign he'd given up on her." Harper caught her breath and gave them time to catch up. "Keep in mind, by this point, it had been over twenty years since her disappearance, but Solomon still didn't know for sure if Sadie Beth was dead or alive. He held out hope she might come home."

"All right. I'm on it. Do we know where she attended college?"

"Brock mentioned he found a sweatshirt in Solomon's closet with *Perkins University Dad* on the front, but that's all I know."

Chief Turner moved toward the door and swiped his card to summon the elevator. "Guess we'd better get to it. We've got a long night ahead."

"We sure do," Harper answered. "This is what Solomon has been waiting for. He's hanging on until we find Sadie Beth."

CHAPTER THIRTY-NINE

Isabella's eyes fluttered open as a nurse removed her oxygen mask.

"Looks like you've bounced back nicely. Your vital signs are good. Can we get you anything?"

Isabella smiled. "I'm starving. Am I allowed to eat?"

The nurse nodded. "Let's start with something light. How about yogurt?"

"Sure. Strawberry sounds good."

Raphael waited on the opposite side of the bed until they finished. "Excuse me, miss? Would you mind bringing a wheelchair?"

The nurse cocked her head. "I beg your pardon, sir. Your wife just gave birth a few hours ago, and it's late. She needs her rest."

"I agree, but we need to visit another patient before it's too late."

"I'm fine," Isabella reassured the nurse, who stared Raphael down before returning with a container of yogurt and a spoon.

"Raphael, what do you have in mind?"

Cradling the baby in his arms, he used the remote to turn up the volume on the television. "I'll show you."

Trailers for upcoming nightly news stories once again showed hundreds of people outside his victim's house.

"Do you recognize that location?"

"Yes, that's Ginger Ridge. The house I pointed out to you earlier, behind the church."

The nurse appeared with a wheelchair and forced a smile.

Raphael waved a thank you and muted the television. "Right. That old man that I hit last week? His name is Solomon Thomas, and he lives in that house."

Isabella's mouth flew open. "No way! I remember him. Such a kind man."

Raphael grimaced. "That's what I've heard. Earlier, I visited him in the ICU. I made a promise to Solomon. If God allowed you and Baby Evie to be okay, I'd turn myself in. So that's what I'm going to do."

Tears filled Isabella's eyes. "Raphael, I'm not ready."

"You know I can't do this without your support. Baby Evelyn must know her father chose to do the right thing. I want you to see Solomon before he passes away. God only knows what will happen afterward."

"Okay. Can you get my robe and slippers?"

Raphael helped her into her robe and brushed his hand against Isabella's cheek. "Like I told Baby Evie, I'm only doing this because I love you."

Isabella rested her hand on his. "Baby Evie. I like that."

Harper ducked into a public restroom and splashed water on her face before returning to room 815. Her plan was to send everyone home and settle in beside Solomon for the night. The two of them had much to discuss.

Propping the door open with her foot, Harper noticed the crowd had thinned out. Judge Lucy was deep in conversation with a man in a business suit with thick, dark hair.

That guy looks familiar.

Presley appeared at her mother's side. "Mom, I'd better run. I didn't realize how late it had gotten. Sydney's mom is downstairs waiting for me."

Harper hugged her daughter tight. "Thank you for coming, kid. Don't know what I would have done without you."

Presley pulled away. "I'll come by tomorrow after practice if you're still here. I love you."

Harper grabbed a cookie and nodded. "Wait. Who's the guy in the corner talking to Judge Lucy? Where do we know him from?

"He's that attorney from the commercials. The GI Joe guy."

"Ahh, yes. 'Let me fight your battle!'" Harper whispered in her tough guy voice.

Presley rolled her eyes. "Mom, you're so embarrassing."

"Good then. Just doing my job." She smirked.

Presley took off, and Harper scanned the latest notes in Solomon's collection on the wall. At his bedside, she laid his hat aside and removed his bow tie.

Harper checked her watch.

Solly, you may not need to rest, but I sure do.

"Visiting hours have officially ended. We must clear the room within the next thirty minutes," Harper announced to the few still gathered.

Judge Lucy motioned her to the corner. "Harper, this is Bart Wilburn, a well-known attorney in Atlanta. Believe it or not, he spent a few years in Ginger Ridge as well."

Harper grinned and reached for his hand. "Of course. GI Joe. Very nice to meet you."

The man offered a sheepish grin. "Marketing teams. Can't live with them, can't live without them. The funny thing is, not a soul remembers my actual name, but they can't forget those dreaded commercials." He shrugged.

"How did you know Solomon? Is he who taught you to dress that way?"

Bart thought for a minute. "Now that you mention it, I should give him credit. My dad did a stint at Fort Bryce when I was eight or nine. I was more into drama and music than sports. I met Solomon at church. We had a conversation about my dad being away for my birthday." Bart dug his hands into his pockets. "The next week, he presented me with army fatigues in my size. Told me I was as tough as my dad, but I'd fight my battles differently because I was so smart. By the time my dad made it home, he had lost a leg. Everything in our family changed. Solomon led the effort to build a ramp on the front of our house. He's the one who showed me what it meant to be gentle and tough, all at once."

"What a great message. That man is brilliant. He saw value in everyone."

"I agree." Bart stepped toward the window in thought.

A stranger entered and all heads turned in that direction.

Harper stepped forward. "I'm sorry, sir. Visiting hours are over."

The middle-aged man wearing a ball cap held up his hand to stop her. "You must be Harper. Rosie sent me. She said you'd want to hear my story."

Harper's mouth twisted in confusion. "I'll defer to Rosie then. She's always right. Please, right this way."

She led him to the window. In the light, she read the writing on his ball cap. "Perkins University? Is that what your cap says?"

"Yes, ma'am. Proud alum and former employee." He reached out his hand. "My name is Spencer Patton. I'm from South Carolina. Sadie Beth Thomas was a friend of mine, and Solomon and I became great friends following her disappearance. He and I spoke weekly on the phone for years. I even visited him a few times. I knew that's what Sadie Beth would have wanted."

Harper's mouth dropped open. "Oh, I don't know what to say. I have many questions about that chapter of his life. Please take a minute to visit with Solomon. We'll get caught up soon enough. Thank you so much for coming."

Spencer took off his cap to reveal a decent head of salt and pepper hair. He inched toward Solomon's bedside and lowered his head.

Detective Sterling burst through the door, chomping hard on a wad of gum. His jubilant voice echoed in the room that had grown quiet after the surprise entrance of the guest from South Carolina.

"Miss Phillips, I launched a search on all missing person cases from the seventies. Once we add DNA info from Solomon, you'd be amazed at what it can reveal."

"Good," she whispered, trying to inspire the detective to lower his voice. "We should get the report back by morning. There's someone I want you to meet. He may be able to provide some answers." She pointed toward Spencer with her head.

Detective Sterling didn't follow her lead. "Great. There's someone I'd like you to meet as well." He stepped aside to reveal a boy about twelve years old wearing a black and gold football jersey. "This is my son, Braxton."

Harper shook the hand of the young man. "Nice to meet you. Another football player in the family?"

Both the detective and his son grinned from ear to ear. "Miss Phillips, Braxton and I haven't seen each other in three years. Tonight, after our story hit the news, his mother drove him here for a quick visit."

Braxton interrupted, "Not only that, I got to meet my Uncle Gray for the first time. I didn't even know Daddy had a twin brother. I've got two cousins in Alabama who I've never met."

"I guess we've got Solomon to thank for this family reunion then, don't we?"

"We sure do." The detective patted his son on the back. "Come over here, Son. Let me introduce you to my dear friend, Mr. Thomas."

Harper motioned for Spencer to join her by the window. "I can't believe you knew Sadie Beth. I believe she's the one Solomon's been waiting for."

Spencer opened his mouth to respond just as the door creaked open. Harper turned her head in that direction, as did everyone else.

Light reflected off a wheelchair as it entered the room. The man pushing the wheelchair appeared as a silhouette against the brighter lights of the hallway.

"I'm sorry, sir, visiting hours are ov—"

Harper's hand flew to her mouth as the light hit the man's face.

Detective Sterling shoved Braxton behind the sofa and crouched down, resting his hand near his ankle.

Bart Wilburn stood from his chair in the corner and took a few steps toward the door.

Judge Lucy's hands rested on her hips. She peeked around the shoulder of Bart Wilburn.

"It's him," they all said in unison.

CHAPTER FORTY

Cam noticed the wheelchair coming through the door. Sitting in it was a young woman holding an infant, but it was the person pushing the wheelchair who caught his attention.

Male, Hispanic, stocky build, shoulder length hair, slight mustache. Remarkably handsome, some might say.

Behind the suspect, Chief Turner and Grayson entered, blocking any escape route.

Cam kept his hand on the service revolver in his ankle holster and threw his other arm in front of Braxton, who knelt behind a couch.

Cam cleared his throat. "Sir, I need to ask you a few questions. What's your name?"

The man held his hands up in surrender. "I'm Raphael Henry." He pointed to the man in a suit. "Ask Bart Wilburn. He knows my story."

Cam cut his eyes to the man in the suit.

The GI Joe guy from the commercials? What's he doing here?

He returned his attention to Raphael. "The question is what are *you* doing here? Why do you keep coming to this room?"

Raphael stepped around the wheelchair, still holding his hands in the air. "You can search me. I brought my wife and daughter to meet Mr. Thomas."

Cam lifted his chin.

Most suspects don't act like this.

He loosened the grip on his handgun and stood to pat Raphael down.

"He's clean," Cam announced. "Okay, let's step aside for a minute and figure out what's going on. Gray, can you walk Braxton to the lobby to meet Miranda?"

"Sure, brother. I'll be back shortly."

Cam hugged his son and waited until they exited the room. He lifted one journal from a table and opened it to the first blank page to take notes.

"Mr. Henry, please start at the beginning."

While Detective Sterling and Chief Turner spoke in whispers to their suspect. Harper wheeled the young lady to Solomon's bedside.

"Hello, my name is Harper. Are you in danger in any way?"

The girl shook her head. "Oh no. Raphael is my husband. My name is Isabella. I saw you on the news earlier. Didn't you used to babysit me and my brother Sergio when we lived in Ginger Ridge?"

Harper gasped. "Isabella Rodriquez? Of course, I remember you. I'm so happy to see you." She reached down to pat Isabella's arm. "I don't know if you are as confused as I am about whatever's going on here, but we can visit Solomon while I admire your baby. She's gorgeous."

"Thank you. Her name is Evelyn. Would you like to hold her?"

"I'd love to. My daughter is sixteen now. They grow so fast."

Isabella handed over the pink bundle to Harper. "Yes, she's a few weeks early, but she's perfectly fine. We're thrilled."

Out of the corner of her eye, Harper noticed that Judge Lucy and Bart Wilburn had joined the circle that surrounded Raphael. No one appeared to be afraid, so Harper returned her focus to Isabella.

"You're the one who introduced me to Solomon, right? We drank lemonade on his porch," said Isabella.

"I sure did. And we walked to the bakery while your father followed from a distance. He was so protective of you."

Isabella smiled at the memory. "He still is. We were actually in Ginger Ridge this morning. Raphael wants me to reopen the Main Street Bakery. The realtor said it's been boarded up for years."

"I have such fond memories of that bakery." Harper smiled. She moved closer to hold the baby as if introducing her to Solomon.

Isabella touched her on the arm. "You know it was an accident, right? Solomon was in the middle of the road at the top of a mountain."

Harper pursed her lips. "Rumors are that Solomon was suffering from dementia. Maybe he wandered off. I'll bet he was terrified."

"This has completely torn Raphael up. He came here to turn himself in. To do the right thing."

"He seems like a kind person, and I know he's remorseful. I saw him here in the chapel the other night. He was so upset."

"Wait, when was he in the chapel?" Isabella asked.

Harper dropped her head. "I can't even remember. Monday, I think."

Isabella laughed in response. "I know what you mean. I can't believe I birthed a baby today. My third! What am I doing up here?" She doubled over in a fit of laughter, holding her stomach.

Harper couldn't stop herself from giggling like a schoolgirl as well. "Okay, you win. You must be more exhausted than I am."

The two ladies laughed until tears pooled in their eyes. The baby stirred in Harper's arms. "This may be unprofessional, but it feels so good to laugh for a change."

"I agree," Isabella said, wiping away a tear.

Harper turned her head and noticed the expression on Solomon's face. "Look, Isabella. I think he's smiling."

Detective Sterling ambled to them. "You ladies okay over here?"

"We must be punch drunk, without the punch. We apologize."

The detective brushed past their playfulness as if he wasn't sure what to do with it. "Listen, I know it's late so we're going to sort this out in the morning. We'll station a security guard outside the Henry's door on their floor and reconvene tomorrow. There's much more to this case than a simple hit-and-run."

Harper met the intensity of his gaze and regained her composure. She turned to Isabella to hand the baby over. "Thank you for letting me hold her. Would you like me to take you to your room while they finish in here?"

Isabella smiled. "That would be wonderful. Thank you."

They said their goodbyes and Harper wheeled her friend into the hall.

Isabella looked up at her. "What do you think is going to happen?"

Harper patted her on the arm. "I don't know, but do you see that impressive group of people circled around your husband?"

Isabella nodded.

"You've got the lead detective on this case, one of the best lawyers in the state, and a judge who is the fairest of them all. Solomon Thomas impacted each one of their lives." Harper pressed the button on the elevator and knelt to face Isabella. "Your husband is in expert hands. I trust Solomon brought them all together for a reason. That's the way he operates."

CHAPTER FORTY-ONE

Harper rested next to Solomon's bed in the rocking chair delivered at her request. In her arms, she held a nameless baby boy with a tuft of black hair and eyes as dark as those of his dazed mother.

The baby was swaddled tight in a blanket that read "For this child, we have prayed." Harper picked it up at the gift shop first thing that morning so he might have something to call his own.

Solomon laid beside her, with machines still doing his breathing for him. Soon, it would be time to disconnect each one of his tubes.

Not yet.

Not until he told her he was ready.

Tap. Tap. Tap.

"Come in," she said, her voice now hoarse after a full night of crying. Her eyes closed as she nuzzled the baby's head.

Brock Timberland poked his head in the door. "Good morning. I see our friend is still with us." He made his way into the room and leaned against the windowsill.

Harper smiled. "Only because I refuse to let him go."

"Should I pretend not to notice the baby in your arms?"

She offered a half-smile. "This happens sometimes when I need to be in two places at once. I blend two urgent needs into one. A young girl abandoned this baby after she gave birth yesterday. I wanted to rock him to remind myself why I choose to do this, but I couldn't leave Solomon's side."

Brock lifted his chin and smiled. "That makes complete sense. Speaking of Solomon, there's still a crowd gathered at his house. We opened the church building for restrooms and prayer groups, and Mayor Martin brought in donuts and coffee this morning. How can I help you?"

Harper shrugged. "You can answer a few questions for me, Rev. Aren't you supposed to be the wise one around here?"

Brock smirked. "You might have the wrong guy. I feel like an imposter most of the time. I have few answers. What I do have are fresh divorce papers. Signed, sealed, delivered, and final. I'd rather focus on others at a time like this, so please, go ahead."

Harper's eyebrows drew together. "I'm sorry to hear that. I don't know what to say."

"No problem. Lay it on me."

Her thoughts exploded into the open.

"Will we ever do enough to make a difference? This week alone, I lost a cancer patient who we believed was on the road to recovery, I'm about to lose the one man who truly cared for me, but I neglected him for the past twelve years, and the young girl in labor who I promised wouldn't have to deliver her baby alone escaped before I returned to her room. What in God's name is the purpose?"

Brock drew in a deep breath as if preparing an answer. Harper never gave him a chance.

"How self-centered am I to hate my memories of Ginger Ridge so much I never went to visit Solomon. I allowed the fear of seeing my father or Julian steal my joy of seeing Solomon? Who does such a thing?"

She stood to pace across the floor, gently bouncing the baby with each step. Brock shuffled out of the way.

"Seriously, isn't it enough I raised my daughter to be a good person? I've kept her from having a baby while in high school. Shouldn't that count for something? Why do I throw myself into this job to get a daily dose of failure in return?"

Brock handed her a glass of water, which she didn't accept.

She kept on. "How have I been so wrong? Ginger Ridge was a great place to grow up. I was the one with problems. Not the town itself. And how could Solomon become friends with my father? Kind people don't befriend mean people, do they? Is befriend even a word?"

Brock settled into a chair in the corner. She stared him down as if seeing him for the first time.

"Here. Hold this baby. I have to go to the restroom."

Brock looked at her in confusion. "Sure. Does he have a name?"

"Yes. I call him Silas. I'll be back in a minute to take him to the nursery. He needs to eat breakfast. You see there? Something I can control. Breakfast."

She handed over the baby and walked into the hallway. As soon as she rounded the corner, she did an about face and poked her head through the crack in the door.

"Hey, Rev, would you be interested in attending a banquet at Harbor House with me next month? I'm the guest speaker, and I prefer a plus one who doesn't freak me out."

Raphael worked through a crick in his neck from sleeping in a stiff hospital recliner as he rushed home to shower and change clothes. He soon returned for a nine o'clock appointment with authorities in a first-floor conference room at the hospital. He entered the room wearing the dark blue suit Isabella bought for his court appearance and a necktie the boys had given him for Father's Day. His heart raced as he shook each person's hand, but he reminded himself to keep his cool.

Judge Weatherly was the first to speak.

"Please take a seat."

Raphael did as instructed, dropping into a leather chair across from the three of them at an oversized table.

The judge laid her glasses on top of a file folder and looked him in the eye. "Mr. Henry, I first reviewed your case as I prepared for your court appearance on Friday. At the time, it seemed an obvious violation with a predetermined outcome. I've since learned there are mitigating circumstances. We've conferred with a team of experts to determine the fairest way of handling your situation under the law."

"I certainly appreciate that, Your Honor."

Bart Wilburn spoke up. "When I met with you on Monday, I admit I came down hard. I gave the best advice I could, but I was rather harsh and left you nowhere to turn."

Raphael tapped the table with the palm of his hand. "I would describe it as brutal, but please, continue."

"Agreed. Since the circumstances have changed, my advice has reformed as well. Do you realize, Mr. Henry, that those in the country illegally who've been charged with felonies cannot be deported?"

Raphael's heart dropped to his stomach. "I did not know that."

"For this reason, it's in your best interest for us not to plea down to a misdemeanor. You will be charged with a full felony." Wilburn cast a glance at Detective Sterling.

"That's correct. An arrest warrant has been issued for voluntary manslaughter. A felony." Detective Sterling smiled as he spoke, odd for someone explaining the details on an arrest warrant. "I'll be taking you into custody over the next week once your wife and baby have been released from the hospital."

Raphael went numb. He pursed his lips. "I understand. I feel terrible about hitting Mr. Thomas with my car, so I deserve to be arrested."

Wilburn intervened. "From there, we will plead guilty."

"Agreed. I am guilty, sir."

Judge Weatherly sat forward in her chair. "During your hearing, after accepting your plea deal, I will recommend a sentence of two years' probation, with an agreement to serve one thousand hours of community service."

Wilburn crossed his arms and leaned back in his chair. "Mr. Henry, I understand you've considered purchasing property in Ginger Ridge."

"Yes, sir. My wife is interested in opening the bakery there. We'll call it Bella's Best. We believe it will become quite a hit."

"We agree with you and believe it to be an excellent proposal," said Judge Weatherly. "Ginger Ridge could benefit from one thousand hours' worth of hands-on attention from a reputable construction foreman. I will assign you to that town, where Mayor Martin will oversee your projects. He's specified you will begin on Main Street with the bakery and then move to the church."

"I'll have the paperwork for you to sign before you leave the hospital," said Wilburn. "Including a renewal application for your H-1B Visa, with a recommendation from Judge Weatherly to proceed with an accelerated path to citizenship."

Detective Sterling was the first to stand as if the meeting had concluded. Bart Wilburn and the judge rose to their feet as well.

Raphael followed suit and his face grew hot. A lump in his throat kept him from speaking.

"Give your wife and baby our best," said the judge.

Raphael responded with a nod, then backed away with tears in his eyes. He burst from the room and raced down the hall.

"Mr. Henry, are you okay?" He heard the voice of Detective Sterling as his footsteps chased after him.

Raphael turned the corner, nearly knocking down a maintenance worker in his path. In front of him were the stained-glass windows of the chapel doors. He jerked them open and darted inside.

He shot to the front of the room and dropped to his knees.

"Thank you, Jesus!" he cried, unable to keep his volume in check. He belted out the lyrics to "Amazing Grace," the first hymn he'd learned in English. Detective Sterling, Judge Weatherly, and Bart Wilburn filed in by the doors with tears in their eyes.

Raphael grabbed Judge Weatherly and twirled her down the aisle as if it was their turn to take the floor at a square dance. Wilburn and the detective chuckled and clapped their hands.

"Oh my. Case dismissed," said Judge Weatherly.

"Case dismissed!" Raphael yelled at the top of his lungs.

Detective Sterling couldn't keep himself from smiling as he took in the sight of one of the most respected judges in their region dancing across the floor with her new felon friend.

A call buzzed through the phone on his hip. He exited to the hallway to answer.

"Hello, this is Agent Stewart with the FBI field office in Atlanta. We've got a match on that DNA in the Thomas Case. The remains of an unidentified female discovered in a ravine at the foot of a trail in the Appalachian Mountains in North Carolina in the early eighties. There were no signs of foul play. It appeared to be caused by a steep fall from an elevated trail."

"Where are her remains now?"

"We've contacted the North Carolina State Police who will escort her remains to Ginger Ridge, per your request."

"We can never thank you enough."

After a cup of coffee and a quick shower in a locker room, Harper returned to room 815 with a temporary sense of composure. A change of clothes brought a better perspective. She owed Brock an apology and explanation. She peeked through the window to find the room had grown crowded once again.

Everyone stood in silence as she entered.

Presley greeted her first, wearing the plaid skirt of her school uniform.

"How did you get here? Why aren't you at school?"

Presley ignored the question. "Mom, I rifled through the items in your closet. The box from your father's attorney? Solomon wrote him letters to let him know we were okay. That's how they became friends. There were pictures of us in your dad's belongings."

Harper pursed her lips. "Of course. That sounds like Solomon."

Judge Weatherly stepped forward, nudging Harper on the arm. "You'll be happy to know we've worked out a plea deal, and we're dispatching Raphael to Ginger Ridge to fix up that old town."

"So, he gets to stay?"

Bart Wilburn interjected. "As a felon, the law requires him to stay. The accident actually benefits him and his family."

Harper smiled. "Only Solomon could pull that off."

Those in the group nodded in agreement.

"Mr. Wilburn, I have a question for you. Granted, I've had no sleep, so take this idea with a grain of salt. Do you, by chance, handle adoption cases?"

Mr. Wilburn shrugged. "It depends on the situation. At this point in my career, I go where my heart leads."

"That's great to hear. I'm going where my heart leads as well. We've got a baby who needs a family and a family who just lost their son. When the time is right, I'd like to discuss the option of adoption with the Higgins Family."

"Sure. We'll work with Child Services to place the baby with an excellent foster family in the meantime."

Detective Sterling folded his arms across his chest and met Harper's gaze.

"I've got even better news. We've located the remains of Sadie Beth Thomas. Once we entered Solomon's DNA into the system, she popped up as an immediate match. She'd been listed as a Jane Doe in North Carolina since her body was discovered in the early eighties. Apparently, she died in a hiking accident on the Appalachian Trail. Not discovered until six years later, she's finally on her way home."

Tears flooded Harper's eyes as she scurried to Solomon's bedside. She kissed his hand.

"Did you hear that, Solomon? We're bringing Sadie Beth home."

The door opened to reveal a team of doctors and nurses as they inched forward. The one in front greeted Harper with a nod. Silent and solemn, the meaning unmistakable.

Each visitor took a moment to say their goodbyes and left one at a time. Harper hugged Presley and asked for a few minutes alone.

"It's time, Solly. Let's see how you do without these machines holding you back," Harper said. She turned to face the window while the technician disconnected each machine and documented the time.

"We'll monitor from the front desk, and give you some privacy," the doctor spoke to Harper and then followed the others out of the room.

The room grew silent. Noticeably absent were the forced breathing sounds of the ventilator.

I hate this.

She remembered a five-year-old Harper teetering up the steps to his front porch and crawling in beside him on his swing. He'd patted the top of her head as she leaned back and closed her eyes.

"Solly, you remember when you said God must have known we both needed a family? Thank you for being mine. Ours. I will love you forever and promise to spend the rest of my life paying it forward."

Harper lowered her forehead to his. Through tears, she hummed the tune of one of their favorite Elvis songs, "Love Me Tender."

She held his hands in hers. "I think we're here now, Solly. Go through those gates. Your family is waiting for you."

EPILOGUE—TWO YEARS LATER

In Ginger Ridge, crowds gather along Main Street in anticipation of the Fourth of July Parade. Mayor Brock Timberland roams through town shaking as many hands as he can while he searches for Harper.

He passes the backside of the church where a vast, covered porch stretches the entire length of the building. Inside, a combination coffee shop and library with tables and cozy chairs scattered about allows guests to chat or read. An old bluegrass hymn plays through the sound system, and the smell of pastries fills the air. Against a brick wall is a table that holds a pitcher of lemonade.

A sign hangs above the stairs that reads: Solomon's Porch.

Across the street, Solomon's home has been expanded and now serves as a museum and visitor's center that depicts the history of Ginger Ridge.

Cam Sterling's brother Grayson, the new fire chief, guides a fire truck into position in the church parking lot and begins to spray water so children can cool off while they wait for the parade to start. Deacon follows the chief step by step until Grayson allows him to hold the fire hose. Chief Sterling assists him from behind, and Brock snaps a photo as he passes through.

Brock passes an older lady he doesn't recognize. She's wearing a flowered dress, fancy hat, and sunglasses, but seems out of place.

"Welcome to Ginger Ridge. I'm Mayor Timberland." He extends a hand. "What's your name?"

"Ingrid. Just stopping in for a visit. I've been hearing great things about your town. I knew someone here once."

"Welcome. Please make yourself at home." Brock grins at the compliment to Ginger Ridge. "Are you looking for anyone in particular?"

"Oh no," she says and starts to back away. "They're long gone."

"Okay, then. You might be safer over here." Brock directs her toward Solomon's Porch to shield her from the growing group of kids scampering through the stream of water from the fire hose.

Brock makes his way to the high school football field, where the police chief, Cameron Sterling, corrals a group of football players, showing them how to maintain their parade lines. Chief Sterling tosses a football to his son, Braxton, who dons a blue and gold Ginger Ridge jersey for the first time.

Brock waves and follows the sidewalk to a row of newly repaired homes a block over from Main Street. A toddler runs into Brock's path.

"Hey there, Little Silas. Someone is ready for the parade this afternoon, aren't you?" Brock picks the boy up and carries him to the porch to hand him off to Roger and Claire Higgins.

"Good afternoon, Mayor Timberland."

"Hello, Claire. Have either of you seen Harper?"

"She was by the creek going over plans for the new Harbor House expansion with Raphael Henry when we took a walk earlier this afternoon. It's been a couple of hours ago."

"Thanks. I'll keep looking. She never carries her phone with her these days."

Brock maneuvers through the crowd to the middle of Main Street, already closed to traffic for the parade. A line of people waits out the door of Bella's Best Bakery, and the grand opening at Bella's Best Diner is going strong at the building next door. The scintillating smell of charbroiled burgers wafts through the entire town.

Brock pokes through the throng to catch the eye of Presley, who is busy waiting tables on the outside patio. A customer asks her about her plans for college.

"I'm headed to the University of Florida," she answers with a grin. "I leave next month, but I'll be home often. You know I can't leave my mother unsupervised for long."

She spins and comes face to face with Brock.

"Do you know where your mother is? I haven't seen her for hours."

Presley shrugs. "Check the cemetery. She never misses a holiday."

Brock snaps his fingers. "Good point."

He gives Isabella a thumbs-up sign as she breezes through. "Congratulations. You've got another hit on your hands."

She crosses her eyes and giggles. "What was I thinking?"

Brock takes the shortcut to the cemetery where he finds Harper standing over the headstones of the Thomas family. Winnifred, Silas, Solomon, and Sadie Beth, all finally together.

Brock keeps his distance and recalls Solomon and Sadie Beth's funeral. After a packed service at the church, over six hundred guests followed those two caskets on foot to their final resting place in complete silence, a moment none of them were likely to forget even though it had already been two years.

Harper stops to pay respects at another grave—that of her father, Major Garrett Phillips III.

Brock waits on a bench until she lifts her head and comes his way.

"I knew I'd find you here. They're ready for us to lead this parade. You know we're running out of time."

Harper grins. "Yes. Wouldn't miss it for the world. Let's do this," she says, as she leans in to kiss his lips.

The End

ABOUT THE AUTHOR

Janet Morris Grimes may not have realized she was a writer at the time, but her earliest childhood memories were spent creating fairy-tale stories of the father she never knew. That desire to connect with the mysterious man in a treasured photograph gave her a deep love for the endless possibilities of a healing and everlasting story.

Janet has served as a featured writer/music reviewer for *Nashville Arts & Entertainment* and *Crossroad Magazines* and a frequent devotional contributor to *Christian Woman* and *Power for Today*. With featured stories in multiple anthologies, including *The Spirit of Christmas* and *Sweet Tea for the Soul: Real-Life Stories for Grieving Hearts*.

A wife of one, mother of three, and Tootsie to four, Janet currently writes from her quiet two-acre corner of the world near Elizabethtown, KY. She has spent the last few years preparing to introduce her novels and children's stories to the world.

Inspiring stories that stretch your heartstrings. An unforgettable combination.

Made in the USA
Monee, IL
27 August 2021